Daily Record

'Fresh, exciting and darkly plotted, this sharp historical mystery plunges the reader into a shadowy and forgotten past'

Good Book Guide

'A crime force to be reckoned with'

Good Reads

'Plenty of colour and action, will engage the reader from the first page to the last. Highly recommended'

Bookbag

'Quietly ....

Shots

Mirabelle Bevan Mystery

Brighton Belle

London Calling

England Expects

British Bulldog

British Bulldog

A Mirabelle Bevan Mystery

Sara Sheridan

CONSTABLE • LONDON

CONSTABLE

First published in Great Britain in 2015 by Polygon, an imprint of Birlinn Ltd.

This edition published in 2016 by Constable

Copyright © Sara Sheridan, 2016

1 3 5 7 9 10 8 6 4 2

The moral right of the author has been asserted.

A CIP catalogue record for this book
is available from the British Library.

ISBN: 978-1-47212-253-7

London EC4Y 0DZ

An Hachette UK Company
www.hachette.co.uk

www.littlebrown.co.uk

This story is dedicated to my Paris helpmates:
Lorne, Lucy and the incomparable Molly. Your
patience with my being a novelist is an amazement.
My, did we trail around the Marais.

Character is formed in the stormy billows of the world.

GOETHE

Prologue

*A thing is not necessarily true just
because a man dies for it.*

6.45 p.m., Monday, 8 February 1954
Brighton

Mirabelle snapped off the light at McGuigan & McGuigan
Debt Recovery and locked the office door. Her breath
clouded in the freezing air as she took the stairs down to the
deserted street. It had been a cold winter and the weather had
been front-page news in the national papers since before
Christmas. Further north the winter skies were crystal clear
and there was heavy snow, but it felt like a long time since the
clouds had parted in Brighton. An unrelenting dampness had
settled over the city. On East Street the sky was forbidding. It
had been dark since five o'clock. Mirabelle often worked late,
especially at this time of year when there was little to go home
to and the office was busy with post-Yuletide commissions.
She looked up and down the street, her fingers already numb
inside her silk-lined leather gloves. If she chose the route along
the front she'd get back more quickly to her flat on the Lawns,
but the seashore could offer no protection from the biting
northeasterly that cut through the city like a shard of ice.
Sizing it up, she turned towards town. The streets were silent
and eerie, the lamplight hazy over the damp pavements.

On Duke Street she realised she was being followed. A man
carrying a briefcase fell into step behind her. She could hear

the segs on his heels clicking on the paving stones, his pace distractingly out of time with her own. She crossed the road, making for North Street, and hazarded a quick glance over her shoulder. The fellow was wearing a dark woollen coat with the collar turned up and a bowler hat. The outfit was respectable enough but she couldn't quite make out his face. Near the corner she loitered, peering into the black window of a ladies' outfitters and hoping he'd pass. He did not. In fact, disconcertingly, he headed straight towards her. Mirabelle stiffened. She wished she was carrying an umbrella – the ideal everyday weapon for seeing off an assailant. Instead she concealed the office keys in her clenched fist in case she had to strike and run. Endeavouring to stay calm, she reassured herself that if she had to she could probably wind him and get away. The man tipped his hat and smiled.

'Excuse me, but are you Miss Bevan? Miss Mirabelle Bevan?' he asked pleasantly.

His voice was educated, cultured even. Mirabelle relaxed a little, though she kept the hidden keys turned outwards. Looking up and down the street, she could see no one else in either direction. The shop fronts were dark, flecked with fine drizzle, caught in movement by the buttery streetlight. She took a moment to examine the man who had addressed her. He was of slight build and sported a moustache. His neck was muffled by a dark scarf and he seemed somehow rather keen. Mirabelle wished someone else was nearby. It wouldn't be the first time a man who owed money to one of her clients had tried to accost her in the street. Further down the road, the door of a pub opened. A watery wash of light leached onto the stone paving and a tall figure in a shabby jacket lumbered out. He turned the opposite way without even looking in Mirabelle's direction.

'I'm Miss Bevan,' she admitted.

'I didn't mean to alarm you,' the man smiled again. 'I intended

to call at your office but there's a good deal of snow up north and my train was delayed. I thought I might as well have a look anyway to get my bearings, and then I saw you leaving . . .'

Now she took a closer look at him, she realised he didn't look like a man who had reneged on a debt, failed to pay his rent, or run up an outstanding bill in a boarding house or any other Brighton establishment. These things could happen to anyone, but you got a nose for people. So what on earth did he want? Occasionally Mirabelle and her colleagues branched into more interesting cases, deserting debt collection for private investigation, but when a special case arose it generally didn't come their way by commission.

'We'll be open again at nine sharp,' she said. Business was business.

'Yes. I see. Only I'm not here about the collection of a debt. It's a more personal matter.'

'You've had a wasted journey, then. We don't take on that kind of thing, I'm afraid.'

The man nodded. 'That kind of thing' meant evidence for use in the divorce courts.

'No, quite. But I don't mean personal to me, I mean personal to you, Miss Bevan. My name is John Lovatt. I'm a solicitor.' He held out his gloved hand.

Mirabelle pocketed her keys and shook it, her hazel eyes unwavering as Mr Lovatt continued. 'The thing is . . . oh, I didn't want to tell you this way, here in the street, but, well, here we are. You've been mentioned in a will. You've been left a rather unusual bequest. Is there somewhere we might go to talk? And have a drink, or dinner perhaps? It's been rather a long day.'

3

Chapter 1

*Where there is mystery
there must also be evil.*

The dining room at the Grand was the obvious choice. Mirabelle hadn't liked to direct Mr Lovatt to the little café where she sometimes ate with Vesta, her office clerk and business partner. The place seemed too scruffy for the solicitor, though the food was tasty. 'Good honest chuck,' Bill Turpin, the office's roving debt collector and third member of the team, called it.

As Mr Lovatt rounded the corner onto Kings Road, Mirabelle realised that she hadn't been to the Grand since the previous year, when there had been a series of grisly murders in one of the penthouses. Mirabelle had come close to being one of the bodies, though no one knew that – at least, no one who would tell.

As the doorman stood to attention, they swept inside. Mirabelle caught sight of herself in a gilded mirror as Mr Lovatt negotiated his way round the exotic potted palms that had recently been installed in the hotel's hallway. She couldn't help noting that next to him she looked as if she was one half of a married couple. Now they were in the light she could see that his coat was well-cut navy cashmere and his shoes were handmade – old but nicely maintained. Mr Lovatt was a gentleman.

'I'm not really dressed for dinner,' she said, looking down at her tailored green tweed suit and fur-lined ankle boots.

'Now, now,' Mr Lovatt scolded good-naturedly as they handed their coats to the bellboy. 'You look fine.'

The waiter showed them to a table and Mr Lovatt ordered for them both.

'Chicken pie,' he said decisively, scarcely reading the menu, 'and I'll have a gin and tonic. Is that all right for you, Miss Bevan?'

Mirabelle nodded. Gin was only her second choice, but the chicken pie sounded appetising. It was good warming food to keep a body going through the chill – better than she would have had at home, where all that awaited her was a tin of soup and a fish paste sandwich. The tailing off of rationing had had little effect on Mirabelle's diet.

As the waiter left there was an awkward silence. Mr Lovatt fiddled with the gold signet ring on his right hand. It was engraved with a shield – perhaps a family crest, Mirabelle thought. She fixed her gaze on the salt cellar, not liking to ask who on earth had died. Mirabelle had been orphaned at a young age. Her mother and father had both been only children and their parents were long gone. She had no family. Mr Lovatt took out a silver cigarette case and offered it across the table. She raised a hand to decline. Lovatt shrugged, then tapped a Dunhill on the box's engraved lid and lit up. It appeared the situation felt awkward to him too.

'Where did you travel from?' she asked at last. That at least might furnish a clue.

'Durham.'

That explained the delayed train. A good three hours north of London, County Durham and its neighbours had seen the worst of the snow. However, the information didn't enlighten Mirabelle about anything else.

'My client became acquainted with you some time ago, as I understand it.'

Mr Lovatt paused as if waiting for confirmation.

'You're going to have to tell me his name,' she said. 'I don't have the least idea who it might be.'

The waiter arrived with two cut crystal glasses. The ice clinked. Mr Lovatt let it settle.

'Bradley. Matthew Bradley,' he said. 'He died just before the weekend – Friday night, in fact. I came as soon as I could.'

The name didn't sink in for several seconds. Mirabelle stared blankly at the solicitor. Then it came to her.

'Do you mean Major Bradley? Bulldog Bradley?'

Lovatt nodded. 'You seem surprised.'

'I am,' Mirabelle admitted. 'He was so young.' Bradley had been her age, or perhaps slightly older.

Her mind flitted back to wartime London. It was nearly ten years since the peace, but her memories still felt fresh. She had met the major twice when he was debriefed late in 1942. Bradley was an escapee. He'd been captured in enemy territory two years earlier – in the weeks after Dunkirk. The Germans confined him to a prisoner of war camp from where he became a serial escapee, and, once he got back to Britain, something of a celebrity. In one particularly energetic run he'd broken out three times in as many months before he finally found a route home.

When Mirabelle ran into him all those years ago he'd been visiting someone in the office down the hall, and later that week she had happened to see him again in a club. The men and women who worked in the government offices – the Whitehall set – stuck together when they went out, though of course no one discussed what they were working on. That night the party had been in Soho. There was a magic show and music, and the major danced with one of the secretaries. She was a plump young thing with auburn hair and watery blue eyes – not the type of girl in whom a man like Bradley might have been expected take an interest, but still. Mirabelle remembered how the major's gaze had seemed too blank as his fingers

lay squat on the curve of the girl's hip. Escapers were the cream of the crop. Fewer than one in a hundred of those captured, Jack had said. Mirabelle's boss had a fondness for calculating percentages.

'You're a bona fide hero,' the pale-eyed girl had cooed.

Dressed in mulberry silk, Mirabelle had caught the words in a lull as the band paused before launching into a swing number. She saw Bradley stiffen, his shoulders moving upwards, his face mostly in shadow.

'Not at all,' he had replied. 'Escaping is ninety per cent luck. All it takes is a sleepy guard or a door left unlocked. All the good men get sent to the front – the ones manning the camps don't have what it takes. Ten to one they're useless. If you wait your chance you're bound to get out.'

Perhaps all men liked explaining the odds, Mirabelle mused. If nothing else Bradley was at least modest. She knew perfectly well that it took a good deal more than just an inattentive guard to get out of a Nazi prisoner of war camp. The girl simpered as the music got going again but Mirabelle thought the major's eyes darkened even more after the conversation. His blank expression had scared her.

'I haven't seen Major Bradley in ten years – more than that,' she said to Lovatt. 'It was when I lived in London. I only met him briefly. I don't think I even knew his Christian name until now. Matthew, did you say?'

'Well, he seems to have remembered you, Miss Bevan. He even knew you were in Brighton.' The solicitor reached into his briefcase and took out a buff cardboard file. Reading from the sheaf of papers inside it, he went on, '"To Miss Mirabelle Bevan of McGuigan & McGuigan Debt Recovery, Brills Lane, Brighton, I bequeath the remainder of my estate on the condition that she accepts the terms contained in the enclosed envelope."'

He extracted a sealed envelope from the file and pushed it

across the table. The skin on Mirabelle's forearms prickled. This felt somehow dangerous. Had the major had her followed? Who knew she was here? Although recently, of course, there had been one or two high-profile cases after which her name had been mentioned in *The Times*.

'But I hardly knew the chap,' she protested.

Mr Lovatt picked up his gin and eyed the woman opposite him. He decided she was not at all unattractive – well dressed and nicely self-contained. It was interesting, he thought. Usually the first question asked by someone who had been left an unexpected bequest was how much. Miss Bevan seemed too shocked to grasp the reality of her windfall. She was about to become if not a very rich woman, then at least extremely well shod.

'Do you know what it says?' she asked, eyeing the envelope.

Lovatt shook his head.

Mirabelle slipped the butter knife through the seal. Inside the letter ran to three pages. The paper flashed between her fingers, showing off her well-manicured nails, painted scarlet by Vesta only the day before. The words crowded together as she unfolded it. Somehow it felt as if this piece of paper was a passport into another world. She didn't want to read it. Why on earth am I in such a panic, she thought. Usually I'd be curious.

The waiter returned holding two steaming portions of chicken pie with cabbage on the side and small boiled potatoes that rolled against the rims of the plates. Gratefully, Mirabelle paused. Controlling her racing thoughts, she returned the letter to its envelope and slipped it into her handbag.

'I'll read it later. In private,' she said. 'It seems disrespectful to tackle it over dinner.'

Lovatt picked up his fork. 'Very wise. I can call on you tomorrow at your office to discuss the matter further, if you like. That should give you time to consider.'

The relief showed in her face.

The pie smelled delicious. At the next table there was a burst of laughter as someone told a joke. Lovatt stared at Mirabelle as she speared a piece of cabbage. He wondered if she was ever going to ask him about the money – Bradley had died one of the wealthiest men in Northumberland.

Apparently she wasn't.

'Have you visited Brighton before?' she asked as she looked up. This, Lovatt decided, was most refreshing. Miss Bevan was genuinely unusual.

'Not at all,' he said. 'I am looking forward to seeing the pier tomorrow. It is renowned, is it not? Brighton Pier?'

'I always recommend the Aquarium to visitors.' Mirabelle smiled.

It was only later, as she slipped the key into the door of her flat, that she recalled the only other piece of information she knew about Major Matthew Bradley. There was a rumour he had specialised in Escape and Evasion at M19. The department had perfected the art of supplying escaped prisoners of war on the Continent with what they needed to escape confinement, outrun their pursuers and, for that matter, avoid capture in the first place.

More than two million compasses and an impressive number of maps had been distributed throughout Europe over the course of the war. Bradley was an obvious recruit – he had, after all, been something of an expert by the time he got home. Unusually for a fellow with a desk job, it was at M19 he'd acquired his nickname. He'd believed there was always a way out and that a chap only had to find it. 'Get out quickly and keep going,' she'd heard him quoted. That certainly had the ring of the solid young man who'd decried the camp guards rather than admit his own bravery. Why on earth had Bulldog remembered her? Worse, why had he come to find her like this – from beyond the grave? The whole thing had an ominous, gothic feel.

Mirabelle shuddered. It was as cold inside the high-ceilinged flat as it was outside. She decided to go straight to bed. Grabbing a bottle of whisky as she passed the drinks cabinet, she poured a slug into her bedside glass. Then she dived under the covers and waited for the bed to warm up before removing her coat, hat and gloves and dropping them to the carpet. The cornicing cast shadows down the wall. Taking a deep breath, Mirabelle drew the envelope from her handbag. With the whisky in one hand and Major Bradley's clear cursive script in the other, she curled sideways into the milky light of the bedside lamp and began to read.

Chapter 2

*Life can only be understood backwards
but it must be lived forwards.*

The next morning the office of McGuigan & McGuigan Debt Recovery was hardly the shipshape place of business that Mirabelle might have liked to present to Mr Lovatt. A distinct smell of wet dog emanated from Panther, the office spaniel. There had been a squally shower as Bill Turpin walked the little dog to work. Now Bill was towelling Panther dry, those on four legs always being of more concern to the stolid ex-copper than those with two.

'Sideways rain,' he was saying. 'I don't mind wind and I don't mind rain. But not together, eh, boy?'

The dog's glossy black coat steamed in front of the single bar fire. Sideways rain or not, they'd be leaving soon on their rounds. Tuesday morning meant a call or two out at Preston Park, and even on a day like this Bill always took Panther for a run off the lead afterwards. Meanwhile, Mirabelle's partner, Vesta, sat at her desk surrounded by samples of chiffon in varying shades of purple.

'I just can't decide between the mauve and the violet,' she sighed as she bit into a biscuit.

Bill pretended not to hear. Since Vesta had got engaged to her American boyfriend Charlie, the arrangements for their wedding had been discussed again and again. Everything, that is, except the date.

Vesta held a long strip of fabric against her face. 'Bill?'

Bill made a noise something akin to a man in pain. 'Very nice,' he managed.

Mirabelle smiled as she hung up her coat. McGuigan & McGuigan frequently felt more like home these days than her flat. Bill was squinting and Mirabelle decided to rescue him. Men, after all, could rarely tell the difference between one hue and another. Jack had been colour blind. Once when she had spent hours getting ready to go out she had paraded in front of him. 'I like you in green,' he had said. 'You look like a very beautiful imp.' She had made the immediate decision not to tell him that her dress was a fetching shade of peach. Jack had been the love of her life. It seemed now, four years after his death, that there had never been bad times, though she knew that wasn't true. Yet all she could call to mind were moments like the one she could see so clearly now – Jack staring at her in the peach evening gown as she made the decision not to correct him, or even to tease him, but to let him believe whatever he wanted as long as he thought she was beautiful. The memory turned in her stomach as she removed her gloves.

'The mauve, dear,' she advised. 'If you really feel you can't run to white or cream.'

Vesta crossed her arms. Her mother was distraught that she wasn't going to wear white, but Vesta was toughing out the family arguments over her wedding, from the colour of her outfit to the fact that she wanted a small party for her big day – a celebration that didn't revolve around tables piled with food and a hundred of her parents' friends arriving to help the Churchills eat it, which was the Jamaican way.

'It's not as if white suits our circumstances,' she tutted. 'And cream is such a cop-out.'

Charlie and Vesta had been sharing accommodation for over a year now. This had been another bugbear for Vesta's parents, although it had also proved an effective bargaining chip. The fact that their daughter was at least about to

legitimise her union meant Mrs Churchill was less likely to criticise her low-key attitude to the ceremony. That did not mean that she hadn't argued vigorously if uselessly in favour of a white dress and a traditional Caribbean party after a service in a church – preferably the one the family attended only a street or two away from their south London home.

Vesta twisted a chiffon scrap around one of her fingers. 'White,' she continued. 'If there's one shade a woman of colour can't wear it's got to be the one everyone expects, hasn't it? I don't want to look ridiculous, and white will only make my skin look even darker. I want to get married our way – Charlie's and mine. Not like a hick from Hicktown, Jamaica. Just the two of us, that's all.'

Mirabelle didn't like to comment, but she couldn't help thinking that if Vesta was hoping to disguise her skin tone she'd need to wear a veil whatever colour she chose.

'Now, now,' she said.

'I'd best get on.' Bill rose to his feet. When Vesta got exercised about her wedding it could go on for some time and he was already out of his depth. He picked up the list of calls that had been left on his desk. The post-Christmas rush of holiday debt had been heavy this year but they'd made a good start and now at least it was on its way to being cleared. There were a few stubborn offenders with whom terms had yet to be agreed, but Bill was methodical in tracking them down. Mirabelle felt proud of what the little team had achieved. The business was making an increasing profit every month – it was an easy mark of success by which to judge her efforts. The ledger balanced. The office was well run.

Vesta pulled herself together. 'Tea?' she offered, casting the fabric samples aside.

Mirabelle nodded. 'Thanks.'

She sat down, unconsciously drumming her fingers on the brown leather desktop as Bill left with Panther at his heel.

Vesta placed a steaming cup in front of her and eyed Mirabelle's manicure for chips.

'What happened?' she asked.

Mirabelle looked up. 'What do you mean?'

Vesta rolled her eyes. 'Honestly! It's always the same when something special comes up. You become very quiet – more distracted than usual. And you drum. Next you'll look at the paper, but you won't really be reading it.'

Mirabelle removed her hand from the desktop and cast a rueful glance at the morning's newspaper sitting on the edge of her desk where Bill always left it. She couldn't pick it up now.

'I received a letter,' she said.

The envelope was nestled in her bag but she didn't want Vesta to read it. Her partner always jumped to conclusions and somehow Bulldog Bradley's missive felt, if not sacred, then certainly personal. 'I'm sending you this,' it said, 'because Jack Duggan once told me you had the conscience of an angel and the sleuthing skills of the devil himself. I hope he was right.' For Mirabelle, the very mention of Jack's name made the letter a private matter – a window into a world that she kept not only closed but also shuttered.

Vesta sat with her head to one side, pulling her thick blue cardigan around her frame. 'Well?' she said.

'Something's come up about a missing person. A man. A soldier.'

Vesta grinned. She longed to take the more interesting cases that were periodically offered to McGuigan & McGuigan but Mirabelle generally vetoed them. She leaned casually over her desk to retrieve her tea and biscuit, and settled down for the story.

'Like a man who has run off and abandoned his missus?' she asked.

Mirabelle pursed her lips. This was exactly what she expected from Vesta, and the truth was that sometimes that way of thinking paid off. It was the reason that the girl was so good

with paperwork – you could hand her a file of drab, seemingly dull information and she'd construct a story from it worthy of a novel. Her instinct for making connections had nailed a case or two in the past. Mirabelle's steely logic and Vesta's vivid imagination were a winning combination. Still, Mirabelle didn't relish the idea of Vesta's mind getting to work on anything that mentioned Jack Duggan.

'Not at all like a man leaving his wife,' she said. 'More like a soldier missing in action.'

'Was he married, this guy?' Vesta said knowingly.

Mirabelle shrugged her shoulders. 'I don't know. But one thing's certain, a chap wouldn't hole up in occupied France just to get away from his wife, Vesta.'

'Occupied France? How long has he been gone?'

Mirabelle told herself that at least this was a sensible enquiry. She paused. Vesta realised she was counting.

'Gosh. It must be almost twelve years,' she said. 'Of course, the most likely thing is that he's dead.'

'A case like that is going to take a while. We'd better put ourselves on an hourly rate.'

Before Mirabelle had a chance to elucidate there was a sharp rap on the office door and Mr Lovatt entered.

'Good morning, Miss Bevan.' He tipped his hat cheerily.

Mirabelle stood up, catching the merest whiff of aftershave. Truefitt & Hill if she wasn't mistaken. There was a familiarity about Mr Lovatt that was comforting.

'Come in,' she said, ushering the solicitor towards a chair. 'Mr Lovatt, this is my business partner, Vesta Churchill. She's our office clerk.'

Lovatt cast a thin smile in Vesta's direction but did not offer his hand. 'How do you do,' he muttered.

Vesta beamed: her standard response to embarrassed Englishmen who were not sure how to behave towards her because of her colour. Her dark eyes flashed.

'Might I make you a cup of tea, Mr Lovatt?' she offered, an unaccustomed twang of Jamaica in her south London accent, inserted simply to underline the point.

Mr Lovatt declined. 'I had an excellent breakfast at the lodging house. Thank you. I came to see you, Miss Bevan, to ascertain . . .' He seemed not to know how to put it.

'Vesta knows about Mr Bradley's bequest,' Mirabelle cut in, mentally ticking herself off for enjoying the solicitor's discomfort. 'She knows about the letter, anyway. You can speak freely.'

'I see.' Mr Lovatt cleared his throat. 'Well, the bequest is contingent on your accepting Mr Bradley's terms, as you know. I wondered if you had had time to consider the contents of his letter?'

'There's a bequest?' Vesta cut in. 'How much is it worth?'

A smile played across Mr Lovatt's lips, as if he had suddenly been dealt the cards he needed to play a royal flush.

'The estate remains in a condition of probate,' he replied. 'Mr Bradley stipulated that you should receive the remainder, Miss Bevan, after his wife's portion, a donation to one or two charitable concerns and of course any outstanding debts that need to be covered, including death duties. At my estimate the sum coming to you will approach ten thousand guineas.'

'Sweet Lord Almighty,' breathed Vesta. It was a fortune.

'Major Bradley was married?' Mirabelle latched onto the information. 'I had no idea. Surely it isn't right that I should be left this money. I mean, Mrs Bradley must be provided for properly.'

Mr Lovatt was not sufficiently indiscreet to admit this had also been Mrs Bradley's position when she heard the terms of her husband's will. She had immediately assumed that Miss Mirabelle Bevan had been Mr Bradley's mistress, if not recently, then at some time in the past. While her husband left her entirely financially secure, Mrs Bradley had enjoined Mr Lovatt to allow her to read her husband's letter to the woman she had immediately termed 'this hussy of Matthew's'. Mr Lovatt had

resisted, though the truth was he had wondered whether it would be a woman of considerably more easy virtue than Miss Bevan that he would meet upon his arrival in Brighton.

'Mrs Bradley is most comfortably off, I assure you.'

'But what must she think?' The words escaped Mirabelle's lips almost involuntarily.

Neither Mr Lovatt nor Mirabelle or indeed Vesta gave voice to the obvious answer. Mirabelle ran back over the evening before – Mr Lovatt pursuing her in the street, eyeing her over the dinner table, and lingering ever so slightly too long as he bade her goodnight in the hallway of the Grand.

'Really, Miss Bevan,' the solicitor insisted. 'I assure you, financially there is plenty to go round. Mrs Bradley and her daughter are well provided for.'

'There is a child as well? My goodness! I shall have to write the poor woman a letter. This must have been dreadfully difficult for her.'

'Quite.' Mr Lovatt restrained himself from saying anything more. Mrs Bradley's feelings, after all, were not his business. Miss Bevan's reaction to the letter she had received was. 'And as to the condition Mr Bradley imposed upon your inheritance – the letter, I mean? I feel bound to enquire . . .'

'It's quite some mystery,' Mirabelle said. 'I can't imagine why he has come to me, or indeed why he waited so long.'

Mr Lovatt reached for his cigarette case. Both women declined as he waved it in front of them before slowly lighting up.

'Might you be prepared to share some of the details?' he asked.

'I was just telling Vesta,' Mirabelle said. 'Major Bradley would like me to track down an associate from his wartime days. He supplies little more than a name and a broad outline of the last time he saw the fellow, which is now of course several years ago. They escaped together from a German prisoner of war camp and appear to have become separated in

17

France on their way back to Blighty. What I don't understand is why the major didn't try to find his friend after the war. I mean, there were agencies for that sort of thing.' She paused as she recalled the confusion that pervaded Europe long after the guns had stopped. 'The major was perfectly well connected and besides that, it's now clear he was a man of some means. If he lost touch with this person why didn't he find him again himself – in his lifetime? The man was a British officer. If he came back to England, it wouldn't have been too difficult. And if the poor chap didn't make it, one way or another it would have been easier to find out at the time than it is now. I don't understand why Bradley didn't just get on with it.'

Mr Lovatt took a deep draw and blew a robust jet of smoke across the desk. 'I might be able to illuminate matters,' he admitted. 'The letter you received and the accompanying bequest were only inserted into the terms of Mr Bradley's will when he knew he was dying.'

'Major Bradley's death was expected? I don't understand. He was still a young man. Why, he can scarcely have been forty years of age.'

'Forty-two.' Mr Lovatt inhaled. 'Cancer of the lungs. Tragic, really. Bradley had always been such a fit fellow. He was a stalwart of the local hunt. He quite threw himself into that kind of thing. In such cases the news of one's own mortality is deeply affecting and it strikes me this bequest might be a matter of conscience. Knowing he had hardly any time left the poor fellow suddenly felt the matter was pressing but realised he wouldn't be able to deal with it himself. That sort of thing takes on a whole new meaning when one is about to face one's maker.'

Mirabelle nodded. 'I suppose that might explain it,' she said doubtfully. The kind of man Bradley had been or at least what she knew of him, mitigated against any delay. Bulldog Bradley had been a bolt of lightning – a man who acted decisively in

the most difficult of situations. The matter was intriguing but it also felt dark. If there was something Bulldog Bradley didn't want to face, Mirabelle couldn't imagine what it might be. She tried to focus on the element of riddle or at least puzzle contained in the letter and ignore the sense of doom that was sweeping over her like dark clouds rolling over open water. Whatever had been going on in Bulldog Bradley's mind, there was only one way to find out.

'All right, Mr Lovatt. I can make some enquiries and see what I turn up.'

'And you'll keep me informed?'

Mirabelle's gaze didn't waver. The letter hadn't stipulated what she should do with the information once she'd uncovered it. But then, on balance, what other course of action was there but to pass anything she found to Mr Lovatt?

'Are you Major Bradley's executor?'

'Yes, I am.' Lovatt smiled and handed her his card.

'All right.'

'Excellent.' The solicitor reached for his hat. 'I'll leave it with you, shall I?'

Chapter 3

Being a woman is a terribly difficult task.

Vesta grudgingly agreed to look after the office while Mirabelle set out to investigate.

'There's no time like the present.' She pulled on her coat, realising with a slight smile that Bulldog Bradley would have approved of the sentiment. She'd have to go up to London. That's where the records were held.

Fighting her way up Queen's Road through the elements, Mirabelle made it to the station in the wake of a particularly vicious burst of icy wind that almost took her breath away. It was too cold to think straight. A sodden newspaper whipped down the hill as she hurried to board the eleven o'clock train. The guard slammed the door behind her. On board everyone was muffled, the men smoking furiously to keep warm. Mirabelle took a seat in a first-class carriage next to a lady wearing a long mink coat.

'Nippy, isn't it?' the woman remarked smugly as she put up her collar. 'And if anything it's worse in the city.'

Mirabelle stared blankly at the window, which was gilded by a sheet of ice outside so that as the train pulled out of the station the countryside passed in a desolate blur of grey, muted green and icy white.

After the war there had been so many displaced people it was impossible to keep track. Prisoners of war, concentration camp victims, those who had hidden the entire length of the conflict, sheltered by friends or even strangers: the world shifted as

peace was declared and from back rooms, basements, attics, sewers and caves survivors flooded out to tell their stories, hoping to be reunited with those they loved. But the world into which they emerged had changed. Whole cities had been reduced to rubble and the maps of Europe had been redrawn.

Perhaps after the war, Mirabelle mused, Bulldog Bradley simply couldn't face trying to find his friend. She wouldn't blame him. It had been difficult to keep going. At the time she hadn't foreseen the toll those first years of peace would take. She remembered the elation when the news came in. Jack had waltzed her across the office in full view of everyone. There had been a chorus of champagne corks. And then they'd realised just how far there still was to go.

The sight of the red brick back yards of Pimlico heralded the train's arrival into Victoria. Disembarking, Mirabelle coughed as she took her first lungful of sooty, biting London air. At the end of the platform a man with one leg busked on his mouth organ playing 'We'll Meet Again'. The lady in the mink coat stalked past him without a glance and slipped into the back of a cab. Mirabelle popped sixpence in his tin.

Outside, hillocks of filthy grey snow melted slowly, seeping into the drains. Passers-by looked like smudges, their dark coats bundled round them and their hats lowered.

Mirabelle cut off the main road for Belgrave Place. The stucco houses in this part of town seemed like greying ice palaces – dank shadows of the era when the streets of Belgravia sported pristine white plasterwork, in the days when there had been money. Panther the office dog was born nearby on Wilton Crescent. Mirabelle looked in the direction of the house as she passed. The puppy was a present two years before from a grateful client. She thought suddenly how different she had felt only that short time ago, when Rose Bellamy Gore had gone missing and Vesta's friend Lindon Claremont was accused of kidnapping her. Then when she came to London it had

meant a painful return to her memories of living with Jack. Now that felt less barbed. She knew if he could see her now he'd laugh at her picking her way past houses where they had been invited to dinner and doorsteps where they had kissed, away from the glare of yellow streetlamps and the not-dark-enough summer skies. Walking through Belgravia no longer felt like betraying his memory.

The skeletal trees on the square were dusted with frost. Above, the clouds sealed a pewter lid over the city. Mirabelle rounded the corner into Grosvenor Crescent to the sound of water dripping onto stone as the sodden snow softened. She smiled when she saw the brass plaque wrapped round a grand column, stamped her feet to remove any ice, and walked through the door of the British Red Cross.

Inside, the hallway smelled of overstewed tea. The reception desk was lit from high above by a single bulb hanging on a wire. A house like this would have had chandeliers in its heyday, but like the wrought-iron balconies that had been scrapped for the war effort the indoor finery had also been stripped away. The buildings that still had their embellishments looked smug somehow – like that woman in the fur coat on the train.

'May I help you, madam?' the secretary at the reception desk enquired.

Mirabelle smiled. She had been trained by the Red Cross during the war – not as a nurse but in emergency first aid.

'I'm enquiring after a displaced person.'

The girl looked too young to remember much about the post-war chaos in which the Red Cross had played such a key part. She couldn't be much older than Vesta.

'Displaced?' The girl checked the word and Mirabelle realised the child was sporting an accent. It was only a slight nuance, but still.

'Yes. Lost.'

'Lost? I see.'

Mirabelle smiled. 'You're Polish.'

The girl's forehead wrinkled as if she had been caught out. Then she nodded.

'Is there someone to whom I might speak? Someone who can help?'

'Give me a moment.' The girl disappeared into the room behind her.

Mirabelle looked up. The building seemed hopelessly old-fashioned. Along the cornice the old wires operating the system once used to call servants remained tacked in place. Here and there a vital wire was cut. Mirabelle wondered how the Red Cross's many activities might be organised from somewhere so close to being domestic. The paintwork was scratched and worn, grubby with a million smudged finger-prints. High above the curl of the grand stairwell, opaque glass had been used to glaze the cupola. It was still taped up in case of a direct hit.

The door opened and Mirabelle felt a wisp of heat from the inner office, or if not exactly heat at least temperate air. If anything the girl who emerged was younger than the Polish secretary but she had an entirely different manner – so fresh that it was as if she had been cut out of a magazine and her Red Cross uniform pasted onto her slim frame. She was wear-ing make-up – something that wouldn't have been allowed in the old days.

'I'm Ann Kettle.' The girl's scarlet lips parted to reveal a set of very white teeth. 'I understand you're looking for a displaced person?'

'Yes. One of our soldiers who went missing in wartime France. Can you help?'

'If you're looking for British military personnel the best place to start is with the chap's regiment, Miss . . .'

'I'm Mirabelle Bevan.' Mirabelle held out her hand. Nurse

23

Kettle shook it, her eyes softening in the wake of Mirabelle's manners. 'I'm afraid I don't know his regiment,' Mirabelle admitted. 'The man was an escaped POW who went off the radar. The chap he escaped with lost him en route home. It occurred to me that after the war, if the chap was still in France, a Red Cross clearing camp might have been his first stop.'

'I see.' Nurse Kettle quizzically tipped her head to one side. 'Why are you looking for him now, if you don't mind my asking? It seems rather late.'

'It is. I'm afraid it was the last request of an acquaintance who recently passed away. He was the other escapee – the one who got out. He never found out what happened to his friend.'

The nurse paused, considering. Mirabelle guessed this was probably not the first time she had heard a story about the derring-do of British troops in wartime. For all her pretty face, the girl had gravitas.

'Well, if this missing person made it out of France, even after the war, his regiment is still your best port of call,' she said flatly. 'But if the chap passed through our hands at any stage, his name will be in our papers. The thing is, the archives are very short staffed. They've just been moved, in point of fact. Here.' She leaned over the reception desk and wrote down an address in Kensington on a scrap of paper. 'That's where they've gone. If you're lucky they'll let you have a look. Though this chap isn't a relative of yours, is he?'

Mirabelle shook her head.

'Well, I hope you find him.'

'Thank you. I'd like to know what happened.'

Nurse Kettle sighed. Her perfect veneer softened a fraction. Knowing what had happened didn't always help. The women's eyes met.

'Anyway, I'll do my best,' Mirabelle said and turned back onto the grey London street, in the direction of Sloane Square.

Chapter 4

One who makes no mistakes, makes nothing.

Vesta answered the telephone with gusto. 'McGuigan & McGuigan,' she trilled.

With Mirabelle away she had turned up the fire while she sorted through the paperwork. The office smelled of coffee and buttery toast with a sprinkle of cinnamon. Vesta's fiancé Charlie worked in the kitchens at the Grand. He kept her well supplied with luxuries and on Tuesdays this was her usual mid-morning snack. Now after lunch she found she was ahead of the game. It had taken no time to prepare Bill's schedule for the next day and get the ledger up to date. She had stopped for ten minutes to make a cup of tea for the poor postman (who was perishing) and have a chat about the volume of mail received by other businesses in the building and indeed in the street. Now she only had the day's bank deposit to make up.

'Can I help you?' she said cheerily into the mouthpiece.

At the other end, Mirabelle's voice sounded as if she was cold. Vesta immediately pictured her friend bundled up in one of the capital's red telephone boxes. In fact Mirabelle had availed herself of the well-appointed mahogany telephone booth in the hallway of the Sloane Square Hotel, but although she was not outside in the worst of the chill, the hotel was hardly balmy.

'Hello, dear, it's me,' she said, 'I need some help.'

Vesta sat bolt upright. Mirabelle was a person who rarely

asked for assistance and was more likely to have help thrust upon her. Recently, however, Vesta had noticed small changes in her friend. Lately, Mirabelle had been perusing the menu without deciding what she wanted immediately when they went for lunch at the little café in the Lanes. It was almost as if she had begun to care about what she had to eat, or at least to notice it. Last week she had given up when the cryptic crossword was particularly tricky and she hadn't seemed in the least perturbed. Vesta was unsure what these changes meant but she instinctively felt they were progress. And here was another change – Mirabelle asking for help.

'I want you to go to the library. This chap who's missing – I think he might be more difficult to track down than I expected.'

'Mmm.' Vesta took a sip of strong sweet coffee and picked up a pencil to make notes.

'His name is Philip Caine,' Mirabelle continued. 'I want you to check *The Times* and the *Daily Telegraph* going back to 1942 when he was captured. See if you can find sight or sound of him – and while you're at it keep an eye out for our Major Bradley, would you? And have a look at what the library stocks in the way of those frightful war memoirs – escapees who got out through France. You know the sort of thing.'

Vesta grinned. It was exactly the kind of book her father liked. Mr Churchill had been stationed in Yorkshire for the duration of the war. 'They didn't think to send a black man into the African desert,' he often joked, after which Mrs Churchill always nudged her husband furiously. She had been grateful he was somewhere safe. Not every family on their street had been so lucky. Unrepentant, Mr Churchill never took the hint. 'The war was my chance to see it,' he would say, smacking his lips with relish. 'The motherland. And there I was, stationed on Monkton Moor like an idiot. I didn't see no action at all.'

'Yeah,' Vesta said now. 'My dad likes those stories.'

'Flick through a few, would you? You never know what might turn up.'

'What exactly am I looking for?'

There was a pause. Mirabelle didn't like to say the word.

'Gossip,' she spat out at last. 'If Caine stayed in France perhaps another escapee came across him on their way down the line. Somebody has to remember. A fellow doesn't just disappear. And as you'll be out of the office, leave a note for Bill, would you?'

'Sure thing.' Vesta stretched one arm towards the coat rack, keeping the phone to her ear.

'Thank you. I might be a while in town but I'll call you back.'

Mirabelle put down the telephone. Vesta was the ideal person to search through that kind of material. Before the women had met, Vesta's place of employment was Halley Insurance, just down the hall from McGuigan & McGuigan. 'Nothing will ever seem dull again,' she had sworn after Mr Halley dismissed her and she came to work with Mirabelle. 'Insurance!' She cast her eyes to the ceiling.

When the women had taken over the business after the unexpected death of Big Ben McGuigan in 1951, Vesta insisted on understanding what she was getting into and spent her first week in the office reading through crushingly boring ledgers and case files housed in the office's filing cabinets. By the following Monday, she was addressing clients by name and was conversant with the details of their accounts. If there was anyone who would find Major Bradley's lost friend in a sea of post-war information, it was Vesta.

Mirabelle checked the slim gold watch on her wrist as she quit the telephone cubicle of the Sloane Square Hotel and approached the reception desk.

'Might I have a piece of paper and an envelope?' she asked.

The receptionist rifled in a drawer before carefully handing over stationery with the hotel's logo emblazoned across the

top. Mirabelle took a seat in a comfortable chair not far from the fire. It was too small a blaze for such a grand hallway but, she told herself, perhaps it was all the hotel could run to. Writing the letter was too important to put off any longer.

Dear Mrs Bradley,

I am so very sorry for your loss. Major Bradley was a passing acquaintance of mine during the war. He was a brave man and much admired. I have to admit to being somewhat astonished by his generous bequest and I wanted to assure you that there was no personal connection between your husband and me, and also that the contents of his letter included a request that I should track down one of his wartime colleagues. I am as yet unsure why Major Bradley appears not to have looked for this person himself if the man's welfare was on his mind. If you ever heard your husband talk of Philip Caine, it would be very helpful to know what he might have said. I am, so far, somewhat at a loss.

I have only just arrived in London on this quest and will not be staying at this hotel. Should you be kind enough to reply, please write to me at my offices: McGuigan & McGuigan, Brills Lane, East Street, Brighton.

My sympathy goes to you at this difficult time.
Yours sincerely,
Mirabelle Bevan

Mirabelle took a postage stamp from her wallet. She stuck it to the envelope, admiring Her Majesty's glowing complexion as she did so. She hoped Mrs Bradley might be able to help, although asking a recently bereaved widow for assistance was an unreliable strategy. In the weeks after Jack died she herself had barely eaten, unsure what day it was or even what time. She had sat, shocked, in an armchair in her living room and his memory had been everywhere – laughing beside the window, throwing a

pillow at her in derision during an imagined discussion, holding her naked as they lay on the floor. The sunshine outside had seemed a betrayal as she willed the ceiling to fall in and end the pain of Jack's being gone. Once, she had walked outside and, blinkered in grief after three sleepless days and nights, had frantically crossed the busy road repeatedly, hoping to be run down. She had ended up weeping on the pebble beach. A widow's instinct was not to dive in with helpful information – that much she knew. Not that she and Jack had married.

Outside, considering a walk might help her to think, she turned left along Eaton Gate. A man in a threadbare coat loitered outside the public lavatory. Mirabelle had noticed him there when she arrived at the hotel. He must have nowhere to go, she thought as she lengthened her stride and slipped Mrs Bradley's letter into the postbox – a sole flash of colour on the corner. In summer this road was leafy but the trees were bare skeletons at this time of year and the grass only intermittent between patches of frozen mud. The railings made the gardens look like prison yards.

A chill wind whipped around her slim ankles as she ran through Bradley's story again to see if she could deduce anything further. He was a sapper – a Royal Engineer – she suddenly recalled as she held him in her mind's eye and deciphered the badges on his uniform. Like many men who had been taken prisoner after Dunkirk, he had been sent to a Stalag – a prisoner of war camp. After trying to escape so many times, he must have been on the Germans' list for a transfer to Posen or even Colditz, where they housed their most troublesome inmates: VIPs and serial escapers. Bradley probably undertook his successful attempt just in time, and having managed to get away with Caine in tow, had made the sensible decision to head into occupied territory. France was their best chance of getting home. There were established exit routes and solid resistance against German forces. The Maquis were adept at

smuggling out information, spies and soldiers. It wouldn't be easy, of course, but elsewhere the odds would have been stacked even higher against them.

Bradley was probably about as ideal an escapee as there could be. The Royal Engineers were practical men, well respected in military circles – there was one, she recalled, who had won a Victoria Cross at Saint-Nazaire. Mirabelle wondered what Major Bradley's field of expertise had been before he became Bulldog Bradley the famous escaper. His regiment built bridges and dockyards, surveyed enemy territory and specialised in bomb disposal. Many of the troops who got out brought back important military information about supply routes, airfields and defensive structures they had seen on their way. Sappers remembered twice as much as anyone else, simply because they understood how installations were built and what it might take to destroy them. Men like Bradley contributed a great deal to the war effort when they got home.

Mirabelle turned her attention to Philip Caine. Bradley was such a huge figure that she found herself assuming Caine was the second man – as if he was only a shadow. It had almost surprised her to learn that the major had escaped as part of a duo. When he got back Bradley's story had been told repeatedly in the press, with no mention of a partner – a man left behind. Escaping in such an arrangement was common enough. In many ways small groups stood a better chance than single soldiers. In his letter, Bradley said he had become separated from Caine en route through France, but that didn't mean the other man had never made it home.

Turning along the back wall of Buckingham Palace Gardens Mirabelle made for St James's. The area was full of military expertise. As she crossed the road the fellow in the threadbare coat caught her eye again. So many people had been made homeless in the Blitz, she thought. She wondered where he was going.

Her own destination was almost in sight: the Army and Navy Club on Pall Mall. London was a mass of private clubs and libraries – a network for those in the know – and perhaps she'd find someone there who could help. The mysterious Caine could have been from any regiment. There were thousands of men in the military but people knew each other by reputation, especially officers, so the Army and Navy – also known as the Rag – was a good place to start. At least it was bound to have a copy of the Royal Engineers List, so she'd get more information on Bradley under her belt.

The tramp followed as she turned onto Pall Mall and Mirabelle began to feel uneasy. She turned and stared at him. His eyes narrowed and he held back, anticipating her movement. She thought of crossing the road to ask him what he was doing but something held her back – the hint of desperation perhaps. His skin was ingrained with dirt; his fingers smeared with the detritus of sleeping rough.

She turned smartly and mounted the steps of the club. What had happened to London? There was something down at heel about the old place. Mirabelle couldn't quite put her finger on it. She shrugged off the uncomfortable sensation of the tramp's gaze and turned her attention to the matter in hand.

The Rag was housed in a fine Victorian building but, she noticed, there was a whiff of old books and cabbage as soon as you entered. The carpet was clean but worn, and the place had the air of a frail old person – a countess gone to seed or an aged baron sitting by a fire, dreaming of happier days. Mirabelle lingered at the reception desk, peering to no avail through the open doors that led off the dingy main hall. There was no one in sight.

'Hello,' she called.

Nothing. She shrugged off the idea of leaving. If nothing else, she didn't want to confront the tramp. If she stayed here long enough, she expected he'd get bored and move on. After

a full minute at reception completely unattended, Mirabelle decided simply to gatecrash. In for a penny, she thought, and, unsure if women were allowed in all the rooms and almost certain that they wouldn't be, she stalked into the high-ceilinged drawing room on the ground floor.

In one corner a curl of creamy paint peeled off the wall below the cornicing and a fire lit in the ornately decorated grate looked set to go out, engulfed by its own ash. Promisingly, however, there were several publications housed on a set of mahogany shelves that entirely covered two of the high walls. Among the encyclopedias and atlases, in a glass dome, a large stuffed penguin had pride of place. As Mirabelle approached she noticed a small note in spidery, fading hand-writing that proclaimed the bird had been sent home from Captain Robert Falcon Scott's expedition to Antarctica. Her eye, however, was drawn to the book propped next to it – a copy of *Who's Who*.

Mirabelle pulled the red leather-bound tome off the shelf and looked up Philip Caine. There was no entry. Major Bradley fared better, and the listing announced he was the husband of Lady Caroline Bland. Though interesting, this was not immediately helpful and Mirabelle moved further along the shelf to the Royal Engineers List that she'd hoped for. Philip Caine wasn't in that either. It had been a long shot, although worth a try: just because Bradley was a Royal Engineer didn't mean his escape partner came from the same regiment. Stalag escape committees paired men according to their talents. For instance, if one spoke German but had poor map-reading skills, he'd be teamed with someone just the opposite. There were, she suddenly thought, a few clues in that. Whatever Bradley's best skills, Caine probably hadn't had them, and vice versa. She filed away this idea for later use and was about to move further along the shelf when a man's voice sounded loud, clear and shocked behind her.

'I say, who on earth are you?'

Mirabelle started but managed a smile as she turned round. The chap in the doorway wore a grey RAF officer's uniform. He was a solid-looking fellow, greying at the temples. His ruddy complexion betrayed him as either an outdoor enthusiast or a toper. Mirabelle held out her hand.

'Mirabelle Bevan. How do you do?'

'How do you do?' he replied.

Neither of them answered the other's entirely rhetorical question and it was Mirabelle who continued the conversation.

'I'm looking for someone. Well, two someones if I'm honest. A Royal Engineer, Major Matthew Bradley and another officer, Philip Caine.'

The man squinted. He removed his hat and gloves and laid them on a side table. He was not as old as he seemed, she realised. Some people simply had a lack of humour that aged the face and this chap was probably ten years younger than the fifty he looked. He turned towards Mirabelle, clearly sizing her up in exactly the same way.

'I don't know what you're talking about,' he said. 'Caine has been dead for years. He never came back.'

'You knew him?'

'Yes, of course I did. Everyone knew Caine. He was a pilot. A very fine one. Not a wing commander or anything, only a flight lieutenant, but he could fly all right. He got shot down in '42, poor fellow. Look, who on earth are you?' The man glanced over his shoulder into the hallway as if he hoped help might arrive and he would not have to deal with this unexpected and irksome woman on club property.

'You're quite right,' Mirabelle admitted. 'I shouldn't be here. The thing is, I was contacted by the solicitor of Major Matthew Bradley, whom I met briefly during the war. Bradley died last weekend. It turns out his last request was that I should look into what happened to Flight Lieutenant Caine. They were friends – escape partners from the same Stalag. They got out

33

together and Caine somehow got lost on the way home. Since I've been asked to track him down, I thought this would be a good place to start. Did you know Major Bradley too? He was quite famous, I think.'

The officer appeared to be deep in thought. 'No, I don't believe I know anyone of that name,' he said at last.

'Bulldog Bradley?'

'Oh, yes! *Bulldog* Bradley. Though I only know him by reputation. Royal Engineer, wasn't he? It seems a long time ago now. I didn't know he'd got out with Caine. Poor Philip. He was a great flier. Never made it home though.'

'Are you sure of that?'

The officer stared blankly. 'Of course I'm sure. What kind of a fool do you take me for?'

'I'm sorry. Please, go on. Tell me, what was he like?'

'Caine? Tall fellow. Thoughtful. The bugger spoke German – excuse my language.'

Mirabelle waved off the apology. German was a valuable escape skill. Between Bradley's practical expertise and undoubted bravery and Caine's linguistic ability the pair must have stood a good chance from the start.

'That's interesting. Where did he learn, do you know?'

'I think there was some Hun family connection. That applied to several of the chaps, of course. The blighter had some French too, I recall. I don't know if that was anything to do with his people.'

'So did Caine have a family?'

'A wife, you mean?'

Mirabelle nodded. The officer sat down in a comfortable leather chair by the dying fire. He clasped his hands and considered the question for what felt like a long time.

'No,' he said finally. 'Though he was engaged, as I remember. They'd known each other as children. I don't think they were cut from quite the same cloth. But once he'd got some

flying hours behind him . . . well, the wings, you see, were damned attractive during wartime. Heroes and so forth. Caine was due to get married that summer. Rush job. But it was like that during the war. If you wanted something you had to seize the day. He never made it to the altar, of course. He must have been shot down the week he was meant to tie the knot, or very close to it. The girl had a title, I remember. Her people were from somewhere up north. She was a rider – a country type and quite a firebrand, as I recall. Made a terrible fuss when poor Caine went down . . . Now, give me a moment . . . it was Lady Caroline something or other . . .'

Mirabelle's heart sank. 'Lady Caroline Bland?'

'Yes. Blow me. Yes, that's it!'

Mirabelle's mind swam. She glanced at the copy of *Who's Who* on the shelf. Lady Caroline Bland was the woman who had married Bradley. This new information meant that she had quite possibly just posted the least discreet letter she had ever written. What on earth would poor Mrs Bradley think? There she was, grieving for a husband who all these years had been wondering what had happened to her erstwhile fiancé. Worse, Bradley clearly felt so guilty about whatever had happened that he effectively employed a complete stranger – Mirabelle – to look for the friend he'd somehow lost on his way home. He'd cut out his wife entirely.

'Well, at least that explains why Bradley didn't look for Caine while he was alive,' she thought out loud.

The officer, pleased with himself, crossed the room and released a decanter of brandy from a locked tantalus. He poured himself a drink.

'One can never get any service round here. No chance of any ice. Might I fetch you something?' he offered.

Mirabelle checked her watch. She doubted there was anything more to be gained at the club. 'No, thank you. I'd best be going.'

As she buttoned her coat, it occurred to her that Vesta would be delighted by the afternoon's revelations. Writing to Mrs Bradley was probably the only thing Mirabelle had done since she met the girl that might constitute a decent piece of gossip. As she glided through the deserted hallway, leaving the RAF officer to drink alone in the club's drawing room, Mirabelle wondered if there was any chance that the postman might let her fish the letter out of the box and start again. Then she realised with a twist of shame that it must have been picked up by now – there was always a lunchtime run. A sheet of half-hearted drizzle showered Pall Mall as Mirabelle stepped onto the pavement. Across the road the tramp loitered. Mirabelle felt her skin prickle as she turned towards Piccadilly.

Chapter 5

I want to be with those who know secret things.

The man had no spycraft. It was easy to tell she was being followed. Mirabelle picked up her pace but he didn't fall behind. Her heels clattered on the icy paving stones and she almost slipped as she turned the corner, righting herself by catching hold of the railings. Further ahead there was a policeman dawdling up St James's Street but she was reluctant to ask for help, instead overtaking him briskly and glancing behind as she did so. Why wouldn't the fellow just clear off?

In a state of mild confusion, Mirabelle found herself on Piccadilly turning sharply left and up the stairs into the Ritz hotel. It was an excellent place to think, if rather grand, and at least the tramp wouldn't be able to follow her. Stepping inside was immediately comforting. The Ritz was unsullied by memories of anyone but Jack – unlike the Savoy, where the year before last she had had lunch with Superintendent Alan McGregor at the end of the Claremont case. It had been pleasant enough, although the vast dining room had been subdued by news of the King's death, which had been announced earlier that day. Still, Mirabelle had been unable to dismiss the feeling that she was being disloyal to Jack's memory by coming there with somebody else. The Ritz was convenient and Jack had believed in hiding in plain sight. With Superintendent McGregor such niceties were not a consideration. There had been no intimate conversation, nothing like that. But still, it had felt wrong.

Today as she strode into the bar at the Ritz it felt like London as it used to be. The velvet seats were carefully placed to allow each table the maximum privacy – the hallmark of a good English hotel, somewhere you'd be left alone. This afternoon there were only two tables in use – both occupied by well-dressed gentlemen drinking by themselves and reading the *Daily Telegraph*. The bar had the air of a shrine – somewhere she could step, even if only fleetingly, into a time when London was at its best and she was in love. She mustn't bring anyone else here, she decided.

'Madam?' The waiter approached.

The whiff of Brylcreem acted like smelling salts. Mirabelle ordered a glass of champagne and settled into a chair in the corner, drawing the pale walls around her like a cloak. She strained to see out of the window but the tramp wasn't in her line of sight. With luck he'd go now. More important, she told herself, was the fact she'd written that dreadful letter. Her stomach churned with embarrassment at Mrs Bradley's anticipated discomfort. When the champagne arrived with a small plate of crackers, Mirabelle picked at them distractedly. Any hope that Bradley's widow might furnish a lead to help her find Flight Lieutenant Caine was over. It was unlikely the woman would even reply. I certainly wouldn't, she thought.

Trying to put aside her horror at what she'd done, Mirabelle focused. After all, that's what Jack would have said. Keep your eye on the ball. She drew her attention back to the matter in hand. What might this new information mean? Bradley was a British hero but so, it turned out, was Caine. Pilots had been revered for their courage: many men were brave (and women too), but not everyone risked their lives in quite such a demonstrable fashion. Now, it appeared she had two heroes on her hands, one of whom stole the other's fiancée while his friend was detained behind enemy lines. Perhaps this shed some light on the major's blank eyes at the nightclub all those years ago,

though it painted him terribly black. The chilled champagne twisted as it went down and Mirabelle repositioned herself in her seat.

What on earth had Bradley been thinking stealing his friend's girl? Had he simply fallen in love with someone forbidden? That was what had happened to her, after all. Jack hadn't loved his wife for years when Mirabelle had taken him on – not that she had had much of a choice. There was no doubt they had been meant for each other. It had felt absolutely right from the beginning. Had it been the same for Bulldog Bradley and Lady Caroline Bland? She considered this as she finished her drink rather too quickly and once more checked out of the window. A cab pulled up at the hotel's front door and she caught a swish of the porter's uniform as he rushed forward with a black umbrella. The tramp was still nowhere to be seen. This investigation felt difficult, like driving in fog. She imagined rolling out the story easily, like unfurling a long carpet, and tried to think where it might lead. Then, leaving money on the table, she stalked into the cold to try to find out.

The post-champagne glow helped distract her from the chill. The man, it seemed, had gone. The crowd thickened near Piccadilly Circus. Flocks of umbrellas concealed pedestrians from each other. At the junction Mirabelle ducked out of the rain and took the stairs down to the Tube. With such a lot to mull over, she hadn't decided which option she would pursue next and as a result she hovered uncertainly at the subterranean crossroads, where the tiled corridors were smeared with grubby melt. One branch led to the eastbound platform, the other to the west.

Then ahead, approaching from a set of stairs, the tramp rounded the corner and stopped, staring. Mirabelle felt suddenly furious. She hadn't fought the war to be afraid of some useless old man. Those days were over.

'Why are you following me?' she demanded. 'What do you want?'

The fellow was sheepish. He held out his palm. 'I need money, lady. I ain't eaten in two days.'

'But you've followed me all the way from Sloane Square.'

'You looked kind. Men don't give a fellow much, but a kind-looking lady . . .'

'You can't go about intimidating women,' Mirabelle snapped in temper.

The man shrugged. 'I just need help,' he said.

Mirabelle turned on her heel. This wasn't her responsibility. How dare he frighten her like that? Reaching into her pocket she fingered the scrap of paper bearing the address of the Red Cross archive, deciding she'd head for Kensington. The tramp leaned against the tiling as if he'd been punched and Mirabelle wondered why she had been so afraid of him. The war was over. It had been over for almost a decade. Why couldn't she let it go? The barrier loomed ahead but she didn't buy a ticket. Guilt twisted in her gut. She withdrew a shilling from her purse and turned back.

'If you want money, just ask. Don't go scaring women by following them about,' she said, and thrust the coin into the man's grubby hand.

He murmured a thank you but Mirabelle hardly heard it. She didn't want to think about the detritus of the war any more. She didn't want to feel guilty, and most of all she didn't want to harbour fearful suspicions about harmless old men.

The roar of the train approaching the platform was familiar. Mirabelle stepped aboard, took a seat, and tried to focus on the puzzle Bulldog Bradley had dropped into her lap as the carriage creaked and rocked its way under London.

If Philip Caine knew he'd lost the woman he loved, might he have given up trying to get home, she wondered? What was there for him to come back to? Heartbreak did strange things to people. She thought about the summer of 1942 – El Alamein and Stalingrad. The Battle for the Atlantic all but won and the

hopelessness of Operation Jubilee – the thousands of Allied troops who died or were taken prisoner in Dieppe. Jack had been restless. And yet, probably knowing very little of the news, Bulldog Bradley and Philip Caine had slipped out of their Stalag and made their way into French territory from where, it seemed, only one of them made it home. She tried to place the day she'd seen Bradley that night in the club – was it August or September? It was impossible to remember. The summer merged into a confusing jumble of air raid shelters and picnics in the park, long hours in the office and kissing Jack in a store cupboard. Recently she had found it difficult to distinguish between one phase of their relationship and another. It seemed as if she'd always known him. Mirabelle sighed. This wasn't helping.

Quarter of an hour later, emerging onto Kensington High Street, she noticed two chauffeurs in uniform smoking and chatting over the bonnet of a Bentley R type. The flower stall at the bottom of Church Street lit the dreary afternoon with a splash of holly. The side streets were unexpectedly steep, and turning the corner she checked the number on her scrap of paper against the figures mounted on the doorways. Here, at least, she hoped she'd find some answers.

The British Red Cross archive was housed in two buildings – numbers 20 and 22. Mirabelle picked her way up the hill past small front gardens with tiled pathways and painted wooden gates. Several of the flowerbeds had been planted with vegetables. She had almost made it to the top when a car emerged unexpectedly from the mews behind, splashed through a puddle and sent a freezing sloop of water over her feet. Mirabelle wished she'd worn her boots and cursed under her breath. Then, steeling herself, she opened the garden gate and knocked on the door. There was no reply, so she knocked again and rattled the letterbox. When that produced no response, she tried the handle.

Inside, the building seemed deserted. It had an air of disorganisation and decay that was becoming familiar. Piles of loose-leafed files teetered on what looked like tea trolleys placed about the hallway. At the bottom of the stairs three filing cabinets had been pushed awkwardly against the banister. Opposite them a spindle-legged table seemed too delicate to bear the weight of several padlocked tin document cases.

'Hello,' Mirabelle called, pushing open the door of the front room, where the disarray continued to such an extent that it took a moment to ascertain that there was nobody inside. She picked up a file and was horrified by a photograph of two stick-thin children, looking up ravenously from a meal of what appeared to be thin porridge. Behind it, two death certificates informed her that one had been called Girda and the other Max, although neither had a surname or, apparently, any knowledge of where they had originally come from. They died in November 1945 at the estimated ages of seven and eight years. They were so small they looked younger, except in the eyes. These children spoke German and Polish, someone had scribbled on the back of the picture – a clue in case anyone came looking and the photograph was not enough. It seemed so scant. Did all these files contain such terrible stories? There was hardly any space to move between the stacks, but could any amount of paperwork be adequate to encompass these tragedies?

Mirabelle returned to the hallway and tried another room, which was in a similar state of disorganisation, but on her third attempt she finally found someone. At the back of the building, in a small room that was in a slightly better state than the others, an old woman wearing a smart navy suit was poking about in a filing cabinet A crumpled handkerchief protruded from the old girl's sleeve and Mirabelle spotted a stain on her lapel that was only partly masked by an amethyst brooch. She was humming as she opened a box of papers, and as she looked

up there was a waft of lavender scent that Mirabelle guessed was comprised mainly of medical components.

'Hello.' She peered myopically at Mirabelle. 'Goodness, I expected someone far younger! What on earth were they thinking?'

Mirabelle laughed. The atmosphere had felt so heavy with history that the old lady's attitude came as a relief.

'Come in, come in.' The woman's accent was northern and she spoke too loudly, which suggested that she was slightly deaf. That was why she hadn't answered the door, Mirabelle thought: she hadn't heard it. 'I'll be glad of the help however old you are,' she continued cheerily. 'It's just you, is it?' She checked the hallway without pausing to let Mirabelle answer. 'Really, we'll need a team of six. I haven't taken on a job this large since I was stationed in Gibraltar.'

'Gibraltar?' Mirabelle raised her voice. 'That sounds like an adventure.'

'I'm Matron Gard.' The woman held out her hand.

'Mirabelle Bevan.' Mirabelle shook it.

'Well, it's high time they sent somebody,' the old lady said, guiding Mirabelle firmly back into the shabby hall and shepherding her into a tiny kitchen located under the stairs. 'Look at you, large as life and I'm sure you're cold too. It's freezing out there. Tea? Well, speak up. Do you take milk? There's some here somewhere.'

'The thing is, I was hoping to use the archive,' Mirabelle said as she took off her gloves. 'I'm looking for a missing person.'

The matron efficiently lobbed some tea into the pot and added a slug of hot water.

'Oh,' she said, sounding dejected. 'My dear, have I made the kind of error that only an old beast can? Do you mean you're not one of the girls they're sending to help? And I was so hopeful.'

'I'm afraid not.'

'I knew you didn't look the type.' Matron Gard sighed.

'Look at your nails. In general, girls who work with this kind of material aren't going to attract a fellow's attention, and that's the truth.'

Mirabelle withdrew her manicured hands from sight. 'Is the archive always so . . .' She wasn't quite sure how to frame the sentence.

'You mean is it usually in such a mess? Oh, yes. I'm afraid it's in the most dreadful state. It outgrew the last place, you see. And then we found these houses at short notice. The records had to be moved in a hurry and you can see the result. There's a saving grace, though only one, I'm afraid – they're organised geographically. That's how they delivered them. As to the rest,' the old lady cast her eyes upwards and Mirabelle momentarily wondered if she was referring to what lay upstairs, 'it's in God's hands. His and the secretarial team's, when they finally turn up. I expected them yesterday. I'm afraid we're really not ready for readers, my dear.'

Matron Gard added a small splash of milk and handed Mirabelle a cup of tea that let off an inordinate amount of steam. 'There's no sugar,' she said.

Mirabelle sipped. Her fingertips were so cold that touching the surface of the cup was painful, and she moved the tea from one hand to the other. Britain ran on tea, they said. At least that hadn't changed.

'Thank you. I was hoping the archive might help solve a mystery. It was the last request of a dying man, Major Matthew Bradley.'

Matron's nose crinkled as if she scented something impor- tant. 'Bulldog Bradley, is it?'

Mirabelle nodded. However eccentric she was, Matron Gard was sharp as a tack.

'He's dead, is he? That's a tragedy. He was one of our finest. But surely he was a young man and handsome? I seem to remember that. Gosh, he went early.'

'Lung cancer,' confided Mirabelle. 'I suppose he must have been thirty when he came out of France. Or close to it. I only met him twice, very briefly. He died last Friday and in his will he asked me to find an old friend, Philip Caine. Flight Lieutenant Caine? Do you know that name?'

Matron shook her head. 'Who is he?'

'He's the man Bradley escaped with. Somehow Caine got left behind in France. They last saw each other twenty miles outside Paris – I don't even know in which direction. I'm not sure why Bradley left it so long to start looking for him – it might be because of some double dealing over a woman, which is the only thing I've been able to find so far. In any case, Flight Lieutenant Caine seems to have been on the major's mind at the end, though they hadn't met since 1942. Caine's probably dead, isn't he?'

Matron Gard put down her teacup. 'Well, I must say, dear, I don't ever like to assume people are dead. If you were that man's mother how would you feel if someone just took it for granted that he was done for?'

'But it's so long ago,' Mirabelle burst out, suddenly passionate. 'The war has been over for almost ten years. If Caine was alive wouldn't Bradley have known? Wouldn't they have run into each other by now? He found me after all this time on a far more sketchy acquaintance. It all seems so long ago.'

Matron tutted. 'Nothing is long ago in an archive. In the records we treat the dead the same as the living. Why, that's the whole point of keeping papers. It doesn't matter if it's a hundred years or only a few weeks. It's all filed away, fresh as the day it went under the covers.'

Mirabelle eyed the nearest boxes. She could see why Matron Gard had been put in charge of sorting out this mayhem. The papers wouldn't dare stay disorganised for long.

'I suppose that's true,' she said, realising that Vesta thought of information in the same way. The files at McGuigan & McGuigan

contained fulsome records. When Mirabelle had challenged Vesta about it, she said you never knew when some small detail might be required. Now the habit seemed comforting.

Matron Gard continued. 'The trouble here is that, apart from the geographical filing, the system is very patchy. It's not even alphabetical yet. Some of it is filed according to date but not much. We'll get to the bottom of it eventually but there is a great deal to do, cross-referencing and so forth.' The old nurse thought for a moment. 'Do you want me to have a look for this fellow?'

Mirabelle found herself grasping the woman's thick fingers in gratitude. It had been a trying day.

'If you have French records . . .'

'French records? My dear. Almost the whole of the upper floor is French.' The matron waved her arm in the air with a flourish. 'The Red Cross had extensive field hospitals all over France. Tell me, what was this man's name again?'

'Philip Caine. Flight Lieutenant Philip Caine. RAF. He was a flier.'

'A pilot? So many heroes. I tell you what, he'll make a very good training exercise. We owe it to the people who died to make sure we record what happened properly. Who knows what information might be useful in the future? These records have reunited families. They've brought together comrades in arms. And – this is very important – sometimes they just let the people who are left know what happened. People don't always get to say goodbye.'

Mirabelle's expression betrayed her and the old lady paused. Fortunately, she was of a breed that would never ask a personal question no matter how much private information passed through her hands. 'I tell you what, when the team gets here that's what I'll start them on. They'll have to go through the lot in any case. We might as well take France first.'

Mirabelle smiled. She restrained herself from hugging the

old woman and instead focused on the information she required. 'He was last seen about twenty miles outside Paris in the summer of 1942. I don't have any more than that, I'm afraid.'

'Don't worry. If he's upstairs we'll track him down.'

'Is there a telephone here?'

Matron's eyes twinkled at the absurdity of Mirabelle's question. 'It might be better if you leave me an address. I shall write to you if we find something.'

'That's very helpful. Thank you.' Mirabelle reached for a pen and paper and decided that when she received the major's money she'd definitely make a donation. The British Red Cross was invaluable.

Chapter 6

There is nothing like a dream to create the future.

Feeling a good deal better, Mirabelle caught the Tube back across town. Perhaps things weren't hopeless after all. Bradley's request was odd but there was nothing threatening about it. If he hadn't mentioned Jack, she wouldn't have become so exercised. Really, it was time she moved on.

A little boy wearing shorts positioned himself on the seat opposite and perched on his heels, smudging the glass with his hot little hand until his mother became agitated and pulled him down into a sitting position. Mirabelle noticed the boy was strapped into a leather harness. Well, really, she thought. Even Panther can heel.

'Don't be a nuisance, Frankie.' The woman smiled apologetically and looked away.

Five minutes later Mirabelle disembarked at Embankment. Rain was dripping from the trees as she cut past Somerset House onto the Strand; the snow had all but disappeared. A thin fog wound across the pavement. Canopies weighed down by pools of rainwater sagged ominously over the shop doorways. A man in a shabby demob suit was smoking on the corner, in conversation with a woman whose winter coat was heavily patched. Mirabelle avoided their eyes. Outside a tobacconist's shop a life-size model of a Red Indian was chained to the railings.

Aware that her footsteps were echoing in her ears, Mirabelle turned along Kingsway and made for the Air Ministry. Matron

Gard had been willing to help, but the sheer volume of paper in the British Red Cross archive meant that tracking Philip Caine that way would take both luck and time, if he appeared in the records at all. This should be a more direct route: the RAF certainly ought to know what happened to one of their captured pilots.

The building loomed towards her, and through the fog she could just make out a jagged straggle of icicles that had frozen where the gutter overflowed. Periodically a thick drip of water plummeted four storeys to land on the pavement with a dull splash. Mirabelle pushed the brass handle of the glazed inner door. At the reception desk an attractive secretary with glossy dark hair held sway – another girl too young to have taken part in the war. Mirabelle wondered momentarily what had happened to the army of secretaries and Morse Code operators that peopled London's offices until 1945. Surely all of them couldn't have married and become housewives? Was she the only woman over thirty who was still single and in gainful employment? She and Matron Gard. Behind the desk, the girl's long legs crossed one way and then another as she studied an appointment diary. Mirabelle coughed.

'Excuse me, I'm looking for an RAF officer who went missing in France in 1942. Flight Lieutenant Philip Caine. He was an escapee.'

'Escapee?' The girl sounded perturbed, or perhaps confused.

'Yes. From a German prisoner of war camp.'

'Oh, I see.' The girl nodded primly, her eyes drawn back to the diary. 'We don't really deal with that kind of thing. I've never had an enquiry like that before.'

'I wondered if someone might remember him. Or if you might hold any records?' Mirabelle persevered. 'Would it be possible to find out who his commanding officer was?'

The girl's lips pursed. Her leg shifted as if she was terribly uncomfortable and this wasn't her concern. 'I don't know.

Lots of men never came home. It's an awfully long time ago, madam.'

Mirabelle felt a sting of anger. People wanted to forget the war; that was only natural. But there was a difference between putting the unpleasantness to the back of your mind and abandoning all duty to the memory of those who fought.

'Is there someone else who might be able to help?' she said crisply. 'The war has been over for some years, granted, but there must still be serving officers who knew the man I'm looking for. He was a pilot.'

The girl glanced over her shoulder. Mirabelle could hear typewriters in full flow and the low hum of conversation. The girl's lips parted. She knew she had to offer some kind of help but it was plain that she wasn't going to do so willingly.

'I think you might do best to contact the chap's regiment directly. Which squadron was your fellow in? I can put you in contact with them, wherever they're stationed. Though it has to be said, several wartime squadrons have disbanded now. They're not needed any more, you see.'

Mirabelle ignored the implication. 'Caine was a flier. A bomber. If you could help me find out his squadron, that would be marvellous. He was shot down over France in 1942.'

The girl's eyes warmed as she took this in. 'Hang on,' she said, figuring it out. 'You're searching for this fellow and you don't even know his unit? Aren't you a relation?' She sat back in her chair, flicking her pencil between long pale fingers. 'If you aren't related to him I can't give you any information. That's absolutely not on.' A cold flash of cruelty pulsed across her gaze. She looked as if she was enjoying this. 'You could be anyone. You could be a *journalist*.' The girl raised her voice as she made the assertion. 'You can't just walk in here and demand an officer's personal details.'

'But . . .'

Mirabelle wasn't sure what she ought to point out first.

What if Flight Lieutenant Caine had no family living? And didn't his escape partner count for anything? She was here, after all, at the request of a bona fide British hero. Suddenly, with a pang, she remembered what it had felt like when Jack had died. The loss turned in her stomach and she felt deflated. She had no real right there, either. If she tried to find out personal details about Jack at the Special Operations Executive, they'd kick her out. Of course they would. SOE made no allowances for women like her. Lovers. Mistresses. Friends. It was only blood that counted, and legal ties. A bit of paper was more important than love.

'You'll have to leave, madam,' the girl said firmly. She licked a finger and turned over a page, directing her attention back to the appointment diary, though a flicker of her long lashes betrayed the fact that she was watching to see if Mirabelle complied.

Mirabelle reeled. Her cheeks were burning and the sense of outrage was building like steam in a kettle. 'Well, really,' she spluttered. If someone had walked into her office during the war and enquired about a member of staff, yes, she'd have given them short shrift, but there was no reason to be rude.

The girl looked up slowly. 'I can't help you,' she said flatly, staring towards the door.

Humiliated, Mirabelle turned on her heel and marched into the freezing street with the words still stinging.

Outside, the cold air slapped her in the face. Jack's face appeared in her mind's eye. Her love for Jack was a shameful thing in the eyes of the world yet they had had eight wonderful years together. It was all so desperately unfair.

Grateful for the drizzle that hid her tears, she turned off Kingsway and passed a beggar sitting in a doorway. He had only one leg.

'Miss.' The man put out his hand.

Mirabelle felt suddenly indescribably angry. Why was there

nowhere for these men to go? Why wasn't the damage caused by the Blitz repaired by now? No wonder she felt haunted by the war – it wouldn't be over until things had been put to rights. She flung a coin at the man and in a flash realised that her fury was directed at Jack's wife – a woman who had been allowed her grief. 'He was mine,' she whispered. The loss curled inwards and it felt raw. What on earth was she doing here digging up this old story? Humiliating herself. She didn't owe Bulldog Bradley anything.

Without thinking she turned into the doorway of a pub. Inside, the regular afternoon drinkers shifted in the gloom as if they sensed new blood. She took a deep breath and realised she was the only woman in the place. The urge to scream or cry disappeared, and dismissing any reservations she stalked to the bar and ordered a whisky. When the single shot appeared the smoky taste revived her. She took out a handkerchief and dried her face.

'It's bitter outside,' the barman said.

Mirabelle was in no mood for small talk. She downed the rest of the malt in one.

'Thank you,' she managed as she pushed the glass back over the bar.

Suddenly she wanted to be back in Brighton – not here in the tatty, uncaring city. She wanted to run a long hot bath and stare at the crackle-glazed tiles on her bathroom wall and sit in the window afterwards and watch the world go by. She wanted to sleep in her own bed and forget that Bulldog Bradley had left her this troublesome bequest and that she'd written a thoughtless letter to his widow. She wanted to forget all of it.

Chapter 7

Happiness is a choice that requires effort.

Mirabelle slept only fitfully. It was still dark when she opened her eyes and for once she felt at peace. The winter dawn stole slowly over the horizon. The bedroom smelled faintly of orange bath oil. She had finished the last of the bottle the night before, that and the whisky, staying up late wrapped in Jack's old dressing gown watching the moon, warmed through by the lazy hot water. Now she fumbled for her watch and squinted, trying to focus on the tiny figures etched on the face in gold. It was only just seven o'clock. Outside the long window the streetlamps flickered and a policeman on his beat crossed the road and stood staring at the ocean. She watched him for a while, then shifted her gaze and caught sight of herself in the ornate mirror propped next to the fireplace. She did not look like the frantic woman she had been in London, but Mirabelle knew that grief and shame lingered only slightly under the surface. Jack was under her skin. He was part of her. She wondered what advice she would give herself if she were a concerned friend. Whatever it was, she doubted she'd take it – good advice was easier to give than to put into action. She'd tried hard to be good in the years since he died, but nothing had made her happy.

In the bathroom she splashed her face with cold water, relishing the shock. Then she pulled her green tweed suit and fur-lined ankle boots out of her wardrobe. Even on good days she rarely bothered with breakfast. There was no question of

eating this morning. Instead, at just past eight o'clock, she left her flat and turned down the Lawns in the direction of town.

First in the office, Mirabelle snapped on the lights. At this time of year the street outside appeared to exist in a permanent state of twilight. Getting back to a normal routine was what she needed, Mirabelle told herself as she looked round. Vesta's solitary cup and plate lay washed beside the sink and a list of Bill's calls for the day was propped on his desk. Several scraps of purple chiffon were folded neatly. Mirabelle pushed them aside and picked up a notepad covered in Vesta's handwriting: notes the girl had made in the library. As expected, Vesta had made a thorough job of it. Mirabelle began to read, although she had already decided that she wasn't going to proceed with her search for Philip Caine. Later she'd tell Mr Lovatt. Meanwhile, the results of Vesta's research were interesting.

Bradley's exploits had been reported in the *Daily Telegraph* and *The Times* alongside more dramatically expressed pieces in the popular press. His engagement was announced in September 1942 and the wedding had taken place three weeks later. After the war his name came up in the court circular now and then, or in connection with his local hunt, just as Mr Lovatt had said. His father-in-law had died in 1951, the same week, she noted, as Big Ben McGuigan. It was strange to think of these people leading their lives in tandem, huge events mirroring each other as they travelled in the same direction without ever meeting. Vesta appeared to have discovered nothing about Philip Caine, but perhaps she hadn't started searching for him yet. Digging up information took time. Mirabelle put down the notepad and stood by the window, staring at the grey paving stones on East Street.

At nine o'clock Bill arrived with Panther at his heel.

'Cold again,' he said cheerily, stamping his feet. 'At least it's stopped raining.'

Vesta, it seemed, had neglected to tell Bill that Mirabelle had even been away. Bill pulled the morning paper from inside his coat and laid it on the edge of her desk as he picked up the list of calls.

'Patcham,' he told Panther, who wagged his tail enthusiastically. 'Quite a sum outstanding in Patcham.' He nodded as he totted up what was due.

'What would you do, Bill, if there was a call you didn't want to make?' Mirabelle asked.

Bill looked up. 'Lummy,' he said. 'What do you mean?'

'You know. If there was something awkward. Something that felt wrong.'

'But it's my job. It's not up to me, is it?'

'It's never happened then?'

Bill considered. 'I don't like it when they ain't got nothing, know what I mean? Before Christmas I had to call to the flats at Carlton Hill. It was a couple. I doubt they was married. The feller owed two quid or something and when the girl opened the door half the floorboards were up. They were using them for firewood, see. You can't get blood from a stone. They shouldn't be giving people credit if they can't pay for it. They was young too – no more than twenty.'

'But you collected the money?'

Bill looked affronted at the idea he might have shirked his duty. 'It's my job, innit? Course I got it. Bit by bit. The bloke managed to get a job soon after and I called him on payday – weeks it took. I let him know I'd leave the girl out of it as long as he promised to get the money back. It was two, three shillings at a time, but he made it. They know they've got to pay. They know they're in the wrong, see?'

Mirabelle nodded. 'And if there was something uncomfortable that was personal? Someone you knew, perhaps?'

'The force knocks all that out of you, Miss Bevan. When I was a copper, or even now, if I had to make a call to an

55

acquaintance it's bound to be worse for them than it is for me. In your personal life you get to do what you like, but at work there's rules, isn't there? You've just got to get on with it.'

Mirabelle lifted up the paper and looked at the headlines without reading them. Bill was right, of course. Bulldog Bradley's bequest was a personal matter; it wasn't mandatory. Wherever Caine had ended up, she didn't need to get upset about it. She had a choice and she'd made the wrong one, but she was allowed to change her mind. Inside the offices of McGuigan & McGuigan things always ended up making sense.

The door opened and Vesta swept in, only ten minutes late.

'Oh, Mirabelle! I didn't think you'd be back so soon. I have great news. Charlie and I have set a date,' she announced. 'Spring, we thought. The last week in April. We reckoned we'd take a run down the coast for a few days afterwards. Charlie likes the idea of a honeymoon.'

'That's wonderful.'

Vesta delved into her capacious handbag and held up a list and more scraps of fabric – this time in an array of soft pinks. 'The trouble is, I can't decide between the peach and the rose petal.'

'I'd best get off.' Bill called Panther to heel and hurriedly swept out of the office. Vesta was oblivious.

'I've seen a couple of things in Hannington's but I hoped you might come with me to help choose,' she continued. 'There's such a lot to organise. My mum's finding it difficult. We asked her and Dad to come down for the wedding but she's told the neighbours that she thinks I've run away and got married on the quiet. She's embarrassed we're not having a big party at church.' Vesta raised her eyebrows. She loved her mother, but sometimes the relationship could be difficult. The Churchills had not approved of many of their daughter's choices. When they first discovered she was working at McGuigan & McGuigan they'd tried to make her come home.

And despite the fact that they liked Charlie, living in sin was unquestionably frowned upon.

When she heard the news that a date had finally been set, Mrs Churchill had been conciliatory but Vesta was well aware that this was because her mother was standing in a neighbour's hallway – the site of the only telephone on their street. The Kellys had been the first to get a television, before the Coronation the year before. Now they'd had a telephone installed, their house had become a veritable Euston Station.

'Whatever you think, Vesta,' Mrs Churchill had said, partly into the mouthpiece and partly in the direction of Mrs Kelly who was standing not ten feet away.

Vesta knew she'd get it in the neck the next time she went home unless the wedding was over and she was Mrs Lewis, in which case it would be too late. For now though, Mrs Churchill appeared resigned, having decided it was better simply to let her daughter get on with it. The truth would just have to be manipulated to make it more palatable in the eyes of her friends and neighbours; that was all.

Mirabelle filled the kettle at the sink and put it on to boil. 'Why don't we pop up to Hannington's at lunchtime?' she offered. 'We might as well make a start.'

Vesta beamed and turned to take off her coat. Mirabelle reached for the teapot. It felt good to be back. Later, she thought, she'd ring Mr Lovatt and tell him that she'd decided not to accept the terms of Major Bradley's will. Perhaps there was a provision to donate the money to charity or maybe it would simply go to Mrs Bradley, to whom, she felt, it really ought to have been bequeathed in the first place. She toyed with the idea of laying her own bouquet of flowers on Jack's grave at the weekend. That might help too.

'Superintendent McGregor called yesterday,' Vesta said as she poured the tea. 'I think he wanted to take you to dinner.'

Mirabelle sighed inwardly. That was another decision she

was going to have to make soon: what to do about Detective Superintendent Alan McGregor. Since the lunch at the Savoy two years before she had allowed him to take her out on several occasions – evenings which Mirabelle guiltily suspected meant far more to him than they did to her. She couldn't continue to lead him on. It wasn't good for either of them. She tried momentarily to decide whether she'd got herself into a pickle or simply into a rut.

'I'll call him later,' she said.

There was plenty to get on with in the meantime.

Chapter 8

Do not grow too wise for pleasure.

Hannington's had not yet put the spring collections on display. Mirabelle and Vesta walked through the main hallway, which was awash with perfume, and up the grand staircase. With one eye on the lush entrance to the fur department, located through a gold brocade curtain festooned with tassels, Vesta led Mirabelle to Evening Wear. A sorry rail of sale dresses languished to one side and a sales assistant was on her knees unpacking a box of full-length ballgowns. The girl sprang to her feet.

'Sorry, madam.' The apology was addressed to Mirabelle.

'No, please. Miss Churchill is only looking today,' she said, tactfully redirecting the assistant's attention. 'Vesta, I think what you need is a cocktail dress, if you're absolutely sure you won't stretch to something bridal.'

'Absolutely.' Vesta grinned. 'But not too racy.'

Mirabelle picked out a slash-necked red dress from the sale rack, but Vesta shook her head. Mirabelle was disappointed – the girl would suit the cut, but then all the colours in the winter collections would probably be too vivid for what she had in mind. Glancing round, Mirabelle could see it was going to be difficult. Vesta sank onto a gilded chair and perused the rails from a distance.

'There was a nice green one the other day, but it's gone,' she said sadly.

'We're looking for a softer colour, a peach, perhaps?'

Mirabelle told the sales girl. 'I wonder, might there be anything in the stock room? Do you know the green dress that Miss Churchill is asking about?'

The girl nodded. 'Yes, madam. It was sold. All the sale stock is on display. We're at a low ebb, but the spring collection will be on the rails in the next few weeks. This is the first of it.' She motioned towards the box she had been unpacking, which contained two dresses in a fetching shade of cream. Mirabelle caught sight of the pastel chiffon scraps Vesta had brought with her and came to a decision.

'I wonder, do you happen to have anything from last season? Autumn, or even summer? As I recall there was a rather nice lemon colour, and a purple. You can't have sold everything. What happened to the rest?'

The assistant hesitated. She looked around, but there wasn't a manager in sight.

'If you could let us see anything you have, we'd be most grateful,' Mirabelle went on.

'I'm not supposed to . . .' The girl spoke in a whisper. 'Usually the gowns go to the warehouse out of town, but what with the snow . . .'

Mirabelle's tone was persuasive. 'The thing is, Miss Churchill is getting married. And she wants a colour.'

Vesta held up her hand to display Charlie's three-stone engagement ring on her finger.

'The bridal department is upstairs.'

'Miss Churchill doesn't like white. Her skin tone, you see.'

The girl lost some of her poise. 'What is it you lot wear then?'

Vesta shrugged. 'Usually we wear white. Just like *you* lot. It's the *worst* colour – I don't want to look like an idiot. Do you have anything? Anything at all?'

The assistant paused as she made the decision. 'It's full length,' she said finally. 'It's not a cocktail dress.'

'Go and fetch it,' Mirabelle encouraged her. 'Let's take a look.'

The girl disappeared behind a red velvet curtain.

'I might have to have something made.' Vesta picked at the chiffon scraps with fluttering fingers as Mirabelle cast her eyes over a display of evening bags. 'That's what you'd do, isn't it? Get something made?'

'Not these days. I don't suppose I'll ever need a wedding dress. Off the rail somewhere like Hannington's can be wonderful, not to mention far more convenient.'

The assistant returned with a dress cased in a thin cotton bag. She undid the buttons and let the skirt cascade to the floor. Vesta gasped. It was a darker purple than she'd thought of – not violet or mauve, more a deep pansy. There was something regal about it. The assistant hung the dress in a changing cubicle and held open the door.

'It's a Ceil Chapman,' she said. 'American.'

'Charlie's American. He's from Delaware.' Vesta smiled as she disappeared inside.

'It's beautiful,' Mirabelle said warmly. 'Thank you.'

The girl blushed. They waited. After the initial sound of rustling silk and shuffling feet there was a long silence. The assistant bit her lip. Mirabelle checked the time. After another minute Mirabelle stepped forward.

'Are you all right, dear?' she tapped gently on the dressing-room door.

Silence. She pushed it open. Inside, Vesta was reflected on all sides, with tears streaming down her face. The dress was a perfect fit, nipped in at the waist and demure around the shoulders. She looked as if the gown belonged to her already and she'd been going to wear it all along. Mirabelle smiled, and reached into her handbag for a handkerchief. Vesta took it.

'It's far too beautiful,' she sobbed.

'Now, now. Nothing is too beautiful for you, dear. It's your wedding day.'

Vesta heaved an anguished sigh and turned to inspect the back of the dress in the mirror.

'It'll be far too expensive,' she said. 'It's from the States.'

'Well, it's last season – I'm sure we can do something. Why don't you let me buy it for you – as a wedding present?'

That set Vesta off again.

'I love Charlie. That's the thing,' she gulped.

'You're supposed to enjoy this, you know. I don't understand why you've been fighting it.'

'I am enjoying it. Really I am. Do you mean it, Mirabelle? It would be the best present in England.'

Mirabelle laughed. 'A teapot is more traditional, but I prefer this by quite some way. Now stop crying.'

Perhaps she'd have dissolved into tears if she'd ever had to buy a wedding dress. She'd have chosen cream. The wedding would have been at the register office, it being Jack's second time around. She'd have picked something knee length with a feathered skull cap, but there was no question what Vesta would be wearing down whichever aisle she chose – the purple dress was perfect.

She turned to the assistant. 'We'll take it.'

The girl shifted. 'It's got no price,' she said. 'It was in the sale but the ticket's fallen off.'

Without hesitation Mirabelle reached into the inside pocket of her handbag and withdrew three white five-pound notes.

'That will cover it,' she said. 'How you account for it is your business.'

The assistant blushed. 'My,' she said. 'Thank you, ma'am. Would you like to have it delivered?'

'No.' Vesta's face appeared round the changing-room door. 'I don't want to leave it behind.'

Coming out of Hannington's and strutting down the drizzly street, Vesta couldn't stop smiling. A boy in a red knitted hat

wheeled a bicycle uphill and she moved the box to let him pass. As the bulky cardboard shifted she could swear she heard the dress crinkling amid reams of tissue paper.

'I'll need to hide it from Charlie, won't I?'

'You can leave it in the office,' Mirabelle offered as they turned into Brills Lane.

The lighting was on the fritz again and the hallway was dull even compared to the natural light outside. The women took the stairs two by two and it wasn't until they reached the top that they heard the telephone ringing. Mirabelle unlocked the door. Vesta rushed inside, flicked on the lights and stowed the Hannington's box behind one of the filing cabinets while gracefully leaning over to pick up the receiver. Her voice sounded absolutely calm – not at all like a woman who had just bought a purple wedding gown and couldn't bear to be parted from it.

'McGuigan & McGuigan Debt Recovery?'

'Miss Bevan?'

The woman's voice at the other end of the line was crisp and to the point. She sounded smartly dressed, Vesta realised, although on reflection she decided not to tell Mirabelle that. She would only be told off for having a vivid imagination. Mirabelle had removed her coat and switched on the fire. The bar began to glow. Vesta hardly missed a beat.

'Please hold and I'll transfer you. Whom shall I say is calling?'

'Mrs Caroline Bradley.'

Wide-eyed, Vesta paused. She covered the mouthpiece. 'It's the widow,' she mouthed, and held out the telephone.

'What widow?'

'Mrs Bradley,' Vesta hissed.

Mirabelle smoothed a loose strand of hair behind her ear before taking the call. Her chest had constricted but she was determined not to let it show in her voice. She took a deep deliberate breath as she lifted the receiver to her ear.

'Mirabelle Bevan,' she said.

'Miss Bevan, I'm calling because I received your letter.'

'Yes, and I must apologise,' Mirabelle cut in. It would be best to get that out of the way. 'When I wrote to you I had no idea of your previous engagement to Flight Lieutenant Caine, Mrs Bradley. I discovered what had happened only after I had posted the letter. You must have had a horrible shock when you read it. I'm most dreadfully sorry.'

'"Discovered" my previous engagement? What on earth do you mean? What kind of "horrible shock"? Miss Bevan, it sounds as if you have been investigating my private life like some kind of seedy snoop. There is nothing underhand here. I want to make it clear I have absolutely nothing to hide. None the less, I don't appreciate your deciding to poke your nose into my business. I don't appreciate it at all.' The woman sounded furious.

'Major Bradley asked me . . .' Mirabelle began, but Mrs Bradley cut her off, clearly more intent on what she had to say than on Mirabelle's response.

'That is exactly what I want to talk to you about, Miss Bevan. Matthew was quite unsettled at the end, I'm sad to say. He wasn't in his right mind. In the circumstances it seems best to discuss the matter in person. I would like to see you at four thirty this afternoon.'

'Four thirty?' Mirabelle was confused. 'Where?'

'I came down at once, don't you see? This sort of thing can't be allowed to fester. I'm staying with an old family friend in Hove. The house is called Moorcroft, at the end of Selborne Road. I won't have it, you know. You can't cast aspersions and rake people's names through the mud in this derogatory fashion. There was absolutely nothing that wasn't respectable about my engagement to Flight Lieutenant Caine. Lots of girls have more than one beau. My late husband must have been confused. I simply can't imagine what he meant by all this.'

'Look, I've decided not to accept the Major's bequest in any case.'

Mrs Bradley didn't appear to be listening. 'Four thirty,' she said decisively and hung up.

Mirabelle sank into the chair behind her desk with the telephone in her hand. She looked at the mouthpiece in dismay. This wasn't what she had had in mind for the afternoon. Vesta pulled two ham rolls from her bag and set them on the table.

'You'll need lunch,' she pointed out. 'Mrs Bradley's here, is she?' Vesta retrieved the telephone from the older woman's grasp and hung it up. 'Why on earth do you think she came down?'

Mirabelle shrugged her shoulders. Surely a newly bereaved widow must have more on her plate than hightailing it to meet a woman her husband had asked to deal with a matter well over a decade old. 'I don't know. I'll have to go and see her, I suppose.'

Vesta picked up one of the rolls and handed it over. 'Go on,' she insisted. 'I'll make us a brew.'

Chapter 9

*The price of anything is the amount
of life you exchange for it.*

Selborne Road stretched south to north into the heart of
Hove. Mirabelle knew the street. The houses just up from
First Avenue had been built in Victorian times. Near the main
road some of them had been converted into shops and flats,
but as the road continued it quickly became residential and the
villas were occupied by the same sector of the population they
had been intended for decades before – Brighton's well-to-do.
Though the architecture wasn't as swanky as some of the
white stucco terraces that had been erected in the town's Georgian heyday, the houses were popular as family homes.

The pavement led steeply uphill. The light was already
fading, and it would be dark soon. When Mirabelle was halfway to the top, the lamps clicked on up the left side of the
street, leaving the right-hand pavement in relative darkness.
It was difficult to make out the name plaques on the houses.
Mirabelle's heart raced as she peered through the gloom,
scanning the front doors for a sign saying *Moorcroft*. Towards
the end of the road all the houses had names rather than
numbers – a sign, she thought, of the residents' aspirations.

Mirabelle crossed the tarmac several times, peering at the
nameplates on either side. Three or four vehicles were parked
in the street, obscuring some of the names. Eventually, dodging one way and another, she located the correct house.
Moorcroft was well maintained. The gate didn't squeak as

Mirabelle pushed it open and looked up at the building. Inside, the lights were on; smoke drifted from the chimney and disappeared instantly, subsumed by the clouds. Over the door the fanlight glowed gold. At least it looks warm, Mirabelle comforted herself as she approached. She was expecting to be berated and only hoped the visit needn't last too long. To her left the tiny front garden was frozen, a few laurels and a brittle rosemary bush holding out against the chill. In the gloom she rang the bell without looking. Inside, nothing shifted for a moment and then a maid appeared.

'Mrs Bradley is expecting me. I'm Miss Bevan.'

The girl stood back and Mirabelle slipped past, handing over her coat. Something is wrong, she thought. There's something I haven't noticed. Oblivious of Mirabelle's unease, the maid laid her things on a chair and led the way upstairs. 'The ladies are in the drawing room.'

Mirabelle followed, trying to ignore the niggling feeling that pulsed in her brain. Instead, she attempted to focus on her surroundings. The hallway was papered in peach with garlands of white and yellow flowers. Above an oak dresser a couple of well-executed landscapes hung on the wall. A pair of brass candlesticks stood on the table in case there was a power cut. The stairs were carpeted in green, held in place by polished brass rods. A hundred other houses on this road and those round it must look the same. There was nothing extraordinary about it. And yet her skin prickled.

Upstairs, the maid opened the door into the warmth of a comfortable room with a bay window. It was decorated in pale blue with an impressive number of colourful paintings on display, many of which were quite modern. The room was in sharp contrast to the more traditional hallway. Someone in the family must be a collector. A fire was roaring in the grate, and on a sofa in front of it, partly obscured by the inordinate number of cushions stacked along its perimeter, sat two

women. One was dressed in a dark brown suit set off by a slim red leather belt. She was smoking a cigarette in an amber holder and holding a cocktail glass in her other hand. She rose to her feet, and Mirabelle's nagging unease resolved itself in a flash of horrified recognition. Her fingers began to tremble as Jack's widow greeted her with a thin smile.

'You must be Mirabelle Bevan.'

The women had never met, but Mirabelle had seen Mrs Duggan a few times over the years, though always in the distance. The woman's tone was cool and superior. She was not in a rush. Her hair had been cut short, Mirabelle noted. It suited her, curling around her ears like an elfin cap. She seemed younger in widowhood – more vibrant. Would Jack have said she looked like a beautiful imp?

'Yes.' She nodded weakly. 'Mirabelle Bevan. That's me.'

'Mary Duggan.'

Mirabelle took in the room in a whirl as it finally sank in that she was standing in Jack's house. She had never been here – never even been close. She was not the kind of woman who stalked her lover, who hung around outside his family home, but she had known he lived in Selborne Road. He had even told her the number, but all the way along the pavement she had focused solely on the names, as if she was determined not to notice the only thing about Selborne Road that mattered. How had she not realised that this had been Jack's home? Her mind flew back to the moments she had stood on the doorstep. There had been no number, she was sure of it, and no family nameplate – only the name of the house. But here it was – the place where Jack had died. His sudden heart attack struck out of the blue on the street outside the front door. With a stab, she realised that she'd walked past the spot without even noticing. He had set out that morning to visit her, as he did every day. But when he died no one came to tell her because no one knew she was there, waiting for him.

Mirabelle tried to stay calm. I must get out of here quickly, she thought.

Her eyes were drawn to the mantelpiece, which housed an ormolu clock and a stack of formal invitation cards. It appeared Mrs Duggan was a sought after guest. There was a photograph of two girls – Jack's daughters. Twins. In the picture they were outside, laughing. It was sunny. The image almost took Mirabelle's breath away. One of the girls looked particularly like Jack – or a slim, younger version of him. Above the photograph, in pride of place, was an oil painting of an old man. Mirabelle wondered momentarily who he might be. He didn't look like Jack at all – perhaps he came from Mrs Duggan's side of the family. She felt giddy.

'This is Caroline Bradley.' Mrs Duggan indicated the other woman – a smartly coiffed blonde with hard eyes, wearing mourning dress.

Mirabelle struggled to control her emotions and realised that she felt sick. 'I'm so sorry for your loss, Mrs Bradley,' she managed. 'I want to say, first of all, that I had no idea when I wrote to you that you had any personal connection to Flight Lieutenant Caine. And I also want to be quite clear that I made no arrangement with Major Bradley. I hardly knew him. I was shocked to hear that he had left this bequest in his will. I hadn't expected it.'

Mrs Duggan stubbed out her cigarette in the ashtray. 'You worked for my late husband, didn't you, Miss Bevan? When he was in London. Poor Jack.'

Mirabelle could only nod. Mrs Duggan sized her up.

'Perhaps I ought to have been in touch with you before. I could have done with some secretarial assistance after Jack died. He left our affairs in a dreadful mess.'

Mirabelle bit her tongue. There was no point in keeping her own counsel all this time only to lose her temper now. She didn't want to hurt Mrs Duggan, or, more important, her

daughters. The girls were, after all, the reason Jack had waited before pursuing a divorce. He wanted them to have finished their education, or at least be living away from home before he caused what would have been a family scandal. Nevertheless, the idea that he might have left his personal papers in some kind of mess was inconceivable. Jack was highly organised.

'I'm sorry to hear that,' she got out. 'I hope you found a way to sort things out.'

'It was a grim business.' Mrs Duggan waved a hand in the air as if flicking away a fly. 'One finds out such a great deal once everything is over, as Mrs Bradley is discovering. She is disconcerted to say the least, aren't you, Caroline? Might I offer you a drink, Miss Bevan? Please.' She indicated a chair.

Mirabelle dropped into the cushions like a ball caught in a large leather glove. Out for six. Mrs Duggan turned to the drinks cabinet and began mixing a cocktail. There was a display of flowers on a side table – all out of season. Then Mirabelle realised they had been dried. The chrysanthemums and hydrangeas must be crisp. She met Caroline Bradley's eye.

'I don't want to take up the Major's bequest,' she said. 'I decided last night. This really has nothing to do with me. I can't imagine what he was thinking.'

Caroline Bradley inclined her head. 'Yes. Matthew was ill. He became unreasonable at the end. It does no good to go digging up the past. But I understand from your letter that you started to investigate, Miss Bevan. I'm curious. Did you turn up anything?'

The tiniest pause hung in the air, hovering in the space between the women – a strange unequal triangle. Then Mirabelle found she couldn't help herself. 'Nothing more than I told you . . . but, Mrs Bradley, do *you* have any idea what happened to Flight Lieutenant Caine? I must say, it does seem odd that he just disappeared.'

The widow's eyes blazed. 'Well, of course not,' she snapped. 'I was horrified when I realised what Matthew had done. No

good can come of it. All this time I assumed Philip was dead. He must be dead. Everyone said so.'

'Did they? I wondered, you see, if Mr Caine had a family. Siblings? Parents?'

'No. Not really. They're all long passed now. Even his brother died. He was RAF too, 52 Squadron. He was shot down in Burma and that was that.'

'But Philip Caine flew in Europe?'

'Yes. The 51st. That was their father's squadron. In the Great War. The old man was obsessed by Zeppelins. Philip was a career flier – not like Pete, his brother. When the squadron was re-formed Phil jumped at the chance to fly with the 51st. He patrolled U-boats for a while. Then he was chosen for bombing raids – pilots with experience were in demand, you see. That's when he was shot down.'

'And his father is dead too? Both his parents?'

'Oh, yes. Old Mr Caine died after the Great War. His mother died shortly after Philip didn't come home. Missing in action. Losing two sons – it doesn't bear thinking about. I suppose there might be some cousins. Miss Bevan, but you can't go raking people's reputations through the mud. I won't have it.'

Mirabelle wondered momentarily to whose reputation Mrs Bradley was referring.

'The Bradleys are old family friends,' Mrs Duggan cut in. 'I know my late husband would want Mrs Bradley's wishes to be respected, Miss Bevan. Especially at this difficult time.'

She handed Mirabelle a glass. Mirabelle sipped slowly. The iced gin slipped satisfyingly over her lips. It was most refreshing. Had there been two Jack Duggans, she wondered? The man who lived here and drank gin cocktails in this comfortable upstairs drawing room and accompanied his wife to at least some of the events denoted by the stack of invitation cards on the mantel. The man whose social circle, unbeknownst to her, included the Bradleys. And her Jack – a man who was

indomitable, clever and brave. A man who drank whisky and waltzed her round the bedroom in her silk negligee before laying her gently on the mattress. A man who loved the airy high ceilings down at the front. Mrs Duggan did not look like a lady who waltzed – certainly not *en déshabillé*.

'It must be difficult,' Mirabelle said. 'There really aren't words. May I ask, how are your daughters, Mrs Duggan?'

'Oh fine.' Mrs Duggan waved a hand. 'They have turned out to be *career* girls. Young women today enjoy that kind of thing. And of course one is so much more resilient when one is younger. Isla is working at *Vogue*. Lilian found a place at the British Museum. The children are all you have left.' She directed the last comment to Caroline Bradley.

'Did they go to college?' Mirabelle asked. 'I know Mr Duggan was very keen that they should have an education.'

'Yes – they left home almost directly after he died. The graduation was last year. Caroline looked after them a good deal while they were at university, didn't you, dear?'

Mrs Bradley finished her cocktail. 'Durham,' she said. 'Fine Art. I'm always happy to keep an eye on a friend's offspring. Weekends; the odd lunch. It was fun really. Perhaps when Jenny is old enough someone might return the favour. Though the poor thing is a bit of a dummy when it comes to school work. I can't imagine she'll go on.'

'How old is your daughter?' Mirabelle enquired politely.

Mrs Bradley deposited her empty glass on a side table. 'Far too young to be worrying about higher education. She's pony mad at present. I was the same at her age. It'll be some time before I need to think of her leaving home. So, Miss Bevan, have we persuaded you?'

'Persuaded me?'

'To throw over this ridiculous quest of Matthew's. Don't you see? It won't achieve anything. I think he was out of his mind at the end. And really, it's too intrusive.'

'Yes,' Mirabelle said. 'I understand.'

'I can talk to Lovatt and see if we can get you a payment – a sweetener, they call it, don't they?' Mrs Bradley offered. 'But the terms of the bequest, I hope you can see now . . . it's simply not on.'

'That won't be necessary. I just feel sorry that it's been so distressing for you.'

'Well, that's a relief.' Mrs Bradley scrambled for her handbag. 'But you must let me give you something for your trouble.' She withdrew her chequebook and a fountain pen.

Mirabelle got to her feet. 'Not at all. I won't hear of it. Please. I have to go home and get changed for dinner,' she lied. 'We're dining out and I don't want to be late.'

The women nodded. 'How nice to have someone waiting for you,' Mrs Bradley said as she put away the chequebook and snapped shut her handbag.

Mirabelle did not contradict her. A sense of relief settled in the room. Jack's widow refilled her glass and took a sip.

'Don't let us keep you.' She reached for the bell. 'Time is marching on. I'll have Alison show you out.'

Chapter 10

*Say what you will, 'tis better to be left
than never to have been loved.*

Mirabelle stumbled down Selborne Road in the darkness. The main road was busy – it was rush hour. Buses were crammed with people on their way home from work. Shops were taking in their displays for the night. Mirabelle felt grateful for the cold. It cleared her head – and not only after the gin. The frozen air felt like silk and she kept going, down First Avenue all the way to the front. She didn't want to go home. Instead, she crossed the road and stood on the grass verge, staring at the vast black ocean and wishing the darkness would engulf her.

Seeing Jack's home had shifted something. Mirabelle understood suddenly that his memory didn't only belong to her. Up till now she had hoarded him. She had considered the Jack she knew to be the only Jack Duggan – the authentic one. This afternoon it had become apparent that Mrs Duggan owned a side of her husband that Mirabelle had never seen. And that man was real as well.

'I was his mistress,' she said out loud. 'That was all.' Jack's death had left her permanently stranded on the wrong side of everything. But then, if he had left his wife and married Mirabelle, would it have made much difference after he died? She'd have been able to admit her grief publicly, but she'd still be on her own. Sometimes things just didn't work out according to plan.

Mirabelle took a seat on one of the wooden benches that

lined the strip of lawn. Behind her the windows of the tall buildings on the front glowed jewel-like out to sea, and above her the moon glowed back. Brighton was beautiful. In the distance she could make out the gaudy fairy lights on the pier and the flashing signs outside the amusement arcades. The front had changed. During the war the beach had been mined and everything had been blacked out. For years it was off limits. Now it had been reopened and taken back into the public domain – not only by the tourists but by the locals too. Further along the pebbles there were still a couple of decommissioned bombs on display – blasts from the past, jokers quipped. During the daytime they were generally surrounded by groups of small boys.

Feeling free, Mirabelle turned to the west and strode away from town. It's my life and I really ought to be living it, she thought as the Georgian buildings slid into Victorian ones and then into a more modern Edwardian style. Soon there were clear patches between the houses and the street lighting became intermittent. The grand pendant lamps overhead were replaced by cheaper versions and up one or two of the streets she could swear she caught glimpses of old-fashioned gaslights. Mirabelle didn't know this side of town. She usually stuck to her own area set back from the Lawns, walking between the flat and the office, and if, at the weekend, she decided to take a stroll, the bright lights and action of the town centre always appealed more than the peppering of residential streets that led away from it. Even when Alan picked her up in the motor, they drove to cosy pubs inland on the Downs or to restaurants to the east of the city, in Hastings or Eastbourne.

She had walked quite some way when she came across a lighthouse. It was now so black she could hardly make out the harbor below it. Only the steady ripple of light on the water allowed her to see at least some of the shoreline. As she listened, the hiss and rush of water betrayed a straggle of boats

moored below. There was nothing in the immediate area bar a row or two of fishermen's cottages, whose windows were mostly dark. She must have walked miles. Suddenly her legs felt tired. She thought of Mrs Duggan and Mrs Bradley, in the dining room at Moorcroft, eating a dinner prepared by Mrs Duggan's cook. Fish, surely – the most appropriate meal for a recent widow. Mirabelle touched her stomach and realised with some surprise that she was famished. Her fingers were so cold she could scarcely feel them. It would take a long time to get back to town. She hadn't heard an engine for miles.

Taking her chances, she continued along the road. Somewhere soon there must be a sign of life, if only she strode out. Twenty minutes on there was another scattering of dark houses. Away from the shoreline she heard a door slam and the sound of feet on paving stones. A murmur of conversation carried on the freezing winter air. Then the coast road veered suddenly inland and following it, Mirabelle was rewarded by the sight of a pub with its windows lit. The sign over the door said *The Blue Dolphin*.

Inside, the room was warm and light. A huge fire blazed in the grate and the heat felt overwhelming at first after the long cold walk. The buzz of conversation didn't abate as she came through the door and saw several people, mostly men, sitting at the tables. The air smelled of beer and something else – the buttery scent of baking. Behind the bar a red-faced man with an even redder scarf tied at his neck nodded as she approached.

'I'm looking for something to eat,' she said. 'And a half pint of stout if you have it.'

The man pulled out a glass and carefully filled it with creamy dark beer, checking the froth meticulously. Satisfied with his work, he laid the glass on the top of the bar.

'We got pickled onions,' he said.

'I can smell something cooking,' Mirabelle said hopefully.

'That'd be Martha's pie. That's our supper. We don't sell food over the counter, miss.'

'Is there a café nearby? Or a restaurant?'

The barman smiled. 'No. There's nothing like that. There's a shop but it's closed by now and mostly it sells tins, in any case.'

Mirabelle tried to hide her disappointment. She picked up the stout and took a sip. It slid down her throat too easily.

'This'll do,' she said, taking a seat at the bar. 'I've walked here from Brighton. Tell me, where have I got to?'

The barman looked bemused. 'Shoreham-by-Sea. You're six miles out of town at least. Cold night like this it'd feel far further. You didn't walk all the way?'

Mirabelle looked down at her shoes, which, without question, were not designed for hiking.

'Yes,' she said, trying not to think about how she might get back to town. There was clearly no point in asking if Shoreham-by-Sea had a hotel, or for that matter a taxi service. She took off her gloves and rubbed her hands together as the door opened and a girl came in. There was a murmur of welcome around the room.

'It's a perisher tonight,' the girl said cheerily.

The barman poured a tot of gin and added some water. 'There,' he said, laying it on the bar. 'That'll always keep an Adams going.'

'Thanks, Dad.'

'Give us a song, Mhairi!' one of the men shouted.

'Let me get my coat off first,' Mhairi objected, undoing her buttons and laying the coat on a stool next to Mirabelle. Then she downed the gin in one before she moved towards the fire. The background hubbub of men's voices faded to an anticipatory silence. Mhairi paused, her cheeks still pink from the biting cold. The hem of her dress was squint, one of her front teeth was missing and she was as skinny as a rake, but she looked regal somehow, and full of grace, as if she was in charge of the room – an impression bestowed by her bearing alone. She began to sing, unaccompanied – just her voice and

the sound of the huge log crackling in the grate. The first notes hung in the air like the chiming of a bell and the girl built the melody from there. As she finished the final chorus the audience burst into enthusiastic applause. She scarcely paused before starting a love song and then a jolly ditty which had the whole room clapping, Mirabelle included. One man stood up and danced at his table. At the end the audience burst into raucous chatter and the barman laid another gin on the counter.

'That was wonderful,' Mirabelle said as the girl came over.

'Thanks. It ain't exactly Covent Garden.'

Mirabelle tried to remember the last time she'd kicked up her heels without feeling weighed down. It had been a while, but here, sitting up at the shabby bar she felt strangely contented. Mhairi Adams hopped onto a bar stool.

'I ain't seen you here before.'

'I walked from Brighton.'

'That's miles.'

'I'm not sure how I'm going to get back.'

'Got carried away, did you? Well, the trains is finished for the night. Ain't you got a fancy man who'd come and get you?'

Mirabelle paused, contemplating the remains of the glass of stout. 'I suppose I have.'

'Thought so.' Mhairi smiled, eyeing Mirabelle's outfit. 'You look like you'd have someone reliable. Someone nice.'

It transpired that Shoreham-by-Sea had a policeman. Constable Shearer was summoned and had no qualms about using police resources to put a lady in trouble in touch with Detective Superintendent McGregor.

'Scotsman, isn't he?' the young constable checked. 'I've heard of him.'

Mirabelle nodded.

'Go on then, Sam. I'm sure the lady doesn't want to be sitting here till closing,' the barman chided.

Sam lumbered off in the direction of his police box. Mirabelle ordered another half of stout and Mhairi stood in front of the fire and sang three more songs. Mirabelle began to daydream about taking a holiday. It would be lovely to have a break.

Almost an hour later, when McGregor arrived, Mhairi had produced a pack of cards and was four games of rummy up on Mirabelle, which meant four shillings. The girl was a capable player.

'I hope that's just friendly,' the superintendent commented as he leaned on the bar. 'Gambling in licensed premises isn't allowed.'

Two men sitting at a nearby table scooped up their dice, and Mirabelle smiled. It crossed McGregor's mind that he'd never seen her look so happy.

'Are you all right?' he asked.

Mirabelle pushed a ramshackle pile of sixpences over to Mhairi, an action which the policeman pointedly ignored. 'I was hoping for a lift home.'

McGregor looked surprised. It would have been far more like Mirabelle to have called him because she'd discovered a body in the cellar or suspected that an old lady was being swindled out of her savings.

'A lift?' he said. 'Right. Maybe we should just have one for the road, eh?' He ordered two whiskies without waiting for Mirabelle's reply. Mhairi disappeared with her winnings, giving a meaningful wink as she slipped behind the bar and upstairs. Perhaps, Mirabelle mused, the lucky girl would be treated to a slice of Martha's pie. She clinked glasses with the superintendent.

'You've never asked for help before,' he said.

'Do you mind?'

'No.'

McGregor stared straight into her eyes and Mirabelle found

she was blushing. The truth was, he'd been waiting for this for months now: a sign that Mirabelle might let him in.

Outside, he held open the car door as she slipped into the front seat. He started the engine and let it run. The exhaust streamed a thick cloud into the pitch-black air and the windows steamed up. McGregor cleared them with the back of his hand and snapped on the headlights, revealing Constable Shearer, fifty yards away on his rounds. As the constable turned the corner, McGregor took his chance.

Mirabelle didn't start as the superintendent leaned in and kissed her. His arm slid across the back of the seat and scooped her towards him. He tasted of whisky and his skin was rough where he hadn't shaved, but Mirabelle kissed him back. As he pulled away she sat there with a bemused expression. She hadn't thought of Jack. Not for a second. And she didn't feel guilty. Not a bit.

'I've wanted to kiss you for a long time, Belle.'

'I won't go any further,' she stuttered, cursing herself for sounding young and stupid. Her fingers were trembling.

'Of course not.'

McGregor put the car in gear and set off towards Brighton. Neither of them said a word. Landmarks loomed in the darkness and disappeared as the car's headlamps passed. Coming into town, McGregor sneaked a glance Mirabelle's way. She was peering out of the window. As they approached the turn-off for Selborne Road she jerked upright in her seat.

'Can we take a detour? Up there?'

McGregor calmly turned the car and slowed the pace. 'What are we looking for?'

'Pull up here.' Mirabelle pointed.

The lights were still on at Moorcroft and the curtains had been drawn. The street was silent, every comfortable home locked up for the night. Mirabelle got out of the car and stood staring at the pavement, where it had happened. The cold

sobered her as she loitered, waiting for the sky to fall in. But Jack wasn't there. He wasn't anywhere. Not even his ghost. In the house next door a light clicked off. A cat stalked past Mirabelle's ankles and jumped across a low garden wall. The frozen air smelled of smoke from the silent, belching chimneys. Life goes on. The thought struck without warning, startling her, but there it was.

Back in the car she smoothed her coat over her knees.

'Thanks,' she said. 'I was just checking on a friend.'

McGregor touched her face lightly. 'You're cold.'

'It's a cold night.'

McGregor nodded. He didn't want to ask more. Mirabelle was always an enigma, and he had the sense that if he pushed her, she'd bolt. He turned the car back towards the main road and wondered if she'd let him kiss her goodnight.

Chapter 11

Suspicion always haunts the guilty mind.

Mirabelle wore her cashmere the next morning. The chocolate brown dress had been a gift from her mother when she went up to Oxford. It was old-fashioned now but very warm and she was glad to find it still fitted like a glove. Turning up East Street she strode out smartly for McGuigan & McGuigan. Vesta was already in. A pot of tea sat on the side ready for action and the office was warming up, the morning edge already gone from the air as the little electric fire did its job.

'Well?' Vesta asked. 'How was the widow?'

Mirabelle peeled off her coat. 'I really don't understand why Mrs Bradley came down. Perhaps in her bereavement she's become irrational. She seemed worried about her good name. Or maybe it was Bulldog's good name. Anyway, it doesn't matter.'

She poured milk into her cup and stirred meditatively. Vesta left her to think and leafed through the first post, sorting the envelopes into separate piles. She placed one stack on Mirabelle's desk, kept the other for herself, and raised a letter opener. 'Race you!'

Mirabelle raised her eyebrows, but as she went to work with the knife she felt a certain satisfaction that she was keeping pace. In the event, though, Vesta finished ahead.

'I'm sure I had more mail,' Mirabelle objected.

Vesta giggled and scrambled to remove the letters and

invoices from the now open envelopes. Once more Mirabelle followed her lead, but only a few seconds into the task she stopped, her glossy red nails hovering over the third in the pile. She held the contents between her fingers – a handwritten letter on thick white paper that ran to two pages. The address written at the top in a clear if old-fashioned hand was the little road off Kensington High Street where Matron Gard held sway. Mirabelle tried to focus. She hadn't expected this. Neither, it seemed, had Matron Gard.

Dear Miss Bevan,

I had not thought to be writing to you so soon but we have been extraordinarily lucky to find a trace of your Flight Lieutenant Philip Caine. He received care in the summer of 1944 in one of our hospitals near Longchamp, Paris. He had suffered wounds consistent with a shrapnel injury. It appears Flight Lieutenant Caine had taken part in the small amount of fighting that ensued when the Nazis retreated from the city. The hospital was run in tandem with the American service – in fact the running and resources were turned over to the American Hospital of Paris some time after VE Day. For this reason the record is incomplete and some papers probably reside in the care of the hospital. I am very happy to tell you, however, that Flight Lieutenant Caine was reunited with his friend Major Bradley and another man whose rank is unclear, a J.M.R. Duggan. Caine was released into their care on 27 August 1944 – around the time, I believe, of the city's liberation. As far as I can make out, he was scheduled to return to Britain thereafter, although it seems he did not report for his transport.

I hope this helps to lay Major Bradley's spirit to rest.

Yours sincerely, Mabel Gard

Mirabelle read the letter twice. She turned the paper over in her hand. J.M.R. Duggan. John Melrose Richard Duggan. Jack. Her mind raced. Jack always said he'd never been to Paris. She certainly couldn't recall him going during Operation Overlord – the invasion of Normandy that had paved the way for the liberation of France's capital. Could there be another J.M.R. Duggan? Mirabelle felt light-headed. No, it was Jack. She knew it. Her heart was quivering. There was no reason to feel betrayed, she chided herself. After all, Jack didn't have to tell her everything, and Paris was not so very far away, but still the revelation stung. Her mind moved on. Bradley's letter had stated he hadn't seen Caine since 1942, and yet here he was back in France tracking down his escape partner in a Red Cross hospital two years later. Mirabelle sighed. If Bulldog knew his friend had survived the liberation, why had he left her the bequest at all? If he wanted her to find Caine why hadn't he told her about this?

Vesta looked up from her own pile of mail, which appeared to consist mostly of invoices. 'All right?'

Mirabelle nodded. Without stopping to think, she reached for the telephone and dialled the international operator. 'The American Hospital of Paris, please.'

Vesta abandoned the papers in front of her and watched open-mouthed as Mirabelle began to speak fluent French. She couldn't follow the words, but she recognised the names: Philip Caine; Matthew Bradley. When Mirabelle hung up Vesta practically jumped on her.

'Where did you learn to speak French?' she demanded.

Mirabelle was staring at the middle distance as if she could see a ghost. 'My mother was French.'

'Do it again,' Vesta insisted. 'Say something else.'

'I'll bring you back a present, if you like. *Un cadeau.*'

Vesta crossed her arms. 'What do you mean? You're not going away again, are you?'

Mirabelle sounded weary as she handed over Matron Gard's letter. 'I've got to go. I can't just leave it like this.'

'To Paris? On your own? Won't that be dangerous?'

Mirabelle laughed out loud. Without fail Vesta always made her feel better.

The boat train left in the evening. Mirabelle packed her small crocodile skin case carefully and caught the three o'clock service to London, which upon examination of the timetable proved to be a quicker and easier journey than trying to make her way to Dover via the coastal route. It had been a long time since Mirabelle had been in France. Before the war, when she was a student, she had made the trip to Paris several times with friends. She smiled, remembering how each weekend had seemed to degenerate into a frantic, sleepless party fuelled by champagne and *foie gras*. Those were the days before rationing, she remembered ruefully, when the graduates of Oxford colleges were expected to go on to rule the world. Now some of them had. She recalled buying shoes on Saint-Germain-des-Prés and having clothes altered by a seamstress in the Marais who had known her mother. It probably wasn't like that any more. After all the fighting it had seen, did Paris wear its scars London style – still painful, if crusted over? How had the war changed the gayest city in Europe?

Arriving at Victoria with time to spare, she glanced at her watch and decided to leave her case in left luggage and call on an old friend. She hadn't expected to see him again. Not after the last time. But it seemed it was a week to revisit the past. She hoped he'd forgiven her.

The sky was a blank canvas, the light failing as Mirabelle walked decisively past the newsstand outside the station. The *Evening Standard*'s headline was scrawled across the news-board: H-bomb Men Seek Safety Plan. She cut across the park towards St James's and slipped along the alleyway that led to

Duke's Hotel. The doorman fussed ahead of her as Mirabelle swept into the hall, checking with a fleeting glance the shelf behind the receptionist's chair. The key to the back room was missing. That meant in all likelihood he was here.

'Eddie Brandon?' she ventured.

The receptionist shook her head. 'We don't have a guest of that name,' she said.

'Never mind.' Mirabelle didn't want to waste time on silly games. 'I'll just wait in the bar.'

Mirabelle wasn't entirely sure how Eddie would receive her. There shouldn't be any hard feelings, but still . . . She drew herself up. At least he had given her a gift the last time they parted – a set of SOE lock picks, which she had put to good use several times since. None the less, it felt slightly awkward to be here. Mirabelle wasn't even entirely sure that Brandon was still stationed in the back room behind the bar. Either way, she reasoned, if he was in London he'd probably still be coming in for cocktails on his way to the park of an evening.

An Italian waiter snapped to attention as she walked in. The man's aftershave was enough to leave her reeling.

'Madam.' He gestured towards a table with a flourish.

Mirabelle declined the invitation to sit down. 'I'm looking for Eddie Brandon.'

'Mr Eddie!' The waiter looked her up and down. It was unusual for a woman to be asking after Mr Brandon.

'I wondered if he might be here. It being time for a drink after work.' Mirabelle checked her watch.

The waiter's expression was that of a naughty child caught in the act of eating sweets before dinner. 'Madam will have a cocktail today, I think? A whisky sour, perhaps?'

He had guessed correctly. A good waiter is practically psychic, she recalled her father saying once. Mirabelle recalled the days when, famously, Italian nosiness had obstructed the

escape of detainees. Perhaps here it was being put to good use. Duke's famously served the best cocktails in London.

'And Mr Brandon usually has something with vodka, I expect,' she said.

Eddie had picked up a good deal while working with Britain's erstwhile allies – the Russians. Covert operations had their advantages sometimes. Vodka was an unusual commodity in Britain after the war, but not if you were engaged in certain negotiations. *Mieux Hitler que Stalin*, many French citizens had thought when their country surrendered. Eddie always said it should be the other way round. 'Fur, vodka and icons,' he would reply when asked for an explanation.

'Come.' The waiter motioned Mirabelle in the direction of the back room, past an elaborate arrangement of fir boughs festooned with blue ribbons. So, she thought, he is still working here. I suppose somebody had to be.

The room hadn't changed much. The padded door was heavy, the walls were painted dark green and the air was thick with the smell of tobacco. Mirabelle took in a portrait of the new queen hanging on the wall and the stack of books on the chiffonier – some, she noticed, written in Cyrillic, as Eddie Brandon, two years older than the last time she'd seen him, sprang to his feet. He laid his slim cigar in a Fabergé ashtray and covered the papers strewn on his desk.

'Mirabelle!' he said, a worried look crossing his smooth features.

The last time they'd run into each other it had ended up costing the department a fortune.

Mirabelle smiled. 'Don't worry. I'm not here to snoop on whatever you're working on.'

'Of course you're here to snoop.' Eddie beamed. 'It's good to see you. Drink?'

Mirabelle nodded. The waiter disappeared. There was no need to order.

'Dreadful weather,' Eddie went on. 'It's been a deadly winter.'

Mirabelle removed her coat. She wasn't going to be diverted into talking about how cold it was outside. 'I came to see you because the most extraordinary thing has landed on my desk and I have got rather swept up by it.'

'So, you're on a mission? You know, Mirabelle, if you ever wanted to get back into the game there are bundles of opportunities. Particularly at present. Things are hotting up in the chilly eastern bloc. We're desperate for women. Plenty of girls volunteered to stand up to the Nazis but fewer seem interested in the Reds. And the fascinating thing is that I reckon Stalin might be worse than, you know, Hitler. I mean in terms of . . .' Eddie drew his finger across his throat to make his point. 'Millions upon millions,' he whispered. 'Really. And some of the experiments they've been running would put Josef Mengele to shame. Blasphemy I know, but if you could read the reports, that's the reality of it. To say nothing of their atomic weapons programme. The Commies are shockingly close to Hitler's vision in some ways. You'd be doing a great deal of good, you know. We're desperate to get information out. We're trying everything.'

'I only work privately now.' Mirabelle sank into the seat on the other side of the desk. 'But this isn't even that. It's personal, I suppose. Tell me, did you ever run into Bulldog Bradley?'

Eddie took a sip of an alarming-looking blue drink stationed at his elbow. 'It's a damned shame. I'm going to his funeral next Monday – somewhere ghastly up north. He lived in Northumberland, you know. Terrible, terrible news.'

'Quite. His wife is beside herself.'

'He has a daughter as well, I recall. It's a tragedy, really. Surviving the war and going down to cancer of all things. And so young.'

The waiter arrived with a generous whisky sour balanced on a tray. He left it at Mirabelle's elbow with a small plate of

nuts that both she and Eddie ignored. Eddie motioned for a refill as the man left.

'I'm glad you knew Bradley,' Mirabelle said. 'That's helpful. Tell me, do you recall how he got out of France in 1942?'

Eddie looked over his shoulder. Careless talk no longer cost lives – at least not careless talk about the war – but old habits died hard. 'Yes,' he admitted.

Mirabelle waited. When Eddie remained silent, she said, 'I'm particularly interested in Bradley's escape partner, Flight Lieutenant Philip Caine.'

'Why?' Eddie habitually answered a question with another question. He who dared might win but he who could get the other person to talk most was best placed.

'I was mentioned in Bradley's will.'

Eddie's eyes gleamed. He was quick to draw the obvious conclusion, and in fact, he took considerable delight in it.

'Nothing of that nature, Eddie. For heaven's sake.' Mirabelle was aware she sounded hopelessly prim.

'Haven't you found yourself a fancy man yet, Miss Bevan? There must be somebody.'

Mirabelle's mind flashed back to the evening before. Was Alan McGregor her fancy man? Truthfully she'd enjoyed the kiss without having the kind of connection to the superintendent to which Eddie was referring. That, however, was beside the point.

'Bradley asked me to find Caine, or at least find out what happened to him. Did you know him too?'

'Yes,' Eddie admitted again.

Mirabelle sipped her cocktail. This was proving an uphill struggle.

'What do you know about him, Eddie?'

'Caine? He was a career flier. His father was in the service. He was a tall chap, as I recall – good-looking. He didn't come out of France with Bulldog.'

'Do you know why?'

Eddie scratched his chin. 'Not exactly. And it'd be Official Secrets anyway.'

Mirabelle crossed her legs. 'So, Caine stayed on for a reason. And,' she patched the information together, 'he spoke German and French. That's probably part of it.'

'He was stationed in France for the rest of the war. He was up to something, but I've no idea what, and I don't know what happened to him afterwards. I can't tell you more than that. I don't cover France nearly so much these days. It's not my bag.'

'Bradley went to bring Caine home in 1944 – after the Germans surrendered Paris. Jack Duggan appears to have gone with him. But Caine didn't make his transport.'

Eddie shrugged his shoulders. As far as Mirabelle was aware Brandon didn't know about her relationship with Jack. No one in London had. But then, she was beginning to realise she didn't know as much about her lover's activities as she thought she did – during wartime and otherwise.

'It struck me as unusual,' she said. 'Jack going.'

There was an unwritten rule about high-level personnel risking missions into enemy territory and Paris had been on the cusp of freedom, but only just. Britain didn't want its finest captured, their rank discovered and information tortured out of them. During the war several officers – real military types – had gone anyway and been shot down; she'd heard of one chap who had simply doctored his uniform and pretended to be his younger cousin. He'd lasted out the war in a POW camp, great chunks of classified information kept safe by his false identity, though he admitted that he had lost considerable sleep over what would happen should his cousin be captured too.

'Jack liked Paris,' Eddie said. 'I went with him after the war once and he trailed me around the place trying to buy something from Dior for his wife. He kept saying how French women were the most beautiful in the world. We almost missed our table at Maxim's over a silk blouse.'

Mirabelle froze. Jack had bought her a Dior blouse – a red one. She didn't know it had come from Paris. In fact, she'd assumed he'd picked it up at Harrods. This emerging secret life of Jack's was unsettling. She had always considered herself Jack Duggan's greatest secret. Now it appeared there might be competition.

'Is there someone I could speak to over there?' she asked as the waiter arrived with Eddie's cocktail.

Eddie picked up his glass and took an eager sip. 'Curaçao,' he said, smacking his lips. 'The thing is, people want to forget the war, Mirabelle. In France they've done that more successfully than here. We're still paying our debts; we can't quite shake it off. It'll be decades. It's different on the continent. The French and even the Germans are better at letting it go. You should see how the Japanese are set. You wouldn't believe it. If I were you I wouldn't go digging up all this old guff. What's the point?'

'Bradley asked me to, so I won't be taking your advice, I'm afraid. He had something on his mind when he died and he wanted *me* to look into it. I intend to track it down, whatever it is. I understand you don't think it's a good idea, but if you wanted to give me some pointers, it would save me time.'

Eddie relit his cigar. 'I don't know how Churchill manages those huge stogies,' he said.

Mirabelle didn't take her eyes off him.

'All right.' He gave way. 'If you must. Though I advise against it.'

'Noted.'

Eddie sighed. 'Near the church at Saint-Eustache there's a street called rue du Jour. Like *soupe du jour*, you know?'

'Near the market at Les Halles?'

'That's the ticket. Look for a woman there – she's notorious. Christine. I heard she set up shop somewhere in the vicinity. I don't know more than that. She was a collaborator.'

'A Nazi collaborator?'

'Yes. That's why she's notorious.'

'But she was really one of ours?'

Eddie nodded. 'We offered to take her out of France after the war but she insisted on staying in Paris. They shaved her head and beat her about a bit. I think it took her a long time to find work and so forth. We owned up to her, of course, but it had gone too far by then and there was a lot of talk about people who had buttered up both sides. She'd probably come quite close to that. It was a tightrope, I expect. Resistance fighters were our bravest – far more so than our own chaps. Fellows like Bradley who got out risked being incarcerated again – that was the size of it. The resisters who helped escapees were shot.'

'And there were women?'

'It was the women who were left behind. Often they ran the lines – in charge of the whole damn thing. Admirable, really.'

'Thanks.' Mirabelle finished her drink. 'I'd best get going.'

'Say hello to the *sous chef* at Maxim's.' Eddie winked.

'All the nice boys like a sailor.'

Eddie saluted. He had started in the Royal Navy, after all.

Chapter 12

The greater the obstacle, the more glory in overcoming it.

It was dark by the time the train reached Dover. Mirabelle settled in the bar for the crossing. As a child she'd visited her grandmother in Paris. The old lady lived in a grand apartment near Parc Monceau where Mirabelle's mother had been brought up. Mirabelle's early memories of the city were the scattered recollections of a child no more than eight years of age. Paris had meant hot milk and bread with jam for breakfast and walking the old lady's poodle in the park. To a child's eye, the capital was no more than an exotic mixture of beautiful displays in the windows of the city's meticulous florists and bistros where waiters fussed over Grandma and called her 'Madame'. Long after the old lady died, in Mirabelle's student days, the city became synonymous with all-night parties fuelled by champagne and intrigue that kept everyone up to watch the sunrise over the rooftops as they walked home along the Seine.

And now, all these years later, she was going back. What would Paris mean to her now? Feeling abstemious she sipped a tomato juice as the motion rocked her from side to side. She found herself daydreaming of golden leaves falling on the park's winding paths as her grandmother's little black dog rushed through them, and, years later, of dancing in a *boîte* – a cramped nightclub that as far as she could recall was somewhere near Pigalle. A jolt woke her unexpectedly and she stretched her stiff limbs, self-consciously realising that she had

fallen asleep. Her mouth was dry. The ice in her glass had long since melted and become a thin layer of watery red on the surface of her drink. The barman, perched on a high stool reading a paperback with a garish flash of orange on the cover, looked up.

'Can I fetch you something, madam? A cup of tea?'

In the old days she'd have been 'miss' and he'd have offered her a cocktail. Mirabelle checked her watch.

'Coffee would be nice, if you have it.'

The barman disappeared into the galley to the rear and Mirabelle could hear him fiddling with a proper coffee maker. Insipid coffee would be unacceptable on a journey to Paris, she thought. Of course it would.

When it came, the coffee revived her, and as she drank she turned her mind to Bulldog Bradley and Philip Caine once more. She had told Mrs Bradley she was declining the major's bequest, and indeed had fully intended to pursue the matter no further, but the knowledge that Jack was somehow involved had changed her mind. The difference was, her search for the truth would no longer be on the major's account; it was on her own.

It seemed the men had come to terms over Lady Caroline. At least, they had done so by 1944. Or had Bulldog come to find Caine because he wanted to apologise to his old friend? And what had Jack been doing there? Quite apart from being a family friend of the Bradleys, he must have had an official function to perform in this story. Had Caine worked under him? But if so, why didn't the flight lieutenant want to come home? As a pilot with a stint in covert operations, he'd have been a hero back in London.

As the train rattled into Paris, the suburbs were shrouded in low cloud. Further along the line the streetlights revealed glossy pavements, wet between showers as the train plunged into the last tunnels before the Gare du Nord. As the

passengers disembarked, the platform was deserted apart from two or three porters who were hastily engaged by those with trunks and piles of suitcases to transport to their hotels. Mirabelle picked up her own case and joined the straggle of travellers emerging into the city's sacred early morning silence. Outside, the papers were being delivered to the newsstand, and a portly woman smoking a cigarette struggled with a sandwich board that declared a security treaty was required for Europe. *Molotov insiste*, the headline said. Molotov demands it. The tall buildings loomed over the street, dark-windowed and forbidding. Still, it wasn't as cold as London. A small rank of taxis was quickly depleted and a trail of prospective fares snaked along the railings to wait for more.

Mirabelle turned her back on them. She crossed the main road, then turned eastwards down a side street. Her footsteps echoed on the early morning air. She didn't know Paris as well as she knew London but at least the city was familiar. She and her Oxford friends had usually shared a suite at the George V all those years ago, but on one occasion the hotel had been full and someone had mentioned a little boarding house near the station. 'It'll be rather fun,' the chap had said. 'It's small, so we can take the whole place over. And there's a piano.' The other students hadn't liked it. The glittering crop of Oxford talent judged itself by its surroundings and preferred its accommodation the grander the better. But the truth was Mirabelle had liked the little lodging house more than its glossy upmarket cousin. Now she turned a corner and her nostrils were assaulted by the smell of baking. A tiny *boulangerie* with a red door and gold writing on the window had its lamps lit. It was still closed, but Mirabelle rapped on the glass and bought two croissants over the doorstep with money she'd changed at Dover.

The hotel came into view round the next corner. In the darkness the building looked just as she'd last seen it – the windows overlooking the street were masked by dark shutters

and the sills were lined with window boxes sporting trailing plants. A sign hung over the door: Hôtel Rambeau. Inside, the lights were off and the front door, encrusted in dusty green gloss, stood locked for the night. Mirabelle put her case down on the pavement and perched on top of it, withdrawing one of the croissants from the brown paper bag and taking a bite. The pastry melted in her mouth: there was nothing in the world like French butter. The flavour took her back to her Parc Monceau days. A rag and bone man drove his cart across the top of the street, the horse's hooves clattering on the cobbles. Mirabelle licked her fingers and rubbed the chalk customs mark off her case. There shouldn't be too long to wait. At half past six, when the light snapped on above her, she stood up and rang the bell. At length a window opened on the first floor and a vaguely familiar face peered out.

'I need a room,' she said in French. 'I've come from the station.'

The man motioned for her to wait. A minute later, when he appeared at the door, she could see how he had aged since the last time she'd been here. His hair had turned completely white and he seemed smaller. But then, it had been twenty years. Her eye was drawn to the blue woollen dressing gown wrapped around his shrinking frame. Its belt was tied in such a complicated knot that she wondered if he would ever manage to untangle it.

The old man peered into the dark street, stroking his unshaven chin. The light of recognition almost sparked in his eyes but not quite. Mirabelle decided not to remind him. She wasn't proud of the nocturnal escapades of her youth. Fired by cocktails, they'd come back from dancing at four in the morning and played the piano, disturbing the entire block. Her friends had found it amusing.

She reached into her bag and pulled out some francs. '*Trois nuits*,' she said.

Three nights should be enough. At the sight of the money the man's face softened. He beckoned her inside and removed a key from its peg behind a little reception desk. Only three rooms were taken, Mirabelle noticed. The hotel was quiet, which was all to the good.

'*Anglaise?*'

Mirabelle nodded.

'*Londres?*'

She nodded again. There was no sense in making things more complicated, and the man might never have heard of Brighton, which, in any case, would be difficult for him to spell when he came to fill in the hotel register. He pointed to the dingy staircase. Mirabelle lingered. She remembered the hotel being prettier. In the old days the hallway had had fresh flowers displayed on every ledge, although admittedly it had been summertime. Now there was only a box of dried lavender on the landing and a row of empty jugs decorating the sill. The old man grabbed Mirabelle's case with a surprisingly firm fist and accompanied her to a room on the first floor.

'*Et voilà.*' He opened the door with as much flourish as he could summon at such an early hour. Mirabelle peered inside. The room was clean and it was to the rear of the building so it would be quiet. The window looked over a courtyard and the bed appeared comfortable. She ran a hand over the turned-down sheet. The French always had good quality linen.

'*Merci,*' she said, removing the key from the lock.

The old man turned to go. Making sure he had left, Mirabelle closed the shutters and laid her suitcase on the bed. She opened the catch and piled her clothes and toilet bag against the pillow, reaching inside the case to carefully flick a switch that was built into the brown taffeta lining. The bottom of the case sprang open, revealing a hidden pocket no more than an inch thick. She had flouted the currency restrictions, changing the permissible value of pounds into francs but also concealing an

additional stash of notes. Paris, she recalled, was an expensive city and government limits on the movement of money were on the tight side. She balanced this with the universal truth that information cost. With a smile, Mirabelle smoothly removed the tidy sheaf of notes and slipped it into her handbag. Then she turned to the enamel sink in the corner and washed the travel stains from her skin. She checked her appearance in the mirror, and, pleased enough with what she saw, picked up a thin scarf from the pile of clothes on the bed and tied it at a jaunty angle – a certain style was mandatory in Paris. Then, nodding at her reflection in the mirror, Mirabelle left the room. If she walked to the American Hospital, she'd get there by nine o'clock when the administration department and archive opened. The hospital was situated in the leafy Seine-side suburb of Neuilly where some of Paris's most prestigious families were housed. It would be a pleasant walk, and if Mirabelle wasn't mistaken she would pass Parc Monceau on her way. She left the room key on the reception desk and slipped back onto the street.

The first watery light of the morning was seeping into the sky. Paris woke slowly, like a giant lumbering to its feet. Mirabelle made her way towards the river. The air felt fresh as she came to the park. Watching the bare trees behind the railings she made out one or two people up early walking their dogs. As if there might be a ghost, Mirabelle decided not to walk inside the gates. In her imagination, her grandmother's old-fashioned ankle-length dresses and laced winter boots passed in a flash of nostalgia. It must have been 1922 when the old woman died. Now Mirabelle kept her distance, skirting the wide pavements at the perimeter of the park. On the other side of the boulevard the houses were ornate, their pale stone carved with panache and thin wrought-iron balconies stocked with terracotta plant pots. Several delivery vans were in evidence and men in suits bustled towards the Métro,

newspapers tucked firmly under their arms. Open-fronted cafés lit braziers outside. There seemed less bomb damage than in London, but in places some of the stone was pockmarked with bullet holes. The Resistance had put up a fight on the streets here and there. At least London had never had to endure that.

Cutting north away from her childhood memories, Mirabelle made for the river. The walk was refreshing and it was pleasant to see people going about their business, children on their way to school and staff smoking outside shops waiting for the manager to arrive with the key. Paris was gloriously green, trees lining the main streets, cutting through the buildings in a swathe, fanning out from the Champs-Élysées.

It was almost nine o'clock when Mirabelle arrived at her destination. As she remembered, the buildings in Neuilly were imposing and the boulevard Victor Hugo was easy to find. The hospital took up almost a block – a brick-built, two-tone complex with ambulances parked in the courtyard. Mirabelle entered the main door smartly and asked a porter for directions to the archive, which it transpired was located in the basement. She took the stairs and was perched on the bench outside the office door at nine o'clock sharp when a flustered chubby woman in a pale blue winter coat arrived in a cloud of floral scent. Her scarf trailed across the tiled floor as she fumbled in her handbag for her keys, pulling off one glove and holding it in her mouth as an unruly blonde curl escaped from the rim of her hat.

'*Bonjour.*' Mirabelle sprang to her feet.

'*Bonjour,*' the woman said, an American accent spread as thickly as peanut butter over her vowels. She removed the glove from between her teeth and smiled, her plump cheeks rosy from the cold and her blue eyes shining. '*Bonjour,*' she tried again.

'Do you prefer English?' Mirabelle asked.

The woman's smile opened into an unimaginably broad grin that was startlingly white.

'Yes please,' she admitted as she turned the key in the lock.

'I rang yesterday . . .' Mirabelle started, just as a slim young man appeared behind her – a chap of a more tidy disposition. He reminded Mirabelle of a filing cabinet with its drawers tightly shut.

'*Bonjour*,' he said curtly, nodding in the women's direction.

'Ah, perhaps this is the gentleman to whom I spoke.'

'Claude?'

The man stiffened as the American woman continued in the worst French accent Mirabelle had ever heard. '*Avez-vous parlé avec cette dame-ci?*' Have you spoken to this woman?

'*Je ne sais pas.*' I don't know, Claude ground out, his expression closing like a steel trap.

The American waved him off. 'Perhaps it would best if I dealt with your enquiry,' she told Mirabelle.

With barely disguised outrage, Claude strutted into a room at the rear of the office and switched on the lights before pointedly closing the door.

'He's French,' the woman mouthed, as if it was a never-to-be-guessed secret and something of which to be ashamed. 'I don't think he likes females at all, you know.'

She removed her scarf and hat and tossed them untidily onto a chair. This action alone was so expansive that it seemed to fill the room.

'It's an English chap I'm looking for,' Mirabelle said. 'He passed through the Red Cross's hands around the time Paris was liberated in 1944, and I understand the papers relating to his injuries and his release might be here. I hope you can help me find him. The man I spoke to said you had records that sounded as if they'd be relevant.'

'Name?'

'Philip Caine. He was Royal Air Force – a flight lieutenant.'

The woman paused. 'I meant *your* name.'

'Oh. Mirabelle Bevan.'

'And you're a relation?'

Mirabelle hesitated She expected her heart to sink but it didn't. Instead, this time she squared up to the enquiry.

'Not exactly.' Her tone was very matter of fact. 'I worked for the chap who was trying to get Caine back to England. He seems to have failed in that. And I suppose you could say that I'm here at the behest of the man who was Caine's escape partner when they gave the Germans the slip. Though that was a couple of years earlier – 1942.'

The unkempt blonde slumped onto a seat in a manner reminiscent of Vesta. 'My, it sounds as if this fellow has quite some story.'

'I'd like to find out more of it.'

'I'm Maisie du Pré.' The woman held out her hand. Mirabelle shook it, her surprise clearly evident for Maisie went on. 'The name is how I got the job. They thought I was French and spoke some English. Instead I'm American and I speak only a little French.'

'The records are in English, are they?'

Maisie shrugged. 'That depends on the nationality of the doctor and the nurses. We have records in just about every language from Hindi, which we can't read, to Russian – we've found a couple of people who can help us with that though the diplomatic service don't like us doing it. An international service is supposed to be a boon. Let me tell you, international records most definitely aren't.'

Mirabelle nodded sympathetically.

'Date?' Maisie enquired.

'August 1944. De Gaulle entered the city on the twenty-fifth or thereabouts. On that day, or close to it, my man was in a Red Cross field hospital near Longchamp.'

Maisie indicated a table set up for six readers. She strode

over and pulled a little cord that switched on a lamp, which in turn illuminated the green leather insert.

'Dinky, isn't it? Wait here and I'll see what I can dig up.'

Moving more quickly than might have been expected, Maisie du Pré disappeared through a door at the rear. Mirabelle removed her gloves and took a seat. She became aware of the clock in the corner ticking. There was something sterile about the office; Miss du Pré was the only lively thing about it. Even with her hat and coat strewn beside her desk, it was like sitting in a mortuary. The clock's hand moved slowly and Mirabelle squirmed in her chair. A full twenty minutes later Maisie reappeared with a large pile of papers that she managed to lever onto the table.

'There were a lot of injuries in Longchamp that week,' she said. 'The Germans mined the roads when they left.'

Mirabelle undid her buttons and slipped her coat over her shoulders. 'Thank you. That's very helpful. Well, I'd best get to work.' She picked up the paper on the top of the pile as Miss du Pré went back to her desk.

Mirabelle wasn't squeamish by nature but the records went into gruesome details of injuries and operations. The hospital had been set up to the west of the city in the open space afforded by the racetrack at Longchamp. It didn't only offer first aid – there was also a surgical unit dealing with gunshot and shrapnel injuries. And it helped the local community. Mirabelle found civilian records – two boys who had contracted mumps and a woman who went there to give birth. While photographers snapped the crowds rejoicing in the streets around the Champs-Élysées as the French reclaimed their city, some poor souls were having limbs amputated or bullets removed. In those last weeks Paris had stood up to the Nazis. There had been widespread strikes and the Resistance had staged a series of incendiary attacks against German targets. In retaliation, as Maisie had pointed out, the Nazis

had mined the roads, hoping to strike the Allies as they arrived. Occasionally a mine hit home. The whole operation had resulted in extensive injuries – not on the scale of an actual battle, but bad enough.

Mirabelle read the medical details of the ensuing devastation for a good two hours before she encountered a familiar name. When she did, it was not Philip Caine, the man she had expected to find. Instead, she turned over a piece of paper and there he was. Jack Duggan. From beyond the grave. His name loomed towards her, his familiar signature on the form confirming that the J.M.R. Duggan in question was the man she had known it must be. The twenty-fifth of August – the day the Germans had surrendered the city. Yet Jack had told her he had never been here. They had joked, she remembered, about her showing him the city where her mother was born. Jack had said he wanted her to be his tour guide. 'You're the one who speaks French,' he had said. Mirabelle had blushed and given a demonstration. 'Well, you'll be in charge when we get there,' he had promised with a grin. 'I'd love to see Paris.' The lie made Mirabelle uneasy. What else had Jack not told her? She rifled through the papers for more information and settled down to read.

Now she knew when Jack had been at Longchamp she could search more accurately by date, and she soon discovered that before he arrived he had sent a communiqué to the hospital, enquiring after the whereabouts of one Mademoiselle Moreau. Curiosity twisted in Mirabelle's chest. Who on earth was she? Soon after that she turned up an accommodation allocation in his name. Jack was quartered near the hospital, put up by the Red Cross in their doctors' quarters. He had been allocated two bunks – numbers thirteen and fourteen. The accommodation block was communal and almost certainly male only – there would be another block for the nurses. So, she deduced, did Jack have Matthew Bradley with him? Had they arrived

together – Bradley in one bunk and Jack in the other? However they got there, the day the men came, Mademoiselle Moreau was under treatment. She had been beaten. The notes detailed several cracked ribs and a broken right arm. The poor woman was also treated for burns on her back and arms. There were three black-and-white photographs of these injuries that made Mirabelle wince. It looked as if someone had attempted to brand Mademoiselle Moreau's back and had stubbed out cigarettes on her arms.

Treatment at Longchamp was swift and the woman signed herself out on the twenty-sixth of August. Mirabelle squinted to read the spidery, barely legible scrawl that, she reasoned, given the circumstances, must have been written using the woman's left hand. Christine Moreau. Christine. Was this the woman Eddie had said she should try to find? Mirabelle checked Jack's bunk allocation again. The day Christine Moreau was discharged Jack retained his two bunks. He stayed at Longchamp for another twenty-four hours.

Moving on, she carefully searched the treatment roster for that week in August 1944, and there he was. Philip Caine. His injuries, it seemed, were relatively slight. He had shrapnel wounds but the doctor bandaged him up and discharged him within six hours. He signed his discharge form in a well-formed hand and left with a bottle of painkillers. Here it was – confirmation that Caine was alive in August 1944. He had given his address as 17 rue du Jour – the street Eddie had steered her towards. That was interesting. Mirabelle turned over the form as she considered. She cocked her head. On the back, scrawled in French, someone had written, 'The British officers were removed and treated for bruising. An orderly had to restrain the patient when he became distressed.' And then one word: *Mal*. Bad? Sick? What did the person who wrote it mean by that? Was Caine in the wrong? Was there more to it than the distress of a man who'd had his fiancée whipped from under

his nose by a friend? Was he sick? Or was he crazy? Lots of men had been damaged by their wartime experiences and ended up removed from the world, depressed, mad or simply violent. Either way it looked as if there had been bad blood over Caroline Bland after all. Caine had struck out against Bradley and Jack so forcefully they'd required medical attention.

Mirabelle suddenly remembered the day Jack had asked her if she'd marry him if he freed himself from his wife. It was the end of August that year – 1944. They had been picnicking and drinking gin all weekend, down near Hampton Court. Jack wanted to get out of the city and they'd put up in a boarding house in East Molesey. They'd called themselves Mr and Mrs Horton, she recalled. It was a sunny Saturday and they hired a boat on the river. Jack rowed and Mirabelle flung herself at him when he'd brought up the subject.

'Yes,' she cried. 'I'd marry you like a shot, you idiot! Don't you know that?'

And as she hugged him he'd cried out in pain.

'What is it? What's wrong?' she asked as the boat rocked dangerously.

'I went riding while I was away, my love. I was thrown.'

It hadn't felt like a lie, but then Jack was adept at managing information. And in his personal life he hadn't seemed the least bit wayward. He must have been in France that week. She recalled that he had waved a hand as if trying to pluck somewhere out of thin air when she asked him where he had been. Perhaps he was reaching for somewhere he could admit to having visited. Up north. That's what he'd said. Up north. Where Caine was from and where Bradley returned to make a home with his wife and child. Mirabelle frowned. It was difficult to accept that Jack had really been in Paris, but it made sense. And he had proposed to her as soon as he came back. Had the liberation of Paris made him sure for the first time that the Allies would win the war? Or had he seen what

fighting over a woman could do? Perhaps he'd learned a lesson and had decided to come clean to his wife. Not then, of course, but later, when the girls were old enough. Either way, that week he decided to mark out his intentions for the future.

Mirabelle had always thought her relationship with Jack was insulated from the war. That it was apart from everything else that had been going on. Now it seemed that somehow he had been prompted to propose by this sordid situation in a field hospital. That meant these people she didn't know – Bradley, Caine and even Caroline Bland – had touched her life. They had changed things. Mirabelle pushed the papers away and looked around the office. Maisie was munching a biscuit as Claude came out of the back.

'*Dejeuner*,' he mumbled, pointing at the clock. Lunch.

Maisie waved him off. 'I'm not hungry.'

Mirabelle got to her feet. 'Thank you so much,' she said, reaching for her coat. 'I found just what I wanted.'

Chapter 13

If we don't know life, how can we know death.

The air was clear as Mirabelle stumbled back onto the street. She walked quickly and it wasn't long before she was back in sight of the river. The cold black water of the Seine flowed wider than she remembered. But then there were so many things that weren't quite as she recalled. The last few days had brought Jack to life – not as the saint of her memory but as a living, breathing man endowed with both good and bad qualities. She decided that if she found Philip Caine she would be interested in hearing his opinion of Jack's character and she'd definitely like to know why he'd attacked Jack when it was Bradley who had betrayed his trust. It was difficult to piece together a clear picture of what had happened. It was as if the three men trailed myriad shifting shadows in their wake.

As she reached the Tuileries, Mirabelle felt tired and flagged down a taxi to take her to Saint-Eustache. A famous church not far from its still more famous cousin, Notre Dame, the building was considered a masterpiece, its high Gothic ceiling a perfect echo chamber for medieval music. As Mirabelle paid the driver and stepped onto the street, a placard propped against the base of a stone pillar announced a madrigal concert that evening. The taxi drove away and Mirabelle sidestepped the house of God and moved in the direction of the network of streets clustered around it. The rue du Jour had come up twice now and Mirabelle wondered what she might find there.

She wasn't far from the huge market at Les Halles, and the air was scented with cooking from several bistros. Between these, grocery shops spilled their wares onto the street with displays of citrus fruits and jars of honey. Three men clustered around a tobacconist's booth, smoking. Next to them the door of a *fromagerie* was wedged open and a whiff of strong blue cheese hung around the entrance. Mirabelle decided she would eat later. At the moment, she had too much on her mind.

The rue du Jour was only slightly wider than a lane. It ran downhill from the main road, with a small fire station halfway along on the left. Number seventeen was a haberdashery, with feathered hat trimmings and brass buttons strung on white threads in the window. Mirabelle paused to collect her thoughts before she stepped inside. Passing a rack of edging ribbons that stretched up to the ceiling, she had to squint to make out a young woman at the dark wooden counter to the rear. She was surrounded by skeins of wool and embroidery silks and appeared to be drinking a glass of red wine as she sewed together the pieces of a child's pink cardigan. She looked up. Mirabelle smiled. The girl's hair was held in place by means of two knitting needles and a crochet hook.

'*Vous cherchez quelque chose, madame?*' Are you looking for something?

'*Une femme,*' Mirabelle said. '*Christine Moreau.*'

The girl removed a knitting needle from her hair and used it to scratch her scalp. '*Non.*'

'*Et un homme,*' Mirabelle pushed on. 'Philippe Caine?'

The girl replaced the knitting needle with a Gallic shrug and a shake of her head.

'*C'est jolie,*' Mirabelle pointed to the cardigan.

The girl picked up the tiny garment and held it against her face. '*La couleur est belle,*' she admitted. It's a beautiful colour.

Mirabelle glanced around. The shop looked as if it had been fully fitted fifty years ago and nothing had changed since.

'*Vous avez travaillé ici depuis longtemps?*'

The girl worked out that she'd worked in the shop for three years – it took a moment. Mirabelle nodded. It was no surprise then that the child wasn't able to help.

'What's upstairs?'

'I live there,' the girl shrugged.

Mirabelle thanked her and turned to leave.

Walking away, she wondered what this area must have been like ten years or so before. The street wasn't far from the Marais, which was as close as Paris had ever got to a ghetto for its Jewish community. It was also the hub of the Parisian Resistance, though the Germans didn't know that – not for sure. They kept their enemies close. Nazi high command based themselves in the ornate splendour of the rue de Rivoli, which ran parallel to the river, or in the houses of French aristocrats around the Palais Royal. It was a different world. The rue du Jour looked quaint today – almost medieval – but a decade ago people must have been terrified on this narrow cobbled street with the occupying forces set on flushing them out one way or another. Mirabelle looked up. Above the shops here there were apartments. Like London, Paris was short of post-war housing and every corner was co-opted for living space.

It started to rain. Drops bounced off the paving stones, and Mirabelle decided to shelter in a café on the other side of the street. It would be a good place to check for information in any case. She hurried inside, settled at a table and ordered *café au lait* and a *croque monsieur*. She fussed over her hat and coat, arranging them to dry a little before looking up and taking in her surroundings. When she did, she saw that the waiter was handsome, but like the girl in the haberdashery, he was far too young and unlikely to have any helpful memories. When he brought her coffee she asked if he knew the name Christine Moreau or Philip Caine, but was not surprised when he shook his head. A man at the next table peered over the top of his

newspaper and looked away. As she took a bite of her sandwich she decided she needed to find someone older to ask.

Outside the window a puddle formed below the kerb. Mirabelle regretted not bringing an umbrella. She finished her coffee and toyed with her food, keeping an eye on the street as people dodged about their business trying to keep out of the rain. A van drew up at a doorway opposite. The driver rolled down the window, flung his cigarette onto the pavement and got out to ring an apartment bell. He sheltered in the doorway until it opened, then ran to retrieve a bale of what looked like printed silk in a fetching shade of red. The roll was only partially wrapped in brown paper; he'd have to hurry to keep the material dry. In the doorway a middle-aged woman accepted the delivery. She was wearing a floral housecoat and had her hair tied up in a cotton scarf. Mirabelle noticed leather cuffs around her wrists and wondered if they were for keeping pins – it seemed there was dressmaking going on in the apartment. In her heyday Mirabelle had had clothes made not far from here, on the rue du Temple. At the next table the man drained his coffee cup and lit a cigarette. He watched idly as the van drove off.

Mirabelle paid her bill. Then, deciding to brave the weather, she pulled her coat round her shoulders and crossed the street to ring the doorbell. There was a hammering sound of steps being taken at a lick before the door opened inwards onto a tiny hall dominated by a rickety staircase. The woman who had just accepted the bale of material stood in the doorway. Yes, Mirabelle thought, she's in her forties. Perfect. Face to face there was something indefinable about the seamstress. Mirabelle's eyes fell to the leather cuffs and she thought there might be more than one reason why the woman wore that kind of protection.

'Christine Moreau?'

The seamstress crossed her arms. 'What do you want?' she said in English.

'I'd like to have something made,' Mirabelle lied. 'I need a dress. You are Christine Moreau? A friend recommended you.'

The woman looked Mirabelle up and down. 'A friend?'

'Yes. In London.'

The seamstress considered this a moment and then seemed to accept it. 'Come in,' she said abruptly, and led the way upstairs and into her workroom.

Inside the studio, Mirabelle looked around. The place was shabby and smelled of dust but it was tidy and warm. A pot-bellied stove stood in one corner next to shelves that constituted a kitchen area, although it appeared entirely devoid of sustenance except for two bottles of Boodles Dry Gin, which stood side by side next to a bottle of cheap red wine. There was a window to the rear but it was caked in grime. A low single bed was covered in boxes of thread, dress patterns and a pile of tiny labels that said 'Made in Paris'. Half a dozen bales of cloth were piled opposite. On the table the dressmaker's tools were laid in a scatter around a silk scarf that she was apparently edging by hand in the grey light from the window.

'It's nice.' Mirabelle motioned towards the scarf.

The woman closed the door behind her, her eyes moving over Mirabelle's outfit as if she was a general surveying enemy troops. She hovered by the coat stand.

'Do you have the material?' she asked. 'For your dress?'

'No. I hoped you might have some I could buy. Red silk, perhaps?'

'A special occasion?'

'A friend is getting married.'

The woman raised her eyebrows as Mirabelle moved over to the corner of the room and touched the bale of material that had just been delivered. The dressmaker cocked her head to one side.

'This colour? It is new – fashionable. Red is unusual for a wedding. Will it be in summer?'

'In spring. The bride is wearing purple. I thought it would

be nice to wear a bright shade as well. Something like this would be perfect.'

'Purple?' The woman looked as if she could not possibly have heard correctly. 'A bride?'

'She is very unconventional.'

'These days the world is upside down. Perhaps it is not unconventional – only modern. Had you considered wearing white to the wedding yourself, madame? Would that not really turn the world on its head?'

Mirabelle smiled. 'I like the colour of this fabric. I thought a pleated skirt?'

The seamstress smacked her lips in disapproval. At first Mirabelle was unsure whether her censure was for the colour or for the notion of pleating. In the end it was for neither. The seamstress took the bale, laid it on the table and rolled it out a few inches.

'This one isn't silk. It is rayon. The colour is bright, but for you, for a dress? No,' she said decisively. 'It will not be good enough. It is to make scarves, you see. It is cheap.'

'Well . . .' Mirabelle said, 'we shall have to find real silk, I suppose, and hope for the same colour. Are you Madame Moreau? I don't know what to call you.'

'You can call me by my name,' the woman said flatly. 'Christine.'

'Ah, so it is you?'

Christine folded away the fabric. Her eyes were hard. 'What do you want? You haven't come here for a dress.'

Mirabelle turned her palms upwards, and stood slightly to the side. People responded to body language without even thinking. It was important to get it absolutely right. She did not want to appear threatening. Jack always said body language made it easy to pretend. You should never trust anyone else's, but always make sure your own sent the appropriate message.

'I want to ask some questions,' Mirabelle admitted. 'I wonder if there's someone you might remember?'

Christine's eyes darted. 'Who?'

'Jack Duggan.'

'Did he send you here?' The woman sounded almost panicked.

Mirabelle shook her head. 'Jack's dead. But you knew him during the war, didn't you? He came to Paris. He met you here. At Longchamp. At the hospital.'

'I met him long before that. Many times. It was all his fault.' Christine sounded furious. 'Jack Duggan was a bad man.'

Mirabelle noticed her fists were clenched. It took some effort to uncurl them. 'What do you mean?' The shock must have showed in her tone, but Christine ignored it.

'I'm glad to hear he's dead,' she spat. 'Glad of it. The arrangement was that he would not return. Well, now he can't. A man like that . . .'

Mirabelle felt fury rising in her chest. 'How can you say that?'

'Ah. You are his wife?' Christine guessed and then, seeing Mirabelle flinch, she changed the assertion. 'No, you were his lover.'

In England no one would say such a thing in company. Mirabelle drew herself up.

'Yes, I was,' she admitted. Saying it felt good. 'I loved Jack very much.'

'And you think he loved you?'

'I know he did.'

'Jack Duggan was not capable of love. Such a grand cause. Did he promise you the world? Did he deliver it? No!' The woman read Mirabelle's eyes. 'Well,' she continued triumphantly, 'that was Jack Duggan. You were betrayed in love, but then he betrayed us all, and we suffered for it.'

Mirabelle's breath became shallow. 'Jack died of a heart attack. Years ago,' she managed to get out. 'But I met him during the war. I worked for him. He would never have done anything . . .' She steadied herself against the table as her voice tailed off. She had lost control of the conversation. She was far too involved now to get the woman to open up. She was betraying herself the more she spoke, but her blood was up

and she didn't care. Jack had made difficult decisions during wartime. That was his job. He ran spies behind the lines and that meant he had to question everything. He had the kind of mind that could play several games of chess simultaneously and still see the bigger picture. But whatever he did, she told herself he'd have done it in a good cause.

'I don't know what you're talking about,' she spluttered.

'Why did you come here, then?'

'A man called Matthew Bradley asked me to.'

This infuriated Christine even further. She picked up a pair of scissors and brandished them.

'Traitor!' she screamed. 'How dare you? Get out! Get out of here.'

Mirabelle clutched her handbag to her chest as she backed away. 'Bradley wanted to find out what happened to his friend. A pilot. A man who didn't go home after the war. He stayed here, I think, and it's as if he simply disappeared. I'm beginning to worry about him. So many brave men . . .'

Christine let out a shriek. She thrust the scissors towards Mirabelle, narrowly missing her face.

'Go to hell! You've come to torture me, but I won't have it.'

She jabbed the scissors towards Mirabelle again as if she was holding off a dangerous animal. Mirabelle made for the door with the dressmaker in pursuit. A bundle of rayon scarves cascaded off the table as Christine brushed past.

'You selfish bloody English! You've had enough of our good French blood! If you want someone to bleed, this time I swear it'll be you. Why didn't they send a man, eh? They haven't changed. Not one bit.'

The woman tightened her grasp on the scissors and kept jabbing at Mirabelle, who dodged left and right before turning and hammering down the stairs. Panting for breath, she burst onto the rue du Jour and raced up the street to get away. Across the road the waiter peered laconically out of the café window.

Mirabelle turned and looked back. Christine was hovering in her doorway, still brandishing the scissors and swearing so fiercely that Mirabelle could hear her from the corner. At least she was not in pursuit. Mirabelle felt a sense of relief as she rounded the top of the road, half running, looking back over her shoulder. Her mind was buzzing. What on earth had Jack done to deserve this kind of behaviour at the mere mention of his name? And Matthew Bradley too. Was the poor woman mad? What had they done to her?

As Mirabelle turned the corner Christine stopped shouting and Mirabelle heard the slam of the woman's front door. She realised that her heart was hammering as she moved towards the church of Saint-Eustache, almost staggering with shock. She lingered for a moment beside the concert notice before pushing herself up the stairs and into the gloomy interior, out of the rain. With shaking hands she slipped into a pew towards the back, holding on to the filial for support. It was early afternoon, and apart from three or four people praying and lighting candles near the altar, the place was all but deserted.

It was a long time since Mirabelle had visited a church for anything but a funeral. It must be three years, she remembered, and then only to speak to a friend, Father Sandor. She wondered what Sandor would make of all this, but of course he was dead. They were all dead. Mirabelle tried to control her breathing. It's what Jack would have told her to do, but the thought of Jack just made her feel more confused. She tried to remember what it had felt like to love Jack without wondering what he was keeping from her, but all of a sudden his image was blurred. There was Jack Duggan who was married to Mary. Jack Duggan, hero of the SOE, who had done something terrible to Christine Moreau. And Jack Duggan, the man who had promised her the world – something she had believed he would deliver. Had she been a fool? If he had lived would Jack only have strung her along? Mirabelle rubbed her face. She felt exhausted.

The church door opened, casting a weak light from the street onto the flagstones and letting in a stream of fresh air. A man genuflected and slipped into the pew behind Mirabelle. She rose, and as she turned she caught the newcomer's eye. It was the man who had been reading earlier in the café on the rue du Jour. He was wearing a Mackintosh now, and a brown homburg, and he appeared to have left his newspaper behind. He smiled and tipped his hat.

'Madame,' he said. His French was accented but Mirabelle couldn't quite make out its origin. 'You appear to be having a difficult afternoon. Are you all right?'

Mirabelle nodded. He held her eye steadily. Suddenly she felt like crying, but she wouldn't do it in company.

'Would you like a drink? I know a bar on rue Rambuteau. It serves good brandy.'

'Thank you, but I want to go home,' Mirabelle replied firmly. Men in Paris were notoriously flirtatious. One mustn't encourage them. Had he followed her inside hoping for an assignation? He clearly thought she was vulnerable and an easy target. Mirabelle drew herself up and moved towards the door without saying goodbye. She had too much on her mind. The urge to sob receded and the puzzle that Christine Moreau presented began to niggle instead. For a start, if Christine hated the English so much why was she still doing business with them? Mirabelle cast her mind back, reconstructing the dressmaker's room in her mind's eye. Yes. The gin. Boodles was a tiny distillery. You could hardly get their gin at home, never mind here. And it was expensive, which was to say overpriced. It wasn't especially good. The bottles must have been a gift from someone. Had Eddie mentioned Christine Moreau because the department was still doing business with her? Mirabelle wondered who the woman was working for. It wasn't Eddie Brandon. His department would know their gin. They would have sent Booth's – High & Dry. At least there were some certainties in life upon which one could definitely rely.

Chapter 14

Timing: judgement of when something should be done.

Outside, Mirabelle headed in the direction of the river. For the first time since he died, she found she didn't want to think about Jack, so she decided to ignore the drizzle and walk for a while as she focused her attention on what she told herself was the real matter in hand. Philip Caine. A cluster of raindrops fell from a tree overhead as she passed. The bright droplets splattered on the paving stone. She needed to think. Turning onto the rue de Rivoli, she halted outside a fancy-looking hotel sporting the French flag over its doorway. Eddie had said that France had recovered from the war more quickly than Britain, but it seemed that wasn't the case for Christine Moreau. Seeing Mirabelle stop, the doorman at the hotel's entrance stood to attention ostentatiously.

'Madame.'

She cast a glance up the street, hesitating only a moment before going inside. Suddenly the instinct to call home was strong – you always reported back, even if, these days, she was her own boss. The thought of the office on Brills Lane was comforting. At least Vesta and Bill were always on her side. McGuigan & McGuigan was gloriously uncomplicated.

At reception she asked if she might make an international call. The porter directed her across the marble hallway to a telephone booth with a frosted glass window, beside a very grand staircase. The booth housed a comfortable velvet chair, a telephone and an overflowing ashtray. Mirabelle was glad to

sit down. She put the ashtray outside on the carpet and closed the door. Being enclosed felt cosy. She regarded the telephone for a moment before lifting the mouthpiece and dialling the international operator, giving the exchange and number in French. When she hung up she had to wait only a few minutes before the bell trilled loudly. Mirabelle pounced on the receiver.

'Vesta? Are you there?'

At the other end Vesta squealed. 'You're in Paris!' she said needlessly. 'What's it like?'

Mirabelle was unsure how to explain her afternoon. 'It's raining,' she said, rather lamely.

Vesta giggled. 'It's raining here too. It's been terrible weather. Gosh, Mirabelle, you sound as if you're only next door. I'm glad you called. I wasn't sure how to get hold of you.'

'Why? What's happened?' Mirabelle envisioned something dreadful. A body. Perhaps two. She wished she was in the office with Vesta making toast and Bill spoiling the dog. That way they could tackle things together. Vesta sounded pleased as Punch.

'I came up with something from the papers. You know, in the library.'

Mirabelle caught up slowly. She hadn't realised the girl would continue her research after she'd left. Brighton seemed distant – certainly more than a day away. Vesta carried on, oblivious.

'I couldn't turn up anything about Philip Caine so I went back to looking for Bradley and decided to keep going forwards to see what happened next. After Bradley got married in October 1942. To Lady Caroline Bland, you remember?'

'Yes.'

'Well. It's the baby, you see – Jennifer June Bradley.'

'What about her?'

'They announced the birth the following June in *The Times* but they didn't give a date, and that's what I thought was fishy.

I mean, you ordinarily say "Last Thursday born to" whoever it was . . . There's usually a date or a day or something. The Bradleys didn't put it like that. The announcement just said, "A daughter born to" or something. So I ordered the little girl's birth certificate and lo and behold she was born on the seventh of February 1943. Now, a baby born that far before its due date would never survive, so the little thing wasn't just early. Do you see?'

Mirabelle leaned back against the wall. 'Yes. If she was born in February that means . . .'

'I know,' Vesta enthused, overjoyed to have uncovered something that constituted gossip. 'It's a cheeky middle name to give her, don't you think? Quite clever. I bet they've been throwing her birthday parties in June all her life. But she's a February baby. The child must have been conceived in May 1942 or perhaps June at the outside. And at that time Matthew Bradley was in a prisoner of war camp in Germany and Lady Caroline was still engaged to Philip Caine.'

'It's Caine's baby,' Mirabelle said slowly. 'Of course. Caine and Lady Caroline planned to get married in the summer, before the pregnancy started to show, but then Caine was shot down over France. At the Army and Navy Club the man I spoke to called Caroline Bland a firebrand. She kicked up an awful fuss when Caine went missing in action. Well, no wonder – she was left in a sticky situation. She must have been beside herself.'

'And then Bradley came home and married her.'

'For his friend's sake.' Mirabelle pieced it together. 'All this time I assumed he was a cad who had stolen her away, but now it would seem he did it to save the woman's good name. I wonder if Caine knew. Do you think the men planned it? And that's why Mrs Bradley came down to Brighton when she heard I was trying to find Caine. She doesn't want any of this coming out. It was years ago – she thought they'd got away

with it and then her husband put the bequest in his will and she was terrified it might all unravel. That's what she meant about dragging people's names through the mud – it was her name she was worried about, and her daughter's.'

'The thing I don't understand,' Vesta said, 'is that if Bradley got out of France and made it home, why didn't Caine too? He had something important to come back to, after all. Something worthwhile. Why on earth did they split up when they were over halfway? Men who escaped tried to stay together.' Vesta had by now leafed through several escape memoirs and was becoming something of an expert. 'Instead of that, only one of them made it, and when he got back he must have hooked up with Lady Caroline immediately – made an agreement, like you said. By my reckoning, he got home late in August and the couple married in the first week of October – that's six weeks at most, perhaps more like five. They could hardly have done it more quickly, what with them having to announce the banns.' Vesta knew the drill – she and Charlie had looked into a church service before they discarded the idea. 'It takes three Sundays, and the wedding was in Durham Cathedral on a Monday. I reckon they tied the knot as quickly as they could.'

Mirabelle's mind whirled. 'You've done a marvellous job. Well done,' she said.

Vesta's grin was palpable down the phone line even at a distance of several hundred miles. 'I'm not finished yet. I thought I'd go back to the library this afternoon. How's it going over there?'

Mirabelle wasn't sure how to put it. 'Well, Paris is lovely. And Caine was alive if not well here in 1944, all right. But I haven't found a trace of him since.'

She didn't want to tell Vesta about being pursued by an unhinged woman brandishing scissors. The story of Caroline Bradley's illicit pregnancy felt comfortably distant and she was glad to be able to focus on that.

'It would be good to know why he stayed all that time in occupied territory – two years,' Vesta mused. 'That's a big decision. I mean, surely he'd have preferred to come home and marry his sweetheart. And why didn't he come home after the war to see her and the little girl? I'd have thought he would be curious.'

'Perhaps it was too painful.' Mirabelle tried to dismiss the uncharitable thoughts about Mrs Bradley that were now passing through her mind.

'How shall I get hold of you if I turn up anything else?' Vesta was nothing if not a grafter.

'Send a telegram. I'm at the Hôtel Rambeau. It's on the rue Lentonnet, close to the Gare du Nord.'

Vesta sounded the words as she noted them down and Mirabelle helped with the spelling.

'I'd best get off. This is long distance.'

'Have a nice time!' Vesta hung up.

Mirabelle loitered a moment in the booth as the line went dead. She imagined the girl underlining the words and then putting aside the notepad. She stared at the telephone, realising slowly that there was no one else in the world she wanted to call. Pulling on her gloves, she emerged into the hotel hallway. Her heels clicked as she crossed the marble and paid the bill in cash at the reception desk. Well, she couldn't help thinking, Mrs high-and-mighty Bradley had found herself in a ticklish situation. She was lucky. Although perhaps ending up marrying someone other than the man she presumably loved might not have been an entirely lucky break. She wondered how Matthew Bradley had felt about it. Had that night in the club in London been his last hurrah? When he had flirted with the pale-eyed secretary had he already booked his Monday morning wedding in Durham? No wonder his eyes had been so blank.

Mirabelle slipped back onto the rue de Rivoli with a shiver.

The rain had not abated and she felt the chill. She asked the doorman to hail her a taxi and tipped him well for doing so. Were wives only lovers who got lucky, she wondered? Some of them were, it seemed. It was unfair. With a flick of her wrist, she directed the taxi to take her back to her hotel. She wanted to draw a bath and get some rest. It had been a momentous day, and now she needed to sift through the information she'd uncovered and think through what to do next. She settled into the leather seat, counting the lamp posts as the car went by, her eye drawn to one or two of the grander shops and to the wide grey sky above.

About halfway back to the hotel, rounding a corner, at the very edge of her field of vision she noticed an old Peugeot following the taxi. Her heart slowed, and then, as if she was on automatic pilot, she directed the driver to turn next left.

The driver objected, telling her it was the wrong way. But she was insistent.

He shrugged and turned left. The Peugeot followed. The car hadn't even indicated. Mirabelle swivelled in her seat.

She asked the driver to turn left again. The driver did as she asked, and when the Peugeot followed once more Mirabelle strained to see who was inside, but it was impossible. The rain was too heavy to make out anything. Barring that, she knew only one way of finding out who it was. She directed the driver to drop her at the Gare du Nord. It would be easy there to disappear into the crowd and watch to see who emerged from the vehicle to follow her. Busy places were friendly places for a woman who didn't want to be seen.

The station wasn't far. As the cab drew up at the concourse, Mirabelle paid the driver and hurried towards the entrance without waiting for her change. The Peugeot halted only a few yards behind and lingered to one side, parked at an angle. It was a good vantage point for peering through the crowd – people with cases and without, businessmen and families. A

small group of schoolgirls in blue uniform coats and red berets clustered together. Mirabelle darted round them and took up a position just inside the station entrance. A moment later the man in the Mackintosh and brown homburg got out of the car. This was intriguing. She had misjudged him. He hadn't been hoping for an assignation after all – even in France this behaviour would be on the keen side. But what on earth was the fellow after if not that? She pulled behind a pillar, out of his sight line, and he ran past her into the station, looking left and right as he went.

Mirabelle slipped out of her hiding place and onto a side street. She waited round a corner, peering towards the concourse. The man came out again about two minutes later and looked around, his arms akimbo. Then he checked his watch and ran back into the station. From her vantage point Mirabelle sighed with relief. He would think she had caught a train. As she turned up the street and headed in the direction of the Hôtel Rambeau she couldn't help smiling. The chap clearly had no training to speak of. The thought drew her attention back to the real conundrum – what had Jack Duggan and Matthew Bradley done to Christine Moreau that was so unforgivable and where on earth was Philip Caine?

Chapter 15

Good clothes open all doors.

When Mirabelle woke it was still dark. She could smell the last of the cheeseboard she'd eaten in her room the evening before – an early dinner. The plate lay on the bedside cabinet. The dregs of a glass of red wine now smelled vinegarish and all that was left of the Camembert was a dry white crust. She fumbled for her watch and the light switch. It was only half past six. She had slept for ten hours. She had needed to. She hadn't even dreamed as she lay under the creamy sheet with its thin over-blanket. The world had disappeared.

Getting up, she poured some water into the sink to wash her face and hands. The soap was homemade. The foam smelled of lavender. Drying her skin on the towel, she turned, cracked the shutter and switched off the electric light. Outside, the little courtyard looked cold but at least it was dry now. She lifted the blanket from the end of her bed and curled up in the chair by the window. Within a few minutes there was a low light in the sky as dawn broke over Paris in an icy roll of peaches and cream. The courtyard was planted with ivy that sneaked up the walls on all sides. There were three wooden tables with chairs placed on the east side where they would surely catch any afternoon sun. That was for a different time of year, when Paris was balmy in June and July before everyone abandoned the city in August because of the heat.

In the hallway she heard movement – a maid perhaps, or someone rising for an early breakfast. The floorboards in the

hallway creaked and then fell silent. Before she slept, Mirabelle had tried to piece the puzzle together. It had whirled round and round in her head, and she had realised that in all the details she had uncovered there were too many stories, too many different points of view. No one had turned out the way she had originally expected. Bradley had married his friend's pregnant fiancée. The men may well have agreed on the plan when they parted in 1942. That alone was strange, but still, for Bradley to keep his word and rescue Lady Caroline was an act of kindness that would have been beyond many men. But two years later Caine had lashed out at him. What was he angry about? And where had he gone?

And then there was Jack. Mirabelle wanted most of all to find out about Jack's dealings in Paris during the war. His secrets. The idea scared her. Christine Moreau had been so furious with him, so hurt and betrayed. What had Jack done to leave the poor woman so damaged all these years later? Mirabelle didn't like to admit it, but it had occurred to her that in some ways she was just as damaged. With a different upbringing or in a different world might she have lashed out that evening in the Duggans' comfortable Hove drawing room? Had Jack really intended to leave Mary and marry her, or had he only been leading her on? Did he plan to keep her as his mistress, and if so had he really loved her at all? Mirabelle knew she couldn't have lied to Jack. She never had. If he had lied to her, or even simply misled her, what did that betoken?

With a shudder as if she was in pain, she tore her gaze away from the little garden and the brightening sky and fumbled in the half-light to pull on her clothes. She fixed her hair in the mirror – a simple chignon, the French way. Her mother would have liked that. It was only just after seven o'clock. Opening the door to the hallway she could smell coffee brewing. Downstairs in the dining room to the front of the building, she gratefully accepted a cup of strong coffee and a small basket of bread and butter with

a smear of dark jam – damson or blackcurrant, it was hard to tell. She ate without thinking, with one eye on the deserted early morning street, still thinking of matters that were long past.

When she judged that the local businesses would be opening their doors, she pulled on her coat and emerged from the hotel's front door to wander along the pavement, passing the *boulangerie* where she had bought croissants when she arrived. The ghost of a breeze chilled the air. Mirabelle was almost out of leads. She had no friends here. Her next call was a long shot and the very last idea she had for turning up some information. She checked behind her to be sure that she wasn't being followed, but the man in the homburg had apparently given up. On the corner, she bought a posy of snowdrops from a flower stall and popped three of the little flowers into her buttonhole. Then she continued in the direction of the Louvre – it was only slightly out of her way. Her grandmother had taken her to the grand old gallery regularly. The old lady understood that a child's attention span was short and had never allowed more than half an hour inside, so it had remained a perpetual treat. She had selected paintings to show Mirabelle that she knew would appeal to a little girl: an angel, a group of fairies and a bright waterfall that split the light into a rainbow.

'Shall we visit our favourites, my little plum?' she cooed. 'It is important to love art, Mirabelle. As you get older it becomes more important. You will see.'

Now, walking the Parisian pavements, it felt right, somehow, to be here. Perhaps that was what the old lady had meant. In a changing world the images framed in gilded wood stayed constant. It was a long time since Mirabelle had visited a gallery. During her London days she had sometimes taken herself to the National. Her favourite paintings in those days were seascapes. Jack liked winter pictures of snowy rooftops and blizzards. They had wandered through the galleries together, hand in hand. Afterwards they headed for Soho and

the privacy of an anonymous restaurant – somewhere away from the demands of Whitehall.

Almost at the Seine, Mirabelle passed through the grand colonnade and hovered at the gallery's heavy iron gates. This building had been a palace once, she thought as she waited. But then, at one time, she had believed herself a princess. It had seemed that way before the world turned and turned again. She peered at the familiar courtyard. The French allowed space between their grand buildings while London piled hers up against each other in an unruly crush.

When the gates opened she was first inside, crossing the courtyard and entering the building ahead of a cluster of tourists. Passing the sculptures in the main hallway, she turned into the first gallery of Old Masters. Mirabelle sank onto one of the benches and stared at a gloomy portrait of an old man. None of the men who concerned her had had the privilege of growing old. Her friend Sandor had been the oldest. He had been the confessor of several senior Nazis stationed here in Paris and had smuggled out information through the Church's own channels. Some of it had even made its way to Jack. No man was all right or all wrong, she thought. The grave eyes of the fellow in the painting confirmed it.

A female tourist came into the room, looked around and asked the attendant where the *Mona Lisa* was hung. The man gave the merest flicker of a glance to confirm that he had been asked this question incessantly for years on end. Then he gave succinct directions to the Salon Carré. Mirabelle wondered what Sandor might have done had he found himself in Paris faced with the conundrum she was trying to unravel. He had talked once about how putting yourself in danger was sometimes the only way. Espionage was a maze. You could never see what lay ahead, you just had to keep trying.

Outside the gallery, she crossed the rue de Rivoli once more and headed for the market at Les Halles. As she got closer she

could see the pavement was littered with cabbage leaves and eggshell. Everyone seemed to be carrying boxes or bags of butchered chickens, root vegetables and bottles of creamy milk. The market opened early and produce was delivered from the country well before dawn, but the traffic was slow in this part of town until midday. A gendarme wearing a cape over his uniform attempted to take charge at the crossroads. His white gloves seemed to glow in the low winter light.

Mirabelle turned away, crossed the main road and disappeared into the cluster of streets that made up the Marais. The last time she had been here many of the shop signs had been written in Hebrew. Today the signs were in French. She passed the Turkish Baths, trying to remember the way she had come on that previous visit, many years ago. In those days she had navigated Paris with her eyes at street level, calculating her route from shop to shop. Now she was drawn to look up to where the ramshackle roofscape met the ever-changing sky. Crossing the rue Rambuteau and turning onto the rue du Temple she hovered, seeking familiarity in the way the street curled to the left, reaching for a long distant memory. A minute or two along she recognised a door. It was painted thickly in black paint that was badly chipped but the old entranceway was still the same, unforgettable as it turned out. You never could tell what would stick. Mirabelle paused before ringing the bell. An old man, rather than the old woman she expected, peered out as the door opened. Mirabelle smiled at him.

'Is there a dressmaker here? A woman who works from her apartment?'

'Yes.' He motioned her to step over the footplate and into the courtyard. 'Her name is Catherine.' He pointed to the stairwell. 'On the second floor. Please, go up.'

Then, with a gruff nod, he retreated into his small office and closed the door. Mirabelle watched through the window as he lifted a coffee bowl to his lips and took a slurp, sitting down at a

rickety table and drawing a copy of *Le Monde* so close to his face that she realised he must be terribly short-sighted. It was still early enough for breakfast. She had risen too soon, perhaps. Beyond the shady entrance, the courtyard was pretty. Colourful geraniums were laid in a row. The plants were flowerless, but it wouldn't be long until spring. Mirabelle entered the stairwell and climbed upwards. The hallway was familiar but she had thought the little studio was higher than the second floor. Nevertheless, she knocked at the door on the second landing. A smell of toasted baguette pervaded the hallway. When the door swung open a thin girl with huge eyes appeared. She could be no more than twenty-five years of age. A small brown terrier tried to push past her leg and she bent down to scold him so that a long curl of her dark hair flopped over her face.

'I'm looking for a dressmaker who made me an outfit some years ago,' Mirabelle said. 'I think she worked on the floor at the top.'

'I'm a dressmaker.' The girl smiled, reaching down to grasp the dog's collar and causing further disarray to her hair.

'This woman was older. She was Jewish.' Mirabelle realised that hadn't come out quite right.

The girl put her head to one side and her hair fell back into place. 'You might mean my aunt. She had a studio here a long time ago. Do you remember her name? Was it Rachel?'

Mirabelle couldn't recall and that now seemed terribly rude. 'I'm sorry,' she said.

'You must have liked the outfit she made,' the girl commented. 'But if it was my aunt then she's not here. She died during the war. Would you like to come in? Is it a dress you're looking for?'

Mirabelle crossed the threshold and the girl closed the door. The dog sniffed Mirabelle's ankles and wagged its tail. Inside, the walls were painted ice blue and interrupted by two long windows. On some days, Mirabelle couldn't help thinking, the sky must match the colour of the room and the windows

merge into the walls. There was a pot of coffee on the table and the room looked comfortable – three or four seats were covered in cushions and a jumbled row of photographs punctuated the mantel. As she walked further in, a little stove sent a wave of warmth across her knees.

'I do need a dress, but really I had hoped to speak to your aunt. She made clothes for my mother, you see, many years ago, and I thought she might be able to help me find out something. There is a dressmaker on the rue du Jour who's about my age, I suppose, and I thought your aunt might know her.'

'Do you mean Christine?'

Mirabelle nodded. She noticed a door on the back wall that opened onto another room facing the street.

'I know who she is.' The girl crossed her arms. 'Everyone knows her. What's this about?'

'I'm trying to find out what happened to someone who went missing during the war. I have to tell you that Mademoiselle Moreau was not,' Mirabelle paused, picking her words carefully, 'helpful.'

The girl laughed. 'I shouldn't think she was. Christine Moreau was a collaborator. There's no love lost there. She mostly takes in finishing – handkerchiefs and scarves. She won't make you a dress, or at least that's not the kind of work she normally does. Most people don't want to employ her, you see.'

'Even now? I thought France was trying to forget what happened. I heard she worked for the British.'

The girl's eyes burned as she shook her head, sending her curls rippling. 'Christine thought people would forget. But some betrayals are impossible to forgive. Here especially. She buttered up both sides but she had a love affair with a German. That's the sort of woman she is.'

'She couldn't have been alone in that.'

'No,' Catherine said sadly. 'Some women will do anything for a glass of champagne and a safe bed. Well, it turned out

those beds were not so safe. Christine Moreau's lover was SS. An officer. Von der Grün. He was an evil man. He had a nose for money. Any hiding place. We'll never get it back, of course.'

'We?'

'My people, Miss Bevan. The Jews. And of course my family too. We weren't rich but we had a few things. My uncle collected paintings – nothing priceless, but they should be ours. My aunt Rachel had some beautiful jewellery. Emerald earrings. People think you're being greedy when you want those things back, but it's not the money, not only that – it's all that's left of them, don't you see?'

'And you escaped?'

Catherine looked as if she might burst into tears. Her blue eyes clouded but she continued. 'Not exactly. I was lucky. I was sent away. In Germany the Jews knew what the Nazis would do. There was at least a little time to try to get out. But in Poland, in France, in Holland – none of us knew they would come so quickly. They were here before there was time . . . I was visiting a cousin in Scotland when Paris fell. It was summer. I never came back – not till after the war was over.'

'I'm so sorry,' Mirabelle murmured, genuinely moved. When the girl came home almost everyone she knew must have disappeared.

Catherine stared at Mirabelle through the burgeoning tears. She wondered what had made her say so much. There was something about this older woman. 'What did you want to ask Christine Moreau? You said you were looking for someone.'

'Yes. A British pilot. Royal Air Force. Philip Caine.'

Catherine shrugged. 'The English left before I came back. I don't recognise the name.'

'What happened to Christine Moreau's lover?'

Catherine looked as if she might spit. 'I don't know and I don't want to know. He probably went back to Germany. Von der Grün. It sounds as if he had a castle. That's what I don't

understand – the Germans killed millions and most of them are allowed to go back to a normal life. A year or two in prison. Even ten years – what's that? And we – all of us – our lives will never be normal again.'

'Why did you come back to Paris?' Mirabelle wondered out loud. 'This place must be the most difficult city you could possibly choose if you want to move on.'

Catherine's eyes sparked. 'I belong here,' she said fiercely.

Mirabelle gazed out of the window. Perhaps she might ask herself the same question about Brighton; perhaps her answer would be the same too. 'Von der Grün,' she whispered.

She didn't recall the name of Christine Moreau's lover. Not from her days in Nuremberg or earlier, when she worked in Jack's office at the SOE. The girl was right – he sounded aristo-cratic. A Dutch officer had made her giggle once with his impression of an upper-class German. 'Not Van Heek,' he had shrieked like a maniac, playing it up for all he was worth. 'Von Heek. One little vowel makes a big difference, Fräulein. A whole estate's worth. The village, my dear lady, and every-thing within it belongs to me on account of that little o.'

The good thing about the aristocracy – German or English – was that they were easily traced, Mirabelle thought. Perhaps she would be able to track him down. If Christine Moreau wasn't prepared to talk to her perhaps von der Grün himself would be more accommodating. Her skin prickled – it was a long time since she'd interviewed a Nazi face to face. She tried to shake off the feeling of dread that crept over her. The war was over, after all, and such a conversation would be illuminat-ing. If von der Grün knew about Philip Caine it would mean Christine had been more on the German side than the British when she played her dangerous game. If he did not, she had been a loyal double agent. As she turned towards the door, Mirabelle found herself curious to find out which it was.

'You've been very helpful,' she said to Catherine. 'Thank you.'

Chapter 16

Curiosity is one of the permanent and certain characteristics of a vigorous intellect.

Mirabelle walked back along rue Rambuteau. Her first stop, she thought, should be the National Library of France. *La Bibliothèque Nationale*. She had almost reached Les Halles when she caught sight of him. The man in the homburg. He was coming out of the market, eating a red apple as he crossed the street – and ahead of her, he couldn't know she was there. Her curiosity piqued, Mirabelle decided to turn the tables and fall in behind. It was only fair –he'd followed her, after all. She kept carefully out of sight as he crossed the road and headed in the direction of Saint-Eustache. The towers at either end of the church's grand façade were clearly visible above the lower roofs of the tenements on either side. The man flung his apple core into the gutter as he passed the church. Mirabelle kept her distance. The pavement widened into a little square and the fellow slowed slightly as he lit a cigarette before cutting down the rue du Jour and disappearing inside the café where she had first seen him the day before.

So, she thought, he's watching Christine Moreau. He must be. She checked her watch. It was still early. There was no sign of life in the dressmaker's apartment, but then yesterday Christine had been embroidering by the light from the window. Mirabelle had no desire to visit Miss Moreau again, but she was curious about what was going on in this little backstreet. Carefully, she peered into the café from the other side of the

road. The man was chatting to another fellow who was sitting at the table the first had occupied the day before. An empty brandy glass was cleared away efficiently and a coffee laid down. These men knew the place, and the waiter, it seemed, knew their order. It looked as if they had been stationed here for some time.

Mirabelle pulled back. Was the man in the Mackintosh part of a surveillance team? If there was a twenty-four-hour watch on Christine Moreau there had to be a good reason. What on earth was the woman up to? Mirabelle turned and walked on slowly, keeping her face out of the men's field of vision, then pulled into a doorway as she heard the door of the café click open. Keeping one eye on the pavement, she fumbled in her handbag as if she was looking for a key. The second man emerged into the street, pulling his coat around him. He was taller than the first but cut from the same jib and, Mirabelle noticed, he wore an identical Mackintosh and a homburg – as if it was some kind of uniform. Often you could tell where someone came from by their clothes, but these outfits were as hard to place as the man's accent in the church the day before. Mirabelle wondered whether they might be American. Were they FBI? Jack had always decried the Americans. Their codes were so simplistic a child could unravel them. During the war the SOE had convinced the Yanks that they should handle that side of things. In fact, they had insisted they handle it. British codemakers stumped the world. The Americans couldn't keep up. 'They're famous but incompetent. FBI. That's what it bloody stands for,' Jack had said. But the Yanks took the criticism of their coding abilities well. Everyone had to give them that. 'They're so damn well balanced it makes you want to push it to see how far you'd get,' she remembered some wag quipping at the Oxford and Cambridge Club. The man yesterday had been incompetent. She'd given him the slip as if it was a first day

exercise and he a rookie. She mustn't get cocky, she told herself. Just because she'd done it once.

It was for this reason that she gave the second man a decent headstart before she set off in his wake. She felt safer following him than the first man – as far as she knew, this one had never seen her. He headed round the corner and Mirabelle kept her distance as she tailed him past the seafood display in the window of *Au Pied de Cochon* and up towards the cafés and restaurants on the main road. He stopped to buy cigarettes from a kiosk, and although she didn't want to get close enough to hear what he said, she wasn't too far away to see that when he smiled at the pretty girl behind the counter, his teeth were certainly not American. The Yanks loved dental work. Their smiles were almost identically perfect, but this man's mouth betrayed a less fastidious approach.

Two blocks along, he turned into a side street and disappeared inside a boarding house. Mirabelle peered through the window as she walked past. A shabby dining room was empty of guests, and beyond it a dimly lit hallway and a staircase were similarly deserted. On the upper floors the shutters were barred. Was there a sitting room to the rear or had the man gone to his room? Mirabelle turned back, stared at the hotel's bashed brass doorknob and decided to risk going inside.

The door was hung so that it opened and closed with a slight wobble. The hallway was silent apart from the ticking of the clock on the wall behind the reception desk. Sporting her best Parisian accent, Mirabelle called out. No one came so she peered over the high-fronted reception and squinted at the register, trying to make out the names. It only took a few seconds. Yes, there was only one party of two men. She smiled. They were booked in as Les Frères Kakarov and had taken the cheapest rooms on the top floor. So the man's accent had been Russian. Brothers, indeed. The Mackintosh and homburg were good choices, she reflected. The disguise had rendered both

men practically anonymous – at least she hadn't been able to guess where they were from. Russians were generally welcome in Paris. Long before the war broke out the city was the centre of the White Russian world as supporters of the Tsar fled the Communists and set up home elsewhere. Tea houses had opened in Passy serving borscht and caviar, and all things Russian had become fashionable for a while. More recently Russia had been an ally during the war, though the French natural sentiment, like the British, was probably to the left of Hitler rather than to the right of Stalin. Still, two Russian men spending some time in the City of Light would be made very welcome. So why were Les Frères Kakarov here? What was Christine Moreau up to?

Mirabelle was still beside the desk when the front door opened behind her and a woman stepped confidently onto the tiled floor of the hallway. She was plump and rosy-cheeked. Her coat was open and she was wearing an olive-green dress trimmed with tatty black lace, which Mirabelle couldn't help thinking would be more suitable for the evening even if it had seen better days. The woman sniffed and smiled at once. When she spoke her accent was from another part of Paris – somewhere poorer.

'I'm looking for the Russian. He wanted me at ten o'clock.'

'Top floor,' Mirabelle replied helpfully. 'He just went up.' She gave the woman a head start and then sneaked upstairs behind her. The stairway was uncarpeted and she tiptoed on the balls of her feet so as not to make a noise. The walls might once have been painted caramel but they had long faded to grey and were unsullied by any attempt to refresh them. The building ran to five storeys and the stairs were steep. Mirabelle's heart pounded as she held onto the banister. Above her she could hear the girl knocking sharply and the Russian's door creaking open and then closing. Encouraged, she picked up her pace. The top-floor landing accommodated three bedrooms; the nearest lavatory

was on the floor below. The skylight was caked in old leaves and grit; cupola would have been too grand a name for it. A brick chimney stack bore down from above. Mirabelle put her ear to the first door, then she knelt down to look through the keyhole and was rewarded with a view of the lady in the olive-green dress removing her attire. The Russian had his hands curled round her frame as she wrestled with a zip. She looked as if she was propped against the bed frame, ready at any moment to fall into place. The room was furnished sparsely and the bed not wide enough to share. Unperturbed, the Russian and the woman he had hired piled on top of each other. The springs groaned. Mirabelle smiled slightly. As long as this continued she was safe from interruption.

She turned her attention to the other two rooms on the landing. A preliminary peep through each keyhole revealed that neither appeared to be occupied, but she wanted to be sure. She slipped her hand inside her bag and removed her SOE lock picks – the ones Eddie had given her. The gift had been tongue in cheek but the picks had come in handy several times. Recently she had remarked to Vesta that they were so much more useful than face powder or toffees, items that seemed to take up most of the room in Vesta's handbag.

The hotel's locks were cheaply made and presented no problem. The first room had definitely not been occupied for days, if not weeks. A thin layer of dust covered the bedside table and the air smelled faintly of turpentine. When Mirabelle put a hand on the single bed it felt damp. The second room must have been used more recently. There was no dust to speak of on the chest of drawers and the window was open an inch. However, there were no personal possessions – not so much as a used match. The wardrobe was empty, and there was nothing under the bed. If the other Russian was staying here he would appear to be travelling light. Perhaps the Brothers Kakarov shared the room next door, using it in shifts.

She let herself out and crept silently back downstairs. She wasn't sure this was getting her closer to Philip Caine, but even though Christine Moreau had chased her off she didn't like to think of any woman being under covert surveillance. Besides, the urge to report back was ingrained. The flow of information was vital. An agent in the field couldn't tell what might be important back at HQ. She'd have to tell someone at home what was going on.

At the reception desk an old man was now perched on a high stool. '*Madame*?' he said as Mirabelle descended the last flight. His voice betrayed his absent-mindedness. He didn't recognise her, but that didn't mean she wasn't a guest.

'*Bonjour,*' Mirabelle replied and walked straight onto the street, looking for a post office. Working from memory, she took a right turn and was shortly rewarded with a fancy set of railings and a blue sign for La Poste. Inside, she headed for the telegraph desk.

'To London, please,' she said. 'Duke's Hotel, St James's.'

The young girl behind the desk sat up straight. 'What name?'

'Edward Brandon,' Mirabelle spelled it out.

She paused a moment as the girl took it down. A telegram was a comparatively public way to convey information. Mirabelle bit her lip. She picked up a pencil to write the message. *Miss Moreau serving gin at home but across the road men drinking vodka.* It was the best she could come up with and Eddie would know whom to pass it on to, or at least he'd be able to find out. She hadn't intended to be a sneak but inexplicably she felt sorry for Christine. No one should remain that hurt for so long, and besides, the Russians weren't allies any more. Neither of the French nor of the British.

'Just sign it from MB,' she said. She hadn't had a code name and she'd never reported to Eddie anyway. Rather wistfully she thought that the last nickname she had had was when her grandmother called her a little plum.

The girl at the desk silently translated the sentence and looked up, raising her brows a fraction. Mirabelle smiled and laid a note on the counter, and the child relaxed, calculating the cost and dispensing change. People often sent inexplicable messages. It was usually because they were trying to keep the telegram as short as possible. Messages were charged by the letter. As things went this was a long one. Mirabelle popped the coins in her purse.

'Good.' The girl tried out her English. 'It goes now. You have a busy day?'

'Thank you.' Mirabelle smiled. 'I'm going to the library.'

Chapter 17

The real voyage of discovery consists not in seeking new landscapes, but in having new eyes.

The National Library of France had an immense and ornate reading room with a vaulted ceiling studded with round skylights that ought to have flooded the place with light even on a dull day such as this, but Mirabelle decided she had never been anywhere so restrained. Even the daylight appeared reticent. Despite the atmosphere, it was pleasant to come in from the cold. She found a desk, laid her handbag to one side, removed her gloves and draped her coat over the back of her chair. The place was busy. Most of the tables were occupied by men wearing tweed suits and glasses, and there was a general air of relaxation. On a Saturday, Mirabelle thought, there were probably lots of hobbyists. The air smelled of musty paper with the vaguest whiff of pipe smoke. The sound of pencils taking notes provided a low scrape and hum, almost like radio interference. Occasionally someone coughed.

Mirabelle left her things at the table and crossed the highly polished floor as quietly as she could to present herself at the counter. She smiled. A wide-faced man of no more than thirty regarded her without lightening his serious demeanour. He nodded curtly and scooped up some small pencils that littered the counter, placing them in a tatty cardboard box to one side. Mirabelle leaned forward and kept her voice low.

'I'm looking for information on a German who lived in Paris during the war. His name was von der Grün,' she said in perfect

French. She might not be interested in seeing Christine again, but she was drawn to the woman's wartime activities. If von der Grün had been Christine's lover, she'd like to know how he fitted into the picture. A good operative would always find out everything she could. In Paris at the same time as Christine and potentially Philip Caine, von der Grün might be connected to the business with Jack and Bulldog Bradley. It was not impossible. If he was alive and she could find him, she'd like to ask him some questions. 'I think he was in the SS,' she added. If the librarian had looked serious before, he now emanated an especially frosty air. Mirabelle was undeterred. 'He must have come from a wealthy family. Von der Grün, you see,' she said helpfully. 'Any information you can help me dig up might be useful.'

It crossed Mirabelle's mind that Parisians were not easy to engage in conversation. Perhaps that was why the Resistance had been so successful. Reticence was clearly a national characteristic, even if the other person spoke French. Such an attitude was a disaster for the success of covert operations, which relied on the unguarded slip, the unconscious choosing of one word over another.

'We do not keep military records here,' the librarian said. 'At least not more recent records. We have a Napoleon archive, if that might interest you?'

'Perhaps there are newspapers from the period? The occupation?' Mirabelle stuck to the point. 'Copies of *Le Monde*?'

The man looked at Mirabelle as if she was a fool. '*Le Monde* was only started at the end of the war. You might like to look at *Le Figaro* or *La Croix*. It makes no difference – during the occupation all newspapers were censored. But you can search on microfiche. The man you're looking for might be mentioned but you will have to keep in mind that the information is unlikely to be accurate. Everything was propaganda.' He waved a hand dismissively in the direction of the back wall, the arc of his arm elegant as Nijinsky's. Mirabelle squinted. She

could make out a short run of microfiche machines, all of which were currently occupied.

'What I really need is a *Who's Who*,' she mused.

'Ah, we keep the reference books over there.'

'Even for foreigners? A German?'

'This is *la Bibliothèque Nationale de France*,' the man said rather grandly, though Mirabelle noted that he sounded only marginally more optimistic than he had about the material held on microfiche.

'Thank you.'

Mirabelle regarded the tall bookshelf that had been indicated and decided to start there. The first shelves were stacked with volumes of the encyclopedia – initially in French and then, interestingly, in English. Further along she found a *Dictionary of National Biography* but the entries only covered the UK. Next to it was a current *Who's Who* – the book she had already consulted at the Army and Navy Club in London, though here it was shelved with several previous editions. Mirabelle pulled over a short run of rosewood steps to peruse the higher shelves. Carefully she climbed upwards, aware that next to the bookcase one of the men had stopped reading and was eyeing her ankles as they passed his line of sight.

The book titles ran from French and Latin to Norwegian and what looked like Japanese. It's a veritable Tower of Babel, she thought. Then her finger landed on a publication entitled *Wer Ist's*. There were several volumes and she took a moment to find the most recent, which was already almost twenty years old, published in 1935. The book was heavy – as she pulled it from the shelf she tottered uncertainly on the steps, unable to see her own feet as she felt her way back to the floor.

'Please.' The reader who had been watching her upwards progress offered his hand, and Mirabelle grasped it. She wished she hadn't taken off her gloves. Holding hands felt too

intimate. She snatched back her fingers as soon as she reached the safety of the floor.

'You're German?' the man enquired in a whisper, seeing the title of the book she was carrying.

Mirabelle felt her cheeks flush with displeasure. 'I'm English.' She cursed herself for sounding as prim as a nanny. But really, what a thing to say.

The man smiled and watched as she hurried self-consciously back to her desk. The book landed with a satisfying thump. Mirabelle's German was rudimentary. Over the years she'd picked up some words and she had a feel for languages. Translation, after all, had been her job before the war. She hoped she'd manage. At first she simply flicked through the pages, realising that the volume was pristine, as if no one had opened it since it had been shelved. But then why should they? It was as Matron Gard had said – material simply sat as fresh as the day it was put away, waiting decades for a single reader, perhaps even centuries.

Reaching the section marked 'Von', which was, of necessity, extremely thick, she trailed the margin with her finger. It transpired there were three entries under 'Von der Grün'. Frederick, Kurt and Wilhelm. Mirabelle discounted Frederick immediately. In 1935 he was already in his late sixties. That put him beyond military service during the war and, she thought, also made it less likely that he was the von der Grün who had been Christine Moreau's lover.

The other two were more promising. Mirabelle turned her attention to them – Kurt and Wilhelm, who were cousins. Both were married and would have been in their thirties during the war and so of military age. Both had titles and estates in the Rhineland. The Germanic system of inheritance, like the French, she recalled, was different from the one at home where only the eldest son inherited titles or property. In Europe brothers and even cousins shared estates.

Nowhere, she sighed, endowed women. These men's sisters would have had to marry to keep their status – a situation of which it was too easy to fall foul. *Wer Ist's* didn't appear even to list women in their own right. Their names only appeared as the wives of the men who merited inclusion. What happened to the spinsters? The unmarried sisters? The maiden aunts? When Mirabelle's parents died she had inherited their money, but only because the Bevans were forward thinking, in possession of a private fortune and there were no titles involved. In that she had been lucky.

Turning back to *Wer Ist's*, she kept reading, sounding the words in her head to help her understand. It was like being a schoolgirl again. Kurt, it would seem, was a member of the Nazi party. Wilhelm was not listed as such but then the book was printed four years before war broke out. Mirabelle squinted. She couldn't quite make out the vocabulary but she thought it said that Wilhelm had a historic claim to estates in a place named Reichsland Elsass-Lothringen. She sounded out the words under her breath. Rhineland was in the south of Germany. It bordered French territory but she hadn't heard of this other place. With one eye on the man who had accused her of being German, she returned to the reference section, pulled out an atlas and returned to her desk. She flicked to Germany and examined the map carefully. She couldn't find a place name that corresponded with the entry in *Wer Ist's* so she tried Austria. No luck. Mirabelle's finger hovered. She turned her attention back to the Rhineland. The map was on a workable scale though the place names were given in French. Still, the places that corresponded to Kurt and Wilhelm's rather fancy titles were discernable. They related to estates very close to the French border and all borders, Mirabelle knew, were fluid. Reichsland Elsass-Lothringen, she repeated under her breath. Elsass. Elsass. Was that Alsace? The French border country had been under German administration in the

decades running up to the Great War. Its heartland was not even a hundred miles from Kurt von der Grün's estate and not much further from Wilhelm's. It was not unimaginable that Wilhelm von der Grün, and perhaps the whole of his family, had a pre-existing connection with France. If *Wer Ist's* listed his claim to titles in what was in fact a foreign country, his forebears might well have been among the occupying forces that had swept into Alsace Lorraine during the Prussian war. Mirabelle smiled. In that case, being brought up close to the border and, particularly in Wilhelm's case, feeling entitled to claim property in France, might well mean the von der Grüns spoke French. And that was a skill the Nazi machine might have found useful.

Flopping into her seat, Mirabelle eyed the bank of microfiche machines against the back wall. There were only three of them and all still in use. She got up and went over, checking her watch. Getting this far had already taken an hour. This was the kind of job she'd usually delegate to Vesta. She peered over the shoulder of one of the current incumbents, seeing how the machines worked. It had been a while.

'You pick up the film over there,' the man hissed. 'And wait your turn.'

'*Pardon*,' Mirabelle mouthed.

She glanced at the banks of little boxes, one of which no doubt contained what she needed, and with a sigh she moved over to take a closer look. The Nazis had taken Paris in the summer of 1940 and that meant Mirabelle had approximately four years' worth of newspapers to examine. Occasionally the presses must have stopped – it was wartime after all – but that still left well over a thousand daily issues. And if *Le Figaro* was anything like *The Times* or the *Daily Telegraph* there would be several editions every day as stories developed. Mirabelle paused. Given that kind of challenge, Vesta would simply start reading through the mountain of material from the beginning. The girl

was habitually interested in everything, but there had to be another way. What would Matron Gard do, Mirabelle wondered.

She ran back over the material she had already uncovered. Catherine had said that von der Grün was in Paris to amass money for the German war machine so it was fair to assume that he'd been involved in the deportation of Jews to concentration camps. Mirabelle tried to remember when that had happened. She knew the deportations hadn't started immediately. It had taken a year, perhaps eighteen months, before the first Jews had been sent away in response to Resistance attacks on Nazi units. The French Resistance was largely peopled by Jewish men who had left Germany in the 1930s. Such a measure was well thought out. The Nazis understood cruelty. They knew how to make a punishment hit home. Mirabelle placed the deportations carefully in time. It had been winter – after Christmas in 1941. The British had had to shore up the spirits of the resisters, some of whom watched their families being sent away because of what they had done. More than a few hadn't been quick enough to hide and were sent to their deaths. As a result there had been a dip in Resistance activities that lasted for months.

Behind her a chair scraped across the floor and a microfiche reader became free. Mirabelle hurriedly picked up copies of *Le Figaro* for December 1941 and January 1942 and popped the first negative into the machine. This, she realised as she scrolled down, was going to take a while.

The light outside was dimming and she had only reached the summer of 1942 when she decided to take a break. The tone of *Le Figaro* was upbeat – the paper had published a *German's Guide to Paris* and its editorials were eager to support the Nazi ethos when the Marais had been cleared. Mirabelle realised she was grinding her teeth as she took in the words. She stopped, looked up and told herself it was only propaganda,

which was certainly not absent from British publications at the time. But British propaganda had humour – its tongue firmly in its cheek. If the British favoured understatement, the editor at *Le Figaro* certainly did not. The endless adulation of the Nazi victories of 1941 turned her stomach. She had seen it with her own eyes from the other side of the Channel. She knew people who'd died in the Blitz and men who'd died in action. Her skin prickled as *Le Figaro* reported British reverses – the retreat into Singapore and its eventual surrender to the Japanese. She remembered a friend of Jack's who'd cried when he'd found out. He had come into the office. 'Now, now,' Jack had said, closing the door to save the man's embarrassment, 'we'll come through it, old boy.' By contrast *Le Figaro* was jubilant – Tokyo and Paris were among a brotherhood of cities basking in the sun of Nazi victories. It felt wrong even to read the words and Mirabelle struggled to keep her attention on the point – there had been no mention of von der Grün. When she got to the sinking of the HMS *Eagle*, Mirabelle looked away. She wondered if there might be somewhere near the library to get a cup of tea. She could do with a break.

Looking up, she saw the man next to the reference section clearing his desk. She didn't want to be misunderstood so she decided to wait till he left. She'd peruse another newspaper. Turning back and focusing on the next *Le Figaro* she caught the date. 12 August 1942. How curious – in her attempt to find out about Christine Moreau's lover she had overlooked the fact that this was more or less the time when Matthew Bradley and Philip Caine must have slipped over the border. They would have been exhausted after the long walk through German territory but excited as they passed into France and the prospect of getting home loomed closer. Mirabelle imagined Caine telling Bradley about his fiancée as they travelled – confiding in his friend as they crossed the potentially deadly terrain. Mirabelle had never been trapped in the field, not really, but as

she understood it, people in such circumstances focused on their families, or at least on the people they loved. That and food, which in wartime Britain, she had to admit, was hardly inspiring. Bradley and Caine would have had to be very hungry before they eulogised Spam fritters or egg powder omelettes. At least in France the food tasted better, though it was probably equally scarce.

Back on the microfiche she noticed that editions of *Le Figaro* were several pages thinner during August. The German occupation had not reduced the appetite for leaving the capital during the hottest part of the summer. Paris's middle and upper classes still made for their country cottages. Suddenly Mirabelle sat straighter. Here he was. Perhaps the dearth of local news was the reason why Wilhelm von der Grün's arrival was noted in the social column. He was SS – a Standartenführer or regimental officer, Mirabelle translated. She thought this was a reasonably senior position although not one that would normally require half a column. She read on. Standartenführer von der Grün was staying in his family home in the 16th arrondissement, it reported. The Standartenführer would be a welcome addition to Paris society. He had always loved the city and was glad to be stationed here for a stretch. I'll bet, Mirabelle thought. It seemed she had been right about the von der Grüns' connection to France. So Christine Moreau's lover had arrived already a wealthy man. The 16th was to the west of the city at Passy. From addresses there near the river you could see the Eiffel Tower. It was not a cheap area and Mirabelle discounted any idea of Wilhelm von der Grün as a down-at-heel aristocrat who had lost his Alsatian title. Well, well. It was only a shame that *Le Figaro* didn't stretch to a photograph. She switched off the microfiche and flicked the celluloid between her fingers before stowing it carefully back in its box. Behind her someone cleared his throat. She had been using the machine for a long time.

'Sorry,' she said, getting to her feet. 'I'm finished now.'

She hadn't meant to hog the facilities. She managed to muster a smile and was set to deliver another apology when she looked round and her face fell. It was the man from the reference section.

'Perfect. Perhaps I could tempt you to a glass of wine, mademoiselle?'

Mirabelle momentarily considered insisting on 'madame', but it seemed petty, and apart from anything else it wasn't true. 'Thank you, no. I'm not finished. I'm looking for street directories now.' Her voice was insistent.

A glimmer of a smile played about the man's lips as if she had said something flirtatious. 'You want to look up a friend's address?'

'No. I need old street directories. Historic ones for Paris. 1942.' Mirabelle gathered her notes and swept her handbag under her arm. 'Thank you.' Dismissing him, she stalked back towards her desk.

The man put on his hat.

'Downstairs.' He pointed at the floor, his voice tinged with regret as if the glass of wine he had planned was certain to have been exceptional. 'You must look downstairs, mademoiselle.'

Mirabelle laid her coat over her arm and nodded a silent thank you. French men were extraordinary. English chaps didn't behave like that – as if in turning down the offer of a drink the course of one's life had been tragically diverted. There was a good deal to be learned, no doubt, from the great French art of suggestion but she had no time now. The library closed in an hour and there was von der Grün's family home to find.

Chapter 18

*I know what I'm fleeing from but
not what I'm searching for.*

The light was fading from the sky as Mirabelle strode along the pavement half an hour later. Along the Seine the low winter sun had disappeared and the air bit her skin with teeth as sharp as needles. With no clouds overhead, it was set to be a particularly chilly night. The stars, however, were spectacular as she headed westwards. It was too late to walk to Passy but Mirabelle wanted to clear her head before she hailed a cab. The words she had ploughed through that afternoon constituted a veritable mudslide of information, some of which was at odds with the way she had imagined Paris during the war. At the time her attention had been wholly taken up by Resistance activities and it was odd to think that for many people life in France's capital had been normal during the Nazi occupation, not entirely unlike the lives of some Londoners at home. The paper had made it sound like a celebration. There had been spring balls and the Opéra had remained open, though it had played mostly Germanic compositions by Schumann, Strauss and Wagner.

Mirabelle's breath clouded as she passed through the pools of streetlight, following the curve of the Right Bank. After ten minutes and with numb fingers, she hailed a taxi and asked to be taken to the address she had found listed in the Paris directory for 1943 under von der Grün's name, 25 rue de Siam. In the current directory the house remained unlisted. It was

almost as if the structure had disappeared. In the shame of post-war recriminations, had the von der Grün family moved? In the cab it was colder than outside, or perhaps that was only because she wasn't moving any more. Mirabelle shuddered and clapped her gloved hands as the driver took a route across the Champs-Élysées, affording Mirabelle a view of the Arc de Triomphe.

'Touristes,' the man said, waving airily towards the edifice and Mirabelle wasn't sure if he was asking her if she was on holiday or whether he was making some comment about the crowds of people jammed onto the boulevard despite the weather.

As the cab passed she caught a glossy glimpse of the Eiffel Tower from the vantage point of Passy and gasped at some of the smart shops in the streets leading away from the centre, with mannequins sporting a froth of tulle skirts and smocked blouses. Paris was getting ready for spring. Further into the 16th arrondissement the streets were quieter. There was a reserve about this part of town. Outside expensive-looking restaurants chauffeurs smoked cigarettes as they waited for their employers to finish their drinks – or, she mused, was it possible that some people were still at the table from lunchtime? The cab drove on. Several grand Second Empire houses with mansard roofs had been converted into hotels. A gaggle of women wearing mink coats emerged from the doorway of one and walked in a diamond-studded cluster, their voices carrying on the chill evening air, excited to be out and in Paris on a Saturday night.

'Touristes,' the cab driver said again, as if no French women would dream of making such a racket.

The rue de Siam was beyond the part of Passy from which the Eiffel Tower could be viewed, and well away from the shops. Close to the Bois de Boulogne, the house was located on a leafy residential stretch not quite as grand as the

boulevards that surrounded it. The driver slowed and Mirabelle peered up at the buildings. The pale stone of which everything was built reminded her of Belgravia, although it was carved more ornately here on the Continent. Maids and artists were no doubt accommodated in the attics, but in the houses themselves the city's most wealthy citizens took up residence. The smoke from a hundred household fires streamed into the clear night sky, though in many of the houses the windows were dark. In Belgravia at the weekend it was the same – people left for the country on Friday night. Mirabelle paid the driver and slammed the door behind her, realising how quiet it was in this part of the city. She could hear the creaking branches of the trees that lined the little street and those around it. Not far away, the Bois de Boulogne had been a hunting ground a hundred years ago and houses this close to it would have been at a premium – those were the days when the von der Grüns owned French territory and presumably decided to invest in a Parisian pied-à-terre. The 16th remained an address for the elite, but these days the old park housed seedy pockets of sex for sale by night and pleasant walks or rides in the daylight hours. The residents of the 16th complained about the night-time activities that were encroaching on their privileged existence, but the open space that the Bois afforded was impossible to contain.

Mirabelle crossed the uneven paving stones to number 25 and surveyed the building. Unlike some of the other houses, which had been separated into apartments, it appeared to be a single residence, and a well-maintained one at that. She stepped backwards. The construction of these houses mitigated against easy access. The windows onto the pavement were girded with elegant yet sturdy iron grilles. Where Parisian aristocrats had stabled their horses Mirabelle couldn't be sure, but there were no single-storey mews to the rear to provide a weak spot in the building's security. With the lights out she couldn't even

guess which room was which. At the front door there was a discreet brass plate. She peered, and smiled. *Comte de Vert,* it said. The name was almost a direct French translation of von der Grün. So, she pondered, after whatever punishment had been doled out to him – the year or two in prison to which Catherine had so stridently objected – the Standartenführer had assimilated, or so it would seem. That explained why the house had apparently disappeared from the street directory – von der Grün had changed his name. It was one way to try to sidestep anti-German sentiment in the aftermath of the war and one that had worked for the British royal family a generation before.

Mirabelle rang the bell and waited. There was no reply and the windows remained dark above her. There was no easy way in. With a sigh she glanced further along the street and seeing a discreet sign for a hotel she walked along the pavement and entered. It would at least be warmer inside, she reasoned. The hallway was floored, rather flashily, in Italian marble and her heels clicked along it. At the reception desk a porter with a waxed moustache looked up. 'Welcome, madame, to the Hôtel Siam.'

Mirabelle enquired after a room – something to the rear of the building so it would be quiet and not on too high a floor for preference, and, she added, she'd need a reservation for dinner. The porter reached for a key and quoted a figure three times what she was paying at the Hôtel Rambeau. Mirabelle nodded. 'But I must eat first. I am terribly hungry.'

With an understanding smile the man emerged smartly from the desk, relieved her of her coat and showed her into a pleasant dining room decorated in shades of peach. The linen tablecloths were so heavily starched that Mirabelle wondered whether they might stand up alone should the tables beneath them be removed. The porter handed her to the old waiter as if she was a long-awaited treasure. It was so old-fashioned that

she felt she was stepping back in time. Her grandmother would recognise this place, surely. The atmosphere in the room was agreeable and Mirabelle's stomach rumbled hungrily – there was a scent of roasted meat on the air. This early in the evening only three tables were taken, all by couples, which meant there was a low hum of conversation and occasional laughter. The women, Mirabelle noticed, were dressed far more appropriately than her daytime suit, but then for all anyone knew she might have been travelling. Her attention was drawn by a blonde in a black cocktail dress whose *décolletage* was scattered liberally with pearls and diamonds. Mirabelle scolded herself – she must focus on the business in hand. The dining-room window opened onto the rear and she indicated she'd like a table beside it.

'I can't see much but it will be pleasant none the less. The moon tonight is beautiful,' she explained, asking for pâté and some chicken, not even looking at the menu. 'And please choose a nice wine for me.'

The waiter nodded and Mirabelle took her seat. He scurried to pour a glass of burgundy.

'I knew this street during the war,' she said, as if confiding in him.

'Difficult times.'

'Yes. A German lived further along this road. An SS officer.' The man looked uncomfortable. 'The wine . . .'

'Yes. It's lovely. Thank you.' Mirabelle laid the napkin on her lap. 'I can't remember the fellow's name. An absolute horror.' She gave a shudder. 'Brün, was it?'

'Von der Grün.'

'Ah. That's it. Number 25.' Mirabelle lifted her glass. So people who lived here knew who he was. 'Well, *vive la France*. Here's to ten years of them being gone.'

The waiter nodded curtly. He didn't want to talk about it.

'Is that a garden outside?' Mirabelle enquired.

'In the summer we serve drinks there before dinner but at this time of year . . .'

'Yes. It is chilly. No colder than London though. Tell me, what happened to him, do you know? The German fellow?'

The waiter shrugged in a non-committal fashion.

'I do not know, madame,' he said and disappeared.

Mirabelle peered once more into the darkness beyond the glossy window. The glass reflected the partly drawn curtain but beyond that there were shadows that suggested the layout to the rear. Two buildings along, over a boundary wall, the back of number 25 sported no lights, though above it there was a breathtaking scatter of stars. Mirabelle wondered if Christine Moreau had come here. Had von der Grün taken her for dinner in the restaurants she had passed on the main road? Had they enjoyed a bottle of wine together – perhaps even in this very room in the Hôtel Siam? And if so, did they have a favourite table? Her thoughts were interrupted by the waiter, bringing a slice of *foie gras* and a basket of soft, warm brioche. Mirabelle smiled. There was no harm, surely, in enjoying herself.

'Thank you.' She smiled at him. 'What a treat.'

After dinner she was shown to a bedroom on the first floor. If the accommodation at the Hôtel Rambeau was serviceable, the room in the Hôtel Siam was a study in luxury. The bed was covered with a quilted satin throw and the bedside lamps were hand-painted with images of kingfishers and daisies. Long windows opened onto a small iron balcony. Mirabelle tipped the porter generously, and locked the door behind him. Not wasting a second, she left a small sheaf of francs on the dresser, switched out the lights and stepped deftly through the open window into the darkness. From the vantage point of the balcony the garden below was beset by light and shadow from the hotel's windows, but beyond that there was only the thick Parisian night. Mirabelle pulled on her coat and more importantly, her gloves. She'd need their purchase to keep hold, she

thought as she tucked her handbag securely in place, manoeu-vred herself over the balcony and climbed into the hotel garden. Dinner sat satisfyingly in her stomach and her curios-ity was lit. Number 25 was only two walls away.

The first was easy enough to scale, even in high heels. The mortar was soft and finding a foothold presented no problem. High above in the house she heard a baby crying. Then she launched herself over the second wall and into the garden of number 25. Dodging between the iron laundry posts she noted that there was a well-maintained herb rockery to one side. The rear gave away no more secrets than that, however. The house was still dark. Mirabelle crept up to the window and peered inside. In the shadows she could make out a kitchen with a pantry leading off it. To the left there was what she guessed was a laundry where a vent protruded from the wall. She tried the back door into the kitchen but it was locked so she turned her attention to the window, which was not. The sash slid open easily. Hauling herself through she caught her skirt on a tap and only narrowly missed ripping the sturdy woollen fabric before she clumsily tumbled onto the floor. The house was silent, a sleeping giant. Mirabelle got to her feet and dusted herself down. She reached over and closed the window.

There was no fresh food in preparation, she noted. No bread on the side or soup on the hob. No one was dining today at number 25 rue de Siam, though the kitchen was clearly in use. A bowl of eggs lay on a shelf and beside it sat some lemons and a few apples. Someone lived here, but they were away. A good opportunity to look round then, she thought as she crept past the kitchen table and out into the hallway. The only sound was the ticking of a clock that emanated from the stairwell. In a shaft of moonlight Mirabelle made out the old timepiece – a grandfather clock on the landing above. Such mechanisms, she reminded herself, required winding on a weekly basis. She mustn't rest on her laurels; there may be staff here.

Carefully, she crossed the hallway and went into what turned out to be a dining room. A pair of Sèvres vases sat on the rosewood table and the walls were decorated with a collection of landscapes in the French style, mounted in gilded frames. The house, Mirabelle noted, didn't feel German at all. On the other side of the hall was a study, and perusing the shelves she noticed several books in English including the latest Graham Greene and several publications by George Orwell. There was a French–German dictionary and a number of books on German military history, including two biographies of Kaiser Wilhelm. In the drawers of the desk she uncovered the usual array of paper knives and fountain pens, elastic bands and paperclips. There was a tailor's bill marked for the attention of Le Comte de Vert, a letter from the Banque de France and a chequebook with stubs made out to a vineyard, a doctor and Maxim's. Mirabelle replaced everything carefully exactly where she found it.

Up the main staircase and past the clock she entered a drawing room where almost every available surface was covered by photographs. Some of them seemed very old and had been taken in the countryside – men dressed in tweeds and carrying shotguns. A beautiful woman stood in a long window, the light clinging to her eerily. She was wearing a Victorian day dress, and Mirabelle wondered what colour it had been. Through the window behind the figure, a street cut to the right in a familiar dogleg. It was London, surely. Mirabelle searched on. To the rear of a table she eventually found a single print encased in a plain silver frame. This, she thought, must be Wilhelm – a man in his thirties wearing an indistinct black collar. The shot was close in, cropped to frame his face so that the details of his outfit were all but obliterated, but still. The man was the right age. It looked the right time. And from what Mirabelle could make out, the dark edges of clothing might well be an SS uniform. He was good-looking and less haughty than she had

imagined. His eyes were intelligent, if steely. On the mantel-piece were pictures of children playing – contemporary photographs of two little boys in school uniform. Perhaps these were Wilhelm's children. He'd be in his late forties now, she supposed. She wondered if he had married one of the women whose photographs trailed across the mantel. Poor Christine Moreau.

Mirabelle sat on a high-backed velvet sofa and it occurred to her that Catherine the seamstress had been right – the house seemed too normal. Surely von der Grün didn't deserve this beautiful, ordered domestic arrangement. Did the war count for nothing? A long window overlooked the street and she gazed at the glassy pavement trying to piece everything together. Then she noticed the woman. She was advancing along the rue de Siam, dressed in a well-cut dark woollen coat and a stovepipe hat (the height of fashion). She was carrying a capacious handbag slung over her left arm. There was some-thing familiar in the way she moved. Mirabelle got up and stood to one side of the window so that she couldn't be seen. Yes, she thought, recognising the figure as it advanced, there was no doubt that it was Christine Moreau. A few feet below the window Christine looked around to check she wasn't being followed. From her vantage point Mirabelle cast an eye along the length of the pavement, but there was no sign of a man in a Mackintosh and a homburg. Then Christine reached into her handbag and extracted a long, thin box, and slid it through the letterbox of number 25.

The sound of it landing with a slap on the black-and-white tiles of the hallway echoed vaguely. Mirabelle stayed at the window, watching as Christine Moreau stalked back down the rue de Siam, before she descended the stairs. The box was wrapped in brown paper and string. Mirabelle unpicked it meticulously – many an amateur had been caught out by rush-ing. Inside, carefully ironed and folded, was a red rayon square

made from the patterned material that Mirabelle had seen delivered the day before to Christine Moreau's workshop on the rue du Jour. The scarf was edged in minute handstitching. A *Made in Paris* chit was sewn along one corner. Nothing was secreted inside the woven satin or the stitching. Mirabelle checked the box but there was nothing else – no note, not even an invoice. Carefully she returned the scarf to its packet, tied the string with the same knot it had arrived with and laid the parcel haphazardly on the floor at an angle as if it had just dropped through the letterbox. Her eyes narrowed. 'My goodness,' she muttered under her breath. 'What on earth is going on?'

Chapter 19

Knowing is not enough.

The next morning, after a night of fitful sleep in the Hôtel Rambeau, Mirabelle walked in the direction of the Marais with church bells ringing across the city on the clear February air. Sunday or not, long deliberation had brought her to the conclusion that there was only one way to proceed and she wasn't looking forward to it. She recalled Bill talking about just getting on with the job, but her heart sank at what might lie ahead as she set out.

At Saint-Eustache the pavement was crowded with Sunday worshippers – women in fancy hats and long gloves making their way inside escorted by less showily dressed gentlemen. A blind man squatted on the corner, begging in front of the door. Around him a scatter of children in matching navy coats with velvet collars played tag before they were rounded up by their mother and marched inside.

Checking her slim gold watch, Mirabelle noted the time as she turned onto the rue du Jour. From the top of the road she could not discern any activity in Christine Moreau's studio. Peering, she caught only a glimpse of the man in the Mackintosh and the homburg sitting in the café over the road. His partner was gone. She smiled – she hadn't been sure if the place would be open. The Russian had removed his hat. At the table he hovered over coffee and a half-eaten croissant, his copy of *Le Monde* held at a distance so he could read with one eye and keep the other on his mark. Mirabelle lingered discreetly

out of sight in a doorway on the other side of the road. When the waiter brought him a fresh cup, the man relinquished the newspaper and focused his attention on adding sugar. Mirabelle took her chance and knocked briskly on the door to one side of number 17 – the stairwell that led to the apartment above the haberdashery. A few moments later the girl from the day before appeared, a thick cardigan wrapped around her for warmth and a pair of men's boots on her feet, which she must have pulled on quickly to answer the unexpected caller.

'*Bonjour, madame.*' She showed no sign of recognition.

'I visited your shop yesterday. I found my friend,' Mirabelle ventured. 'Christine Moreau? She has a studio further down the street.'

The assistant's face opened into a grin. 'Oh, yes,' she said. 'We aren't open, you know. It's Sunday.'

Mirabelle smiled apologetically. 'The thing is, there's a man sitting in the café over there. I don't want him to see me visiting Mademoiselle Moreau. I wondered if you'd be kind enough to let me go the back way?' Mirabelle gestured towards the shop. 'I'd be terribly grateful. Is it possible to get through to the rear?'

The girl looked in the direction of the café. 'Men? They're nothing but trouble, though the trouble can be . . .' She searched for the word. 'Glorious.' She settled with a smile.

She let Mirabelle inside. The shop was dark. At the counter the girl had evidently finished the pink cardigan and was engaged in trimming a sea-green felt cloche hat with a matching ostrich feather. It was propped carefully on the edge so the feather tumbled over. Mirabelle couldn't help thinking it looked rather smart.

'You have talent.'

The compliment was waved off as the girl led the way into a tiny back room that opened onto the rear of the terrace.

'There,' she said, producing a key. 'He won't see you going this way.'

'Thank you.'

Outside, the back of the terrace was quite different from the well-kept gardens to the rear of the rue de Siam. As the girl opened the door Mirabelle reeled at the stale whiff that emanated from a rotting outdoor toilet, the walls of which were almost overgrown with thick ivy. The buildings on all sides, which were presentable enough from the pavement, looked as if they were crumbling privately back here where no one could see them. Window frames were split and stains sullied the stonework where the long iron pipes had occasionally burst. Mirabelle could hear hens clucking in a yard further along. In its favour, each yard was separated from its neighbour by ramshackle fencing, much of which had fallen into such disrepair that Mirabelle could step over it. It would be easy to find a way through.

'I'll leave the door open,' the girl offered. Mirabelle thanked her and set off.

There was something dispiriting about this flipside of the rue du Jour. At Christine Moreau's building cobwebs trailed from the sills, quivering in the breeze. The paint on the back door was peeling and the yard was completely overgrown, apart from a track that had been worn from the back door to the *pissoir*. A bucket with a huge hole in its base lay uselessly among the weeds. Mirabelle knocked and waited. There was no reply, but then it was quite possible she hadn't been heard. She scrabbled among the wood sorrel and dandelions to find some gravel, and stepping back threw it at the rear window of Christine Moreau's apartment. It hit with a raucous scatter. A few seconds later a shadow appeared in the grimy window above. Mirabelle raised her gloved hand but Christine Moreau snapped shut the thin curtain and withdrew. Mirabelle threw another handful of tiny stones against the glass but nothing stirred. This was going to be difficult. It wasn't surprising Christine didn't want to see her, but Mirabelle wanted answers.

She removed her SOE picks from her handbag and got to work. Not for the first time she thought the picks were the best present anyone had ever given her – she should have thanked Eddie properly when she'd seen him, if only she'd remembered. The lock was heavy but not difficult to manoeuvre, and in a few seconds she slid it aside and slipped through a small back room, which appeared to be all but derelict, and into the narrow hallway. Taking the stairs she rapped on the door to Christine's rooms on the first floor. There was no keyhole to tinker with, so there must be a bolt on the interior, but that afforded no easy way inside. What on earth did Christine do to lock the place when she left? Perhaps she had a padlock. Well, Mirabelle decided, there's nothing for it. I'll have to talk my way in. She put her hand on the wall and gathered her thoughts.

'Christine,' she called. 'Please.'

Silence.

'Christine. I need to speak to you. The men outside don't know I'm here. That's why I came from the back. Please. Let me in.'

This was going to be tricky. She'd need to tempt the woman somehow. Mirabelle moved her weight against the door jamb and took a deep breath. Her fingers tingled. She knew the only weapon in her arsenal was to be completely honest, but she'd never voiced these things before. Not to a soul.

'You were right yesterday.' She spoke loudly so the words would sound clear through the door. 'I was Jack Duggan's lover all through the war. And after it too. He promised the world – that's what you said, isn't it? Well, you were right: he promised it to me. The whole shebang.' Mirabelle was alarmed to find her throat becoming tight. She struggled against the feeling that she might cry. 'The thing is, he lied, Christine, and I'm only just realising that. I'd never have lied to him. I couldn't have. But now I'm here, the more I find out the less I know. Really, it's been a terrible trip. Jack meant everything in the

163

world to me and now I'm finding out he wasn't honest.' The admission left her scrambling in her handbag for a handker-chief, furious with herself as the tears seeped out. 'I loved him, you see, and the thing is he's been dead for years and I can't let him go. It's as if I'm waiting for him. It's as if he's going to come back any minute. I can't believe he came to Paris and I didn't know. But you knew. That's why I've come. I need you to tell me about it. Please. I want to understand.'

She felt she couldn't breathe as the words tumbled from her lips – a hideous admission of her failure. She'd been so naïve. Jack hadn't loved her enough. Her shoulders dropped, and tears streamed down her cheeks, but no sound emanated from the studio. Now she'd started, though, Mirabelle found it diffi-cult to stop. 'I want to know what he was doing here.' She kicked the skirting board behind her in frustration. 'Because now I don't even know if he ever really loved me. I don't even have that any more.' She gulped. The silence felt heavy on the air. She waited, but there was no response. Christine Moreau simply didn't care. Why should she?

Slowly, Mirabelle regained control of her breathing. Her gloves were wet where the handkerchief had proved insuffi-cient. Leaning against the wall, she blew her nose and pulled herself together. There was still no sign of life inside. She sniffed, her cheeks burning with humiliation as she turned towards the head of the stairs. 'The war may have left you scarred but I'm scarred too. I hadn't realised how badly.' She was about to leave when the sound of a bolt being drawn stopped her. Christine Moreau opened the door. She didn't meet Mirabelle's eye.

'That's Jack Duggan for you,' she said. 'That's British SOE all over. You'd better come in.'

The studio looked much as it had the day before. Mirabelle hovered awkwardly inside the doorway. She had only indulged herself in this kind of passionate outburst once before, when

she was nine years of age and had told her mother she wanted to read a book that had been deemed unsuitable. In her mind it had been vital at the time to know the story – the ensuing temper tantrum had been an outcry against a child's lack of autonomy. She couldn't even remember the name of the book now. Only the cover – a hand-drawn flyleaf in black and white. Thinking back, it must have been a ghost story. Edgar Allan Poe. Her mother had been right. On that occasion Mirabelle hadn't felt exhausted once she finished shouting but now she found she could scarcely drag herself into Christine Moreau's room. Such outbursts were for children, and then only for badly behaved ones. Her limbs felt heavy, as if they were trying to discourage her from continuing on this quest. Christine went to the dresser and pulled out one of the bottles of gin. She poured two glasses and added water from a jug.

'Here,' she said.

Mirabelle was about to object that it was too early, but what was the point? Gin was better than bourbon, at least. Better than vodka, for sure. She took the glass and downed it. Christine beamed and followed suit.

'There,' she said, and gestured that Mirabelle should sit at the table. 'We give them everything, don't we, and then they just disappear. Poof! They ignore us, yes? They want to pay us off? Money? Pah! Money is nothing.'

Mirabelle sank onto a chair. She was intrigued. 'What happened?' she asked.

Christine's eyes blazed. 'The history of the Resistance is written in men's names,' she spat. 'Our noble Frenchmen saved the country – that's what they say. Our noble Frenchmen were in German prison camps for most of it. Our noble Frenchmen saved their backs. They ignore us women now. So many women. And we were brave, you know. Us and the Jews. The ones who had fled from Germany. Between us we were the meat and bones of the French Resistance. Many of us died.

They were my friends. But now when they write the history, they lie, Miss Bevan. They talk about the glorious Frenchmen because Frenchmen want to believe they saved the country from the Nazis, and so we are sidelined. We will be forgotten, you'll see. They are creating a legend and legends endure. *Vive la France.*'

Mirabelle nodded. After her speech at the door she found herself tongue-tied for a moment. Her eyes fell to the scissors with which Christine Moreau had pursued her onto the street the day before.

'And I turned up and quoted the worst of them.'

A smiled played around Christine's lips. 'The very worst,' she said stoutly. 'We didn't do it so they would raise a monument in our memory. We did it for our country. For our children. But now it's over there will be no monuments to our achievements. That is clear. And they will only tell the stories of the men. Jack Duggan and Matthew Bradley were happy for that to be the case. They could have stood up and told the truth, but they didn't. They could have saved me, and instead of roaring like lions they squeaked like cowardly mice. The British!'

Mirabelle drew her attention back to the point. 'But you still work for us, don't you? The British, I mean.'

Christine looked nonplussed. 'Why do you say that?'

'I saw you. Last night. In Passy.'

Christine's expression betrayed no information. 'And that, I imagine, was not a coincidence,' she said smoothly. 'What were you doing in the 16th? I don't believe this is all about Jack. Who travels so far in search of a dead man? Who are you working for, Miss Bevan?'

'I'm not working for anyone. I haven't lied to you. Bulldog Bradley left me a letter when he died. He wanted me to find out what happened to Philip Caine. That's what I'm doing here. But it's cast up so much about Jack . . .'

Christine was a woman of long experience. She waited to see if Mirabelle would cry again. There was never any point in talking to someone who was crying. Mirabelle bit her lip and tried to focus. Christine Moreau controlled her body language minutely, she noticed. It was impossible to tell if Matthew Bradley and Philip Caine meant anything to her, just as it was impossible to guess what she had been doing on the rue de Siam last night.

'Would you like another drink?' Christine offered, crossing to the cabinet.

Mirabelle shook her head as Christine poured another measure of spirits and watched Mirabelle's eyes playing on the bottle. Slowly she added water.

'This is the only British thing I enjoy. They used to send it over during the war. At first I thought it wasn't as good as brandy. There was no good French brandy for months at a time. No brandy. No coffee. Pah! But once I started on gin I got used to it. It is originally a Dutch drink, of course.'

'Not that one,' Mirabelle said pleasantly.

'Well, anyone can make it.' Christine dismissed the implication. She took a small sip and sat down again. 'You don't have to worry about Jack Duggan. He told me about you once. Not by name, of course, but it must have been you.'

Mirabelle's heart stopped. 'Jack? What did he say?'

'He said he had found someone who made sense of the difficult things. The things he had to do. Someone worth fighting for. It must have been you, mustn't it? Men don't talk about their wives that way.'

'When? When was he here?'

Christine thought. 'It was when Bradley got out.'

'1942?'

'Yes. In the summer. We managed to run him through Bilbao. At that time it was the quickest way. Jack went with him.'

'Did Jack come often?'

'I don't know. I saw him perhaps half a dozen times. Maybe not even that. It was dangerous.'

Mirabelle nodded. 'I wasn't aware he had come to Paris at all.'

'We were up all night, waiting,' Christine said. 'They left in a rubbish cart. That was how we did it.'

'And that's what he said?'

Christine nodded. 'The men often talked about home. About what made it worth the risk.'

Mirabelle looked out of the window but she could scarcely see through the glass. By 1942 Jack hadn't yet told her that he loved her. That came later. A dim picture show played in her mind's eye of Jack laughing in the punt that day on the Thames in 1944. Of her promising to marry him as soon as he was free. Of him years later, one sunny day, giving her the key to her flat on the Lawns and carrying her over the doorstep into the empty high-ceilinged apartment. The room had been full of light. He had promised that one day they'd live there together.

Oblivious, Christine continued. 'I will not say Jack Duggan didn't betray me. I'll not say he couldn't have helped me when the Germans left Paris. Suddenly, when they didn't need us any more, the British vanished.' She gestured as if the entire British nation was a wisp of smoke that had blown out of reach. 'Your lover came to see me when I was in hospital at the end of the war. They had admitted I was a resister but people didn't believe it. It wasn't enough. There had been reprisals because of what I had done. My lover was German. Jack offered me money to leave. "Why not go to one of the Spanish islands? Majorca? Just for a while,"' she mimicked, then her tone hardened. 'I risked my life for my country. All of France was dancing in the streets and I was supposed to skulk off as if I was ashamed. But I was proud. I wanted to tell them what I'd done even if they didn't listen. And he wanted me to pack a bathing costume and sit on a Spanish beach? I would rather . . .' She

reached for the words but finding none adequate she pulled off one of her leather cuffs and rolled up her sleeve. All down the length of her arm Christine Moreau's skin was pockmarked – the injuries Mirabelle had seen in the raw in the Red Cross files at the American Hospital.

'They burned me. They branded me,' she said. 'And they shaved my head. My hair grew back, of course, but . . .'

Mirabelle made herself take it in. The skin had healed but the surface looked more like tree bark made of flesh than the arm of what must have been a very beautiful woman.

'I'm so sorry,' she whispered.

'You're quite right. The scars are on the inside too. We cannot help who we love. You know that as well as anyone.' Christine shrugged. 'And I loved von der Grün. I couldn't stop myself. But I didn't agree with his politics. I worked against the Nazis and I hoped I could have it all. If you stake a lot and you fail, you lose everything. That's the truth.' She pulled her sleeve back into place.

'And Philip Caine?' Mirabelle ventured. 'He was in the same hospital as you, wasn't he?'

Christine nodded. 'I met him long before that,' she admitted. 'Of course, Jack Duggan and Matthew Bradley enraged him too. He took a long time to even take it in properly. For the men who'd been away it was difficult to find their homes changed and their people gone.'

'You mean Caine's fiancée? Is that what they fell out about?'

Christine's eyes darkened. 'No. Not that. He wished the girl well. No. He couldn't believe that they hadn't told him about his mother. While he'd been in France his brother had died in action and as far as everyone back in England was concerned, Philip was missing presumed dead. The old woman lost heart. She died. There was a suggestion that she had taken her own life. They couldn't have told her what Caine was doing. He knew that in his rational mind. The story had to be that he was

simply missing. But still . . . his whole family was gone, you see. His brother, his father, his mother – everyone. Bradley had promised to look after his people. His fiancée and his mother. He knew he'd never be able to own his daughter. The old woman was all he had left. Bradley let him down.'

'And that's why he attacked them at the hospital.'

'Duggan and Bradley came to take him home, but there was no home to go to.'

'He lived here, didn't he? On the rue du Jour?'

'During the occupation. On and off.'

'And he was a Resistance fighter?'

Christine stared into the middle distance. 'A spy. Caine was more of a spy – you know, an agent,' she said. 'I don't want to talk about it.'

Mirabelle took a breath and would have pushed the other woman to say more, but she knew she wouldn't talk about her war either. Not about some of the things she'd done. Christine was being very generous in letting her in this far.

'Have you been spying too? Is that what you were up to last night?'

Christine's lip pursed only slightly. 'The Russians are watching me,' she said in a matter-of-fact tone. 'That is the last time I will ever make such a trip. Now it is my job to keep them watching me for as long as I can.'

'You're going to keep them busy?'

'I will walk in the park and make conversation with strangers. It might take them a month to realise that there is nothing going on now. It might take them three months. If they are watching me it's two less Russians who are available to watch somebody else.'

'And von der Grün?'

Christine shook her head. 'I think you ought to go now, Miss Bevan. You should leave by the rear.'

The window that opened onto the back of the building still

had its thin curtain drawn. Mirabelle slung her handbag over her arm and rose. Christine had said that Jack loved her, and yet that wasn't enough to fill the void left by his death. She wanted to know what he had been doing here. She wanted to know what had happened to Caine.

'You must go.' Christine shooed her off.

'Thank you for the gin. For everything.'

'OK. Sure thing.' Christine smiled, betraying a glimpse of the fact she had drunk two double gins only shortly after breakfast, if indeed she had eaten at all.

'OK,' Mirabelle repeated as she made for the door.

Now, that was interesting.

Chapter 20

One cannot answer for his courage when
he has never been in danger.

On the main road, Mirabelle caught the Métro to Passy from Les Halles. The market was abandoned today, a gendarme walking his beat past the empty stalls. The street behind him was strangely deserted – after only a few days in Paris the Sunday silence already felt strange to Mirabelle as she descended into the station. The Métro seemed more complicated than the tube in London, but perhaps Mirabelle was simply more familiar with the ins and outs of the Northern and Piccadilly lines. She slowly read the map and boarded the right train. The journey allowed her time to think, and when she emerged from the station at the other end she turned away from the Eiffel Tower in the direction of the Bois de Boulogne. Jack always said if you let someone talk for long enough they'd tell you far more than they meant to. Christine had said a great deal this morning and Mirabelle dwelt on that. For a start, it seemed Christine's love affair with von der Grün was over. She had talked about him in the past tense. He must have gone back to his wife. Mirabelle wondered if without the war and its immediate aftermath, Jack and she might have gone their separate ways. It hadn't felt that way. If anything they had become closer as the affair progressed. She wondered if von der Grün stood trial for his crimes. Not every Nazi had merited Nuremberg, but courts had been set up across Europe. She must check.

Last night the darkness had cloaked some of the grandeur of the great tree-lined boulevards of the 16th arrondissement. Now in the cold winter sunshine Mirabelle smiled at the elderly women walking their lapdogs. An enticing whiff of coffee emanated from the open door of a bar and she decided to stop and allay the effects of the gin. She sipped a café crème at the bar, Italian style, and continued on her way. The key to it all was here somewhere among these streets, she thought. Paris knew.

At the rue de Siam it appeared that number 25 was occupied again. Smoke streamed from the chimney and the lights were on in the hall. When Mirabelle rang the doorbell, a maid appeared and bobbed a prompt curtsey.

'Is your master in?'

The girl looked over her shoulder. No doubt the butler should be the one to answer the bell.

'Are you alone?'

The maid nodded.

'When will they return?'

'*Ce soir,*' she said. This evening.

Mirabelle thanked her and headed up the street. She'd come back later. It was something to look forward to. It would be interesting to meet the man Christine Moreau had loved. Perhaps the delivery of the little packet the night before betokened the fact they still had a connection. She hoped von der Grün would betray himself – that she'd be able to read him.

On the main road Sunday service was over and the congregation was in the process of leaving church. Most people set out to walk home but one or two had brought cars and chauffeurs. Neighbours stopped to greet one another and a bottleneck formed around the priest, who was shaking hands with his congregation at the church door. Mirabelle followed the movement of the crowd, blending in so perfectly that an elderly gentleman wished her well this fine Sunday. She shook

his hand and passed on. Several people walked in the same direction, and it wasn't until they arrived at their destination that she realised they were making for the cemetery.

At the gate a young girl stood at a flower stall, selling lilies and ivy wreaths. Without hesitation Mirabelle moved through the iron gates past a stone relief commemorating the soldiers of the Great War and she took the path to the left. While her college companions slept in all those years ago she had stayed up to make an early morning visit to Paris's largest cemetery, Père Lachaise, to lay flowers on her grandmother's grave. That was on the other side of town. She wondered fleetingly if anyone was tending the old woman's plot now or if the grave had been taken over by weeds. Père Lachaise would look after it, she comforted herself. Here in Passy the gravestones were tidy. The cemetery felt like an enclave, surrounded by chestnut trees. Flowers were piled up on the stones commemorating Debussy and Manet. White lilies framed two plots occupied by members of the Romanov family – Russian royalty. Next to the Grand Duchess there was a private plot with a row of picture frames containing images of the people who were buried there – all one family with a long Russian name. A row of stones and some greenery adorned the grave of Georges Mandel, one of the male French Resistance fighters so greatly resented by Christine Moreau.

Mirabelle sat on a bench and stared in the direction of the Trocadero beyond the boundary of the cemetery walls. A couple passed on their way to the gates, discussing where to have lunch. The woman's arm was slung casually through her husband's.

'Not le Châtelet,' she said. 'Last time the soup was terrible.'

Mirabelle smiled at such domesticity. They passed out of earshot as a man with an American accent showed his son around – a strange outing for a child, Mirabelle thought.

'It's the only cemetery with a heated waiting room,' the man said, acting the tour guide.

'OK,' the little boy replied with gravitas, as if he was taking in this strange detail and memorising it.

Mirabelle sat a little straighter. 'OK,' Christine had said. 'Sure thing.' As if it was natural to use the phrase. So, it might be assumed that Mademoiselle Moreau was working for the Americans. A smile played around Mirabelle's lips. Yes, it would be like the Yanks to supply Boodles Dry Gin – they were generous but in her experience they generally missed the mark.

She stood up. All things American resided not far from here, in the 8th arrondissement. There was an embassy and a grand ambassador's residence. She cast a glance at a Napoleonic ossuary – such a strange custom, but then Paris was famous for its catacombs. As she turned to leave she was already planning a route westwards. It would divert her for the afternoon until von der Grün came back to town.

When the man touched her, it took her a moment to recognise there was a firm hand on her elbow. It was so unusual to be accosted in that way that she didn't understand immediately what was going on. Then she turned, and let out a cry as a man in a Mackintosh closed in. With a strong grip on both her arms, he guided her along the path. Her mind swam. It was the man from the library – the one with the seat next to the reference section.

'What are you doing? Get off me!' she snapped, kicking him as hard as she could.

The man produced a handkerchief and thrust it in her face. 'She always gets upset here,' he said to a woman who had turned from the grave she was tending.

Mirabelle tried to pull away. She wanted to shout, but the fabric smelled of chemicals and whatever they were had made her woozy. Her diction suddenly slurred and she was having difficulty keeping her balance. She leaned into the man's side

in order to stay upright and he steered her along the path. It was an odd sensation, trying to get away at the same time as toppling towards him.

'*Ma pauvre*,' the man said as if he was comforting a grieving widow.

'You can't . . . I'm a British citizen,' Mirabelle managed to get out, but her voice was too low to be heard by anyone other than the person she was trying to escape from. 'No,' she said again, gasping for breath and hearing the word come out as a moan.

The man laid a firm hand on her waist as he guided her through the gate. The flower girl nodded as if she understood how upsetting it was to visit the cemetery. Mirabelle opened her mouth, but no sound came out. She felt suddenly as if she might fall asleep, and no amount of knowing that she mustn't could overtake the feeling that was sweeping through her limbs. She was vaguely aware of a car pulling up and the man lifting her inside. The seat was upholstered in red leather and the interior smelled of half-eaten apples and crumpled newspaper. She felt her body sway as the engine drew away from the kerb. Remember how long they drive and if there are twists and turns. Listen for noises that can identify the route. She tried to remember the drill, clinging on to it as if she was a swimmer about to go under. Then an image appeared in her mind's eye of Jack smiling. She relaxed. And after that everything went black.

Chapter 21

Adversity is the first path to truth.

When Mirabelle came round she was in a bare room with no windows apart from a grubby skylight, the outlook from which informed her that it was late in the afternoon, probably close to dusk. A bare light bulb was switched on, illuminating worn pine floorboards and chipped plasterwork. Against the wall her handbag lay open where they had rifled through it. Her limbs felt stiff and she was tied to the arm of the high-backed chair in which she was sitting, secured by means of a long rag. The man must have been half-hearted about detaining her because he had only tied her right wrist, leaving her left hand free to pick at the knot. She started on it immediately.

'Miss Bevan.' The voice came from behind her. It sounded amused.

Mirabelle squirmed, but it was impossible to turn round. She couldn't see him. She let go of the material. Then she manoeuvred her jaw, checking she could move it before she tried to speak. Her throat felt dry, and she thought that standing up would only make her more groggy. It was probably to her advantage to stay seated until she recovered from whatever had been on that piece of cloth. This did not temper her outrage.

'Well,' she said, 'I don't know what you're thinking. Kidnapping is illegal. I'm a British citizen. You're in the process of causing an international incident.'

The man walked into her line of sight and slowly lit a cigarette. He held up the packet. *Disque Bleu*. 'Do you smoke?'

'Not really.'

He smiled. 'So British. Any other nationality would say yes or no, but you British are so charming. So indirect. "Not really"!'

'Please untie me.'

The man kept the cigarette between his lips and leaned over her, pulling at the knot until it unravelled. Up close Mirabelle could ascertain no clues as to his identity from his appearance. There was something overwhelmingly neutral about him. His accent was so perfect that it wasn't there all.

'I can see we're going to get on,' he said.

Mirabelle rubbed her wrist. So, she reasoned, he was trying to befriend her. That kind of interrogation was old-fashioned even by the time she left the SOE. It was far more effective to keep your distance and build up real trust by not lying to a prisoner. Most people would talk eventually with a prod or two, if only you knew how to listen. This over-friendly rigmarole was ten years out of date and the man was acting as if he hadn't snatched her in public. That was interesting. She'd have thought that he might threaten her. He could have replied to her outburst that international incident or not, he had the power of life and death and that no one knew where she was, and for that matter no one need ever know. He could have threatened her with truth drugs. It always amazed Mirabelle how afraid people were of truth drugs. It was as if they couldn't really trust themselves, as if they were terrified the barbiturates would uncover a truth they weren't aware of. She knew better. If it was old-fashioned play-pretend chums he wanted, she'd play along.

'Thank you.' She smiled, rubbing her wrist. 'What's your name?'

'You can call me Albert.'

It wouldn't be his real name. He'd chosen something that made sense in English and French as well as Russian.

'Where am I?'

'Paris, Miss Bevan. I didn't bring you far. You've been sleeping, that's all.'

'Sleeping? That's one way to put it. What do you want?'

The man looked vaguely amused. His eyes lingered on Mirabelle's ankles. 'I want to know why you're here. What brought you to France?'

'I came to your attention because I visited Christine Moreau. Is that it?'

Albert nodded.

'Well, there's no secret. Miss Moreau is an old acquaintance. She made a dress for me in the 1930s, when I visited Paris with friends. I hoped she might make me another, but I fear she doesn't take on that kind of work any more. Your Mackintosh is like a uniform, monsieur. You and your colleagues. If you spotted me, I spotted you just as quickly.'

Albert squatted so that his face was level with hers. Mirabelle caught a whiff of spirits and stale coffee on his breath beneath the tobacco.

'That's interesting. Why would you notice us? Did you already know we were here? Were you looking for us? Most people don't register people like me, Miss Bevan. Or people like you, if it comes to that. Do they?'

'A lady on her own always notices what a gentleman is wearing. When two gentlemen are wearing exactly the same thing, it catches the eye. That's what brought you to my attention.'

'Gentlemen!' His voice was scornful.

'You think me bourgeois? Well, you're quite right, I expect. I fear I have stumbled into something that is quite beyond me, Albert.'

'Not beyond your capacity. My colleague lost track of you the other day. You're clever, Miss Bevan, I'll give you that.'

'Dodging someone at a railway station isn't cleverness. It's training. And my training came from a time when your masters and mine were allies. It has been quite a while.'

'You knew who he was?'

'At first I thought American.'

Albert looked unamused. 'And then you realised?'

'The teeth.' Mirabelle opened her lips. 'Americans, you see, have perfect smiles. Alas, your friend does not.'

He laughed. 'I begin to like you, Miss Bevan. But the idea you're not working for the British doesn't hold water, I'm afraid.' He drew Mirabelle's lock picks from his pocket, and dangled them in front of her. 'Standard issue.'

'A memento of times past,' she admitted. 'But I'm not who you're looking for. I don't know anything.'

Albert paused just long enough for it to become clear that he didn't believe her. Mirabelle let his silence hang in the air. When convincing someone, you must let them make up their own mind. Albert changed tack.

'You went back to see Mademoiselle Moreau today. And that has made me curious. Tell me, what did you talk about? You two ladies? Tea and cucumber sandwiches, no doubt. Is that what you're going to have me believe?'

'The war. We talked about the war. I was in London and she was in Paris. Where were you, Albert?'

He ignored the question. 'And the house you called at on the rue de Siam on the way to the cemetery?'

'I went to visit an old friend.'

'A friendship from wartime as well?'

Mirabelle nodded. 'Yes. They weren't at home.'

Albert backed away, leaning against the wall opposite the coom that cut a slice out of the room. He put the lock picks in his pocket. 'No, I don't think so. You're going to have to come up with something better than that.'

'There is no more. It's the truth – a lousy cover, I agree. But

that's the nature of it. I don't even know why you're here – or why you're interested in Christine Moreau, come to that.'

'Do you believe in coincidences, Miss Bevan?'

Mirabelle answered honestly. 'No. Not more than one at a time.'

'Neither do I.' Albert stubbed out the cigarette, crushing it against the bare wood with the sole of his shoe. 'You English like a puzzle, don't you? It is part of your national character. Crosswords. Guessing games. Well, I shall pose you a riddle. This woman almost never leaves her studio. And yet she is receiving secret information and passing it on.'

'Information about what exactly?'

'Classified information.'

'From whom?'

Albert shifted on his feet. 'I don't know. But I know where it's coming from. It's coming from behind our borders.'

'And what do you believe she is doing with it?'

'Selling it, of course.'

'To whom?'

'Anyone who will pay her. You British perhaps.'

'I see you have not ascertained Miss Moreau's feelings towards her erstwhile compatriots. Yesterday she chased me out of her studio brandishing a pair of scissors because I even mentioned the British.'

'The Americans, then? The French? Anyone who has money.'

Mirabelle's eyes narrowed. 'Yes. I understand why you're watching her. There she is, in that tiny studio, working her fingers to the bone, reduced to piecework. I can see why you think she's making a fortune as the hub of an international network. Perhaps you ought to have kidnapped her instead of me. I certainly don't have the information you're looking for, Albert. Perhaps you ought to search her studio if you're convinced she's a spy.'

He cast her a withering look. 'It's all standard. She buys the

cloth from a factory in Poland. The invoices. The remittance. The sales. The orders. There is no radio. No telephone. Nothing. A bale goes in, two hundred scarves come out. An exporter in Calais deals with the shipment. But the trail of information leads to her – she is the axis of it.'

'Well, stop her supply. Stop everything going in and coming out. You can do that, can't you?'

Albert smirked. 'And then we will never find out how she is doing it. It would be like taking apart an engine and not being able to put it together again.'

'Poor Christine,' Mirabelle sighed, thinking quite the opposite. It would be fun to drive Albert round the twist – she had a vision of Christine picking particularly eccentric people to talk to on her outings to the park. 'You've got her all wrong, you know.'

'She is bourgeois – just like you.'

'There is no crime in that. Not here, anyway. Christine Moreau was a Resistance fighter. She is a patriot.'

'She took a Nazi lover.'

'She fell in love. Ill advisedly, I'll grant you. But she is a brave woman. She fought for her country despite her involvement with an SS officer, and that takes guts.'

Albert lit another cigarette and blew out the smoke energetically as if he was obliterating Christine Moreau's past.

'And then you turn up. The first person in months to visit the studio. And you visit her twice in short order. Do you see why you came to my attention?'

'I'm afraid there is no mystery. On my first visit we ascertained that Miss Moreau knew a friend of mine, someone who is sadly now dead. I visited her a second time to talk more about him.'

Albert appeared to lose patience. He moved across the room as if the story had offended him. Then he grabbed Mirabelle's arm and forced it against the chair as he retied the

knot, this time twisting the rag around both wrists. His jaw was set, as if he wanted the fabric to cut into Mirabelle's skin. Mirabelle wondered if he was really angry or only trying to intimidate her.

'I'll be back later,' he said.

'You can't . . .' she spluttered.

'I'll bring food.'

'Don't be ridiculous.'

'You will talk.'

'We have been talking.'

'I'll make you talk.'

Behind her, the door slammed and the key turned in the lock. Mirabelle listened. There was no carpet outside – only a set of wooden stairs by the sound of it. She wondered how long he might be. In his place she'd leave the subject at least an hour before coming back, if not several hours. Often waking someone in the dead of night confused them and they said more than they meant to. In any case, when Albert returned she'd have some warning. The stairs made a dreadful racket.

She struggled against the knot, working her hand backwards and forwards. Then she tried using her teeth to loosen it. He should have tied her with rope; the piece of old linen had far too much give to be effective for long. She remembered reading an interview with Bulldog Bradley during the course of which he said you had a better chance of getting away if you escaped early. The sooner the better, he'd advised, giving examples of men who had got away while the Nazis were waiting for transport to take them to the Stalag. She smiled as the knot began to loosen. She pulled one hand free and then the other. She took a deep breath and stood up, only realising when she got to her feet that Albert had removed her shoes. If he thought that was going to deter her, he had another think coming. Her stockings had ripped at the ankle. Annoyed, she grabbed her handbag and checked inside. The sheaf of

banknotes was still hidden in the inside pocket. Her notebook was missing, but she hadn't used it while she'd been here. From memory, the last list had been for shopping – meat paste for sandwiches, milk to make tea and a bottle of bleach with which she intended to clean the bathroom. Albert would ascertain little from that. She sighed, remembering he'd taken the lock picks.

Her eyes flew to the door, and, legs shaking, she limped over. Getting to her knees, she looked through the keyhole. The key was in the other side but the bottom of the door was too well fitted to allow the old trick of pushing the key out onto a piece of paper that could then slide back through the gap. Then Mirabelle heard a movement on the other side. It sounded as if someone was turning the page of a newspaper. She stood up carefully and stepped back. Albert had taken the stairs but someone was still out there on guard. It was lucky they'd taken her shoes – she'd moved all but silently as she investigated the room. Then, as she looked up, she realised there was another way out.

The skylight was rusty. Mirabelle stood on the chair and pushed hard, and the old window opened with a crack. The freezing night air hit her in a wave. She waited, ready to jump back down if the man guarding the room came to investigate the noise. Nothing. Above, the sky was dark and the view from the top of the building afforded a spectacular view of Paris at night. Albert had told the truth – he hadn't brought her far. From here she had a clear sightline to the Eiffel Tower. Stretching in all directions, Paris's streets were well lit. The lead roofing was wet. Here and there it reflected a dim glow from the lights on the other side of the street. Sticking her head out as far as she could, Mirabelle surveyed the roofscape. The building was at least five storeys high. There was a flat area running along the top of the roof above the skylight, which was set upright into the eaves; if she could climb the

slanted part that led to it she'd be able to survey the whole terrace and, she hoped, find a way down. She looked back into the room and took Bulldog Bradley at his word. This was the first opportunity she'd had to get away and she wasn't going to let it pass.

With her handbag pushed up over her shoulder, she took her weight on her arms and pulled herself out until her bare feet were balanced on the freezing iron gutter. She turned slowly and closed the window. Then, telling herself not to look down – or at least as little as she could – she focused on the surface beneath her feet. Thank heavens it wasn't raining. Climbing in bare feet would be far more dangerous if the surface was being sluiced as she moved. She held on to the frame of the skylight as she carefully manoeuvred herself upwards. Her bare soles allowed a little purchase, though the cold nipped and her toes soon began to ache. At last she laid her hands on the edge of the flat area and hauled herself up.

As she tried to calm her breathing she surveyed the scene. As she had hoped, the flat area ran the length of the terrace, all the way to the end of the street. Unfortunately, she could see no easy way to the ground. There was no hoped-for fire escape. Thick soil pipes punctuated the sheer drop at the back, plummeting to the black gardens below, but they were mounted tightly against the masonry and without a rope it would be all but impossible to use them to make a safe descent. At the front, however, there were slim ornate iron balconies running across the top three floors. Mirabelle lay flat, pulling herself over the edge to try to make out which windows had lights on and which lay dark and were therefore presumably vacant. She chose the unlit window second from the end – the one that was furthest from her captors. Carefully she took up a position over it, made sure her handbag was secure and allowed herself to slip back towards the gutter. Gingerly she tested it with her foot. The iron was riveted into place, completely secure.

Mirabelle paused. She tried not to think about what would happen if she missed her mark. They'd call it suicide – a woman tumbling from this height onto the pavement. How long might it take them to identify her body, she wondered fleetingly, and then pushed the thought out of her mind. Taking a deep breath, she folded her fingers over the ledge and lowered herself into the night air, suspended directly over the balcony on the top floor. There was a moment of relaxation, strangely, when she simply dangled, and then, closing her eyes and realising she was unable to breathe, she let go and dropped onto the iron fretwork. Her hands were trembling and her ankles had taken the strain but she realised with some surprise that she had made it. The room within was dark and she couldn't make out the interior. Stumbling to stand straight, she tried the window but the catch was locked, so using her handbag to shield her from cuts she broke the glass with her elbow and reached through.

The room was warm. She pulled herself inside onto a thin strip of carpet and only just managed to quash the feeling that she ought to fall to her knees and give thanks. How foolish, she chastised herself, deliberately turning her attention to her surroundings. A quick inspection of the stove in the corner revealed embers that had burned low. Mirabelle warmed herself in front of them. Her feet felt as if they had been immersed in ice. Looking around, she found a pair of men's socks beside the bed and pulled them on, rubbing her soles to get her circulation going. When she could feel her toes again, she rooted further. A pair of tan leather riding boots three sizes too large were stowed in the lower part of a cherrywood dresser. She pulled them on and took an experimental step or two. It was better than going barefoot, she told herself as she laid a banknote on the bed. She wasn't a thief and the man who lived here would have to repair the window and replace his socks and boots. A summary inspection of the room

betrayed the fact the poor fellow, whoever he was, was short of funds.

She tried the door. It was locked and she could find no key. Carefully she removed a pin from her hair, thankful that Albert had left her hat in place. She decided not to look in the small mirror that was mounted beside the bed and tried not to dwell on how ridiculous she must appear in her woollen day dress, tweed jacket, men's boots and little hat. The red nail varnish applied so meticulously by Vesta at the beginning of the week had chipped in places. It was as if her outfit had been made up of random jigsaw pieces. She sighed. Then she knelt at the door to pick the lock. It wasn't a difficult job. She'd done this kind of thing before.

Chapter 22

Man is made by his belief.

Detective Superintendent Alan McGregor had never visited France. For that matter, he'd never been outside Great Britain. Once he'd cleared customs at Dunkirk, he'd spent some time admiring the stamp on his passport and reading the declaration on the inside cover. He wondered if anyone would ask to inspect the stamp now he was in Paris and was faintly surprised as he strode unobstructed out of the Gare du Nord and looked around. It seemed somehow too easy to have boarded a train and then a boat and now to be here, in the French capital. He wasn't sure what he had expected, but the network of roads around the station and the tall Parisian tenements did not look as foreign as he had feared. The damp February air felt the same in Paris as it had in Brighton and emerging onto the street he had attracted no particular attention, which meant he did not look outlandishly different.

He pulled a guidebook from his pocket. *On Foot in Paris* had been the only publication available at short notice. He'd considered himself lucky that the stand in Victoria was open on a Sunday. He had spent the journey perusing the book's pages but now he had actually set foot on French soil – or at least pavement – he realised that he had not memorised the map upon which he had marked the location of the Hôtel Rambeau. This wasn't how McGregor had hoped to spend the weekend. He'd envisaged a game of golf and perhaps taking Mirabelle for dinner somewhere nice down the coast and

indulging in another kiss. When he dropped into McGuigan & McGuigan Debt Recovery on Friday afternoon he'd been flabbergasted when Vesta told him where Mirabelle had gone.

'What the devil did she want to go to Paris for?' he'd demanded.

Vesta grinned. 'A missing airman. RAF. He was a flying ace during the war.'

McGregor looked offended as Vesta stirred the tea in the pot and cast around for biscuits. 'Well, he's been missing a long time,' he managed to get out. 'Why did she have to go now?'

'That's just what I said,' Vesta agreed heartily as she poured. 'I've been trying to get hold of her, actually. I phoned her hotel but I think she was out.'

'What do you mean? She was either out or she wasn't.'

'The fellow who answered was French. I've no idea what he said. I couldn't even leave a message.'

McGregor drank his tea with a quiet slurp.

'It's all right for Mirabelle,' Vesta added. 'She's fluent.'

The superintendent's eyebrows rose slightly.

'Her mother was French, you see,' the girl continued. 'Which explains Mirabelle's style. They say French women wear clothes terribly well. I don't know when she'll be back.'

Vesta was deliberately taunting the superintendent with this information, hoping it might propel him into action. Unaware that Mirabelle and McGregor had kissed earlier in the week, she found the way the couple had been circling each other ever since they met most frustrating. She proffered a biscuit.

'Huntley and Palmer, eh? Thanks.' The superintendent sighed. 'So, what did you want to speak to Mirabelle about? Office business, was it?'

Vesta put down her cup and leaned forward. 'She'd asked me to look into something, so I went to the records office and dug up some old papers. I thought she'd find them interesting, that's all. I'm nervous to trust them to the post. I

mean, it's abroad. And to telegraph the information would cost a fortune.'

McGregor dunked his biscuit. 'I learned a bit of French at school,' he admitted.

'Go on!' Vesta's face lit up. 'You never! Say something.'

McGregor put down the cup and the biscuit in preparation for a demonstration. '*Ou est mon parapluie*? That's "Where is my umbrella?" And *Je voudrais deux billets, s'il vous plaît*. That's "I'd like two tickets, please."'

Vesta's dark eyes twinkled mischievously. 'Well, then, you could go and help Mirabelle, couldn't you? Speaking French and all. We didn't do any of that at school.'

McGregor found himself staring at the teacup in front of him. The station had been quiet of late and he had leave he ought to take – weeks of it. Paris for a day or two might be nice. He imagined Mirabelle in front of the Eiffel Tower wearing a beret at a jaunty angle. He'd like to kiss her there, looking just like that, he thought, and then he blushed at his presumption.

'I suppose I could deliver those papers of yours,' he had said. 'Where did you say she was staying?'

Glad to be off the stuffy train at last, McGregor crossed the main road in the direction of rue Lentonnet. He paused as a bus passed and he met a female passenger's eyes for an instant as it speeded south towards the city. The evening air was fresh, and passing one or two bistros he realised he was hungry. The interiors glowed orange and smartly dressed waiters delivered appetising plates to the tables. There was a smell of roasting meat on the air. However, casting an eye over the menus on display, the superintendent realised he had no idea what was on offer. What was *agneau*, he wondered, and *moules*? The French language classes at Corstorphine Primary hadn't covered those. Two men stood smoking in a doorway, their

conversation sounding like a babble. It had been a long time since Mademoiselle Keltie had put him through his paces in the schoolroom, and even then French conversation had dealt mostly with how to buy tickets and discuss the weather. The two sentences he'd hazarded in front of Vesta were the only ones he could remember with much clarity. Now that he listened to French being spoken by, well, the French, the language was faster than he recalled – a rough and complex jumble of indecipherable words.

Coming to a halt in front of the Hôtel Rambeau, McGregor wondered if Mirabelle was inside, and if she was, whether she would be pleased to see him. Through the window he could see an old man settled at the reception desk, reading a paper and smoking a pipe. He paused, surprised to find himself nervous as he turned the handle and stepped inside.

'*Bonsoir, monsieur.*' The man looked up.

McGregor was instantly tongue-tied. '*Un* room,' he managed to get out. 'I am looking for my friend. An *amie*, Mirabelle Bevan.'

The old man squinted. He removed his glasses and said something incomprehensible.

'Mirabelle Bevan,' McGregor repeated. '*Ici*?'

The man nodded and said something incomprehensible again. McGregor wondered if it was the same thing he'd said before or if it was something different. In either case, the old fellow had at least nodded, which indicated that he might be in the right place.

'All right.' He thought for a moment. '*Ou est* Mirabelle Bevan?'

The man shrugged and said something that McGregor suspected was about women in general. He motioned towards the rack of room keys. McGregor checked his watch. It was six o'clock.

'*À quelle heure*?' he asked, getting into the swing of things.

The old man laughed. McGregor felt deflated. He pulled

out the francs he'd exchanged at Dover and pointed towards the remaining keys.

'*Pour moi?*' he tried.

The old man took down a key, handed it over and efficiently removed a note from between McGregor's fingers. He handed over his pen and motioned for McGregor to sign the register. Then he sounded out the strange name.

'McGregor.'

'*Je suis Écossais.*'

'Ah. Glasgow.' The old man grinned.

'*Oui.*' McGregor did not correct him. Instead he tried to procure a drink. 'Whisky?'

This was an internationally recognisable term. The old fellow came out from the reception desk and led the superintendent into a room that was laid ready for breakfast. Disappearing into the back, he returned a few seconds later with a short glass of amber liquid.

'*Et voilà, monsieur,*' he said.

McGregor took a sniff. It didn't smell too bad. He motioned into the hallway and up the stairs.

'I will go to my room,' he said slowly and loudly. 'I will wait for her.'

Mirabelle peered onto the street from the front door of the house in the 8th arrondissement. She couldn't make out anyone suspicious along the pavement. An old woman walked a dachshund on a lead, dawdling to match her pace to the dog's tiny legs. Occasionally a car drove past. Her heart pounding, she stepped out and walked towards the house where she'd been held. The old boots felt heavy and loose. They were well made, but it was like walking with her feet encased in boxes.

Above her head the lights were switched off on the first two floors, but further up the windows were lit. She stepped back to gaze up at the skylight she'd escaped through. It had seemed

higher from above than it did from the street. At the doorstep a row of bells was unmarked by names. Anyone visiting this house would have to know already which bell to ring. Mirabelle walked as unobtrusively as she could towards the end of the road, noting that she had been held on the rue de Courcelles. It was an address to be avoided in future.

She turned in the opposite direction to the elderly dogwalker just in case and strode past some chic boutiques. Tomorrow she'd buy new shoes, and in the meantime there was nothing to be gained by returning to Christine Moreau's studio or seeking out anyone who might help at the American Embassy. Christine knew she was being watched, and if she was working for the Americans they must know too. Mirabelle contemplated a return to von der Grün's house on the rue de Siam but that, surely, would be the first place her captors would put under surveillance when they realised she had gone. Reporting to the British Embassy would almost certainly result in a rap on the knuckles and being sent home on the first available train. The British would want any information she uncovered, but as soon as they had it they would certainly view her as a loose cannon, and a loose cannon was never welcome.

Mirabelle tried to think what Jack would do in this situation. She envisioned him, papers splayed across the desktop in front of him, his hands clasped together as he thought. When he was struggling with a problem a deep furrow appeared between his eyebrows. It was impossible to know how long she had been followed, she reasoned. So the first thing she must do was move and keep moving and not go back to anywhere she might already have been seen. She stopped at a phone box and dialled the number of the Hôtel Rambeau. The bell rang several times before anyone answered.

'Hello,' she said in rapid French. 'It's Mirabelle Bevan. I've been called home suddenly. Will you ship my case, please? I

have to leave at once. You can send it to the left luggage office at Victoria – I'll pick it up from there.'

The old man sounded uncertain. 'But your husband has arrived,' he said.

Mirabelle's heart almost stopped. '*Mon mari?*' she said, a vision of the man in the Mackintosh looming in her mind's eye.

'Yes. Monsieur McGregor.'

If the old man was suspicious of what must look like a romantic assignation, his tone didn't betray it. Mirabelle's eyes darted. It was a relief not to feel alone, she realised, but she was mystified as to why McGregor was here and worried that he might be in danger.

'McGregor? You're sure?' she checked. 'No other man?'

The old man stifled a laugh. 'How many men are you expecting, madame?'

Mirabelle ignored that. 'Put him on, would you?'

'A moment.'

It took longer than that. Mirabelle shifted inside the phone box as she waited. The Parisian streets were glossy with rain and all but deserted. It was Sunday, after all. On the corner two teenage boys burst out of a bar and paced down the street discussing music loudly. A taxi drew up and the driver pulled out a copy of *Le Monde* to read as he waited for his fare. Mirabelle wondered how much good Christine Moreau had done over the years. That was the difficulty with covert operations – sometimes it was only years later that you realised what the operation had achieved, and often the people involved never knew. When you were a small cog in a larger machine, the outcome was beyond you. She wondered what information Christine was handling and how on earth the woman was getting it in and out. She had foxed the Russians, and that of itself was admirable.

There was a rustling sound at the other end of the line.

'Hello?' McGregor's voice brought her attention to the matter in hand.

'Superintendent,' Mirabelle greeted him. 'It really is you. Are you alone?'

'Yes.' He sounded quite proud of himself. 'Vesta sent me with some papers she wanted you to have. She dug them up in the library or the records office or something, and wasn't sure about posting them.'

'What do they say?'

'I have no idea. They're upstairs in my case. In an envelope.'

Mirabelle allowed herself a smile. McGregor was about as far from a covert operative as one might hope to get. It clearly hadn't occurred to him to open the envelope and see what was inside.

'Are you hungry? Can I take you for dinner?' he continued.

Mirabelle decided not to explain where she had been or what she'd been up to. She'd have to meet him away from the Hôtel Rambeau in any case – it might as well be at a restaurant, though not everywhere would be open on a Sunday night.

'There's a bistro near the Louvre,' she said. 'It's along the colonnade at the Palais Royal. There's an enclosed courtyard there. A sort of park.'

'Right you are.' McGregor's voice sounded uncertain.

'You'll need to take a taxi,' Mirabelle advised him. 'Check you're not being followed. Do you know how to do that?'

McGregor grunted in the affirmative.

'Get the cab to drop you at the Palais Royal. We'll meet at the Bistro Florentine. I'll be waiting.'

Chapter 23

Let food be thy medicine and medicine be thy food.

Mirabelle had to admit the location was romantic. The courtyard was flanked by a wide sandy gravel path round a long lawn which was lit by old-fashioned wrought-iron lamps that cast a diffuse honey-coloured light over it. A fountain rose at the centre and a couple of statues punctuated the grass on either side. Lines of chestnut trees, devoid of their leaves at this time of year, must provide welcome shade in the summer. A long colonnade enclosed the courtyard and running along it there were little cafés and grocery shops that served the apartments above, though most were dark-windowed in the evening. On the side that opened towards the Louvre the shops sold souvenirs and antiquities. This was where Mirabelle entered, slipping past the displays of fossils, unframed miniatures of Napoleon and postcards of the *Mona Lisa*. The courtyard would be an easy place to spot anyone following McGregor. The structure made it difficult to hide – there was nowhere to get lost in the ordered layout. If you walked in, you could be seen as soon as you moved past the line of trees.

While much of Paris seemed deserted this Sunday evening, the courtyard was relatively busy. Lights shone from the upper floors. As Mirabelle arrived, she could make out residents moving in the bright rooms – serving dinner, preparing clothes for the following day, listening to the radio or simply reading. An elegant woman in a long chocolate-brown coat and a fur hat overtook Mirabelle and tripped into one of the passageways that

led to the apartments. Mirabelle eyed the woman's high heels enviously. Perhaps the riding boots would put paid to the superintendent's romantic ideas once and for all, she thought sadly. It was strange, now she came to think on it: the truth was that she didn't want McGregor and yet she didn't want to give him up either. Paris provided shelter from such decisions. Brighton seemed so far across the Channel it was almost a dream.

The Bistro Florentine was lit mostly by candles and heated by means of an open fireplace beside which logs were neatly stacked. Flames flickered in the grate as a dapper waiter showed Mirabelle to a table for two by the window, which was partly steamed up. She slid her hand across the damp glass to clear it, ordered a glass of red wine and settled down with one eye on the yard. It always struck her as odd that one minute one might face the risk of kidnap or plummeting from a five-storey building yet not long after the world felt entirely normal and all that was left was a sliver of adrenaline in the bloodstream. No one would guess the kind of evening she'd had or what she had been up to. It seemed strange to slip so easily back into normality. The wine tasted smooth, almost buttery, and she gulped it down. McGregor was not far behind her. He entered through the arch she had come in by and she watched as he strode along the colonnade looking for the right place. He seemed taller than she remembered. He was a fine-looking man, if a little scruffy, and in Paris scruffiness seemed somehow more acceptable to her than it had been in Brighton. Out of context, Mirabelle considered Alan McGregor with fresh eyes. When he noticed her gazing through the candlelit window he smiled and waved. Inside he didn't greet Mirabelle with a kiss, like a Frenchman, but instead put his hand on her shoulder.

'Are you all right? Why did you think I might be followed?'

'Were you?'

'No.'

Mirabelle pondered that to anyone looking it would be apparent they weren't French. But then, why would anyone be looking? 'Are you sure?'

'Yes. I'm sure. I've a good ten years on the force, remember.'

'I know. I'm sorry.'

'I'll have one of those.' McGregor directed the waiter's attention to Mirabelle's wineglass.

The man hovered.

'*Encore deux verres du vin rouge,*' Mirabelle translated.

McGregor took off his hat and coat and sat down. He was wearing a blue woollen scarf that matched his eyes. Mirabelle tried not to notice but the superintendent's face held the light somehow.

'Vesta said you had the lingo down pat. Your mother was French, is that right?'

'Yes. She was brought up here. In Paris, I mean.'

'It's a beautiful city.' McGregor had taken a taxi as instructed and had spent the trip staring out of the window at the glories of the French capital. 'Vesta said you were looking for somebody. Have you found him?'

'Not yet.'

'Well, this might help.'

McGregor withdrew a manila envelope from his inside pocket. Mirabelle's name was written on the front in Vesta's scrawl. As she tore it open she felt a sudden nostalgia for the office on Brills Lane – the endless tea and the comforting rhythm of keeping the ledgers. Inside the envelope was a set of handwritten notes. McGregor picked up his glass and drank.

'That's good,' he pronounced. 'Very nice.'

Mirabelle laid the papers on the table. In the low light it was difficult to make out the words formed by Vesta's untidy hand. The page was headed *Mrs Ida Caine's Last Will and Testament* and below it was a list of worldly goods: a house a mile outside the dramatically named village of Pity Me in County Durham

and a car, an old Morris 8 series. There was some jewellery: a string of pearls valued at £26 and a diamond ring worth about the same. The relics of a woman's life. Mrs Caine had died in January 1944. In only a few months she could have had her son home again, Mirabelle thought sadly. She had passed away thinking that she'd lost everyone. No wonder Caine had been furious when he heard.

After carefully copying the items contained in Mrs Caine's estate, Vesta had continued. Mirabelle lifted the paper and squinted. She cocked her head to one side as she read.

'But they can't have actually done that.' The words came out in a low whisper.

'What is it?' McGregor looked up from the menu, which he was examining with a bemused expression.

Mirabelle's eyes returned to the page as if she couldn't quite believe what she was reading. Her mind buzzed, making the connections. In the absence of close family, her sons being missing in action, Mrs Caine's property had been bequeathed to her cousin. That was normal enough, but this wasn't just any cousin. During wartime the estate must have languished unexecuted, because no British solicitor would dream of contacting a German with the news that they'd inherited a good deal of property in England. What had Mrs Caine been thinking? The situation itself was interesting – a legal conundrum – if not entirely a surprise. Almost since the beginning Mirabelle had known of Caine's German relations. *Some Hun family connection*, the RAF officer had said at the Army and Navy Club – on his mother's side, it would seem. No, what made Mirabelle's mind pulse was that the cousin Mrs Caine had named was Wilhelm von der Grün. She read the name again to check that was really what it said. On the lines below, Vesta had carefully copied out von der Grün's titles, the ones Mirabelle had read at the National Library in *Wer Ist's*. The girl had written 'sounds posh' in brackets at the end.

Mirabelle sat back in her chair. The titles meant there was no mistaking the identity. It wasn't simply a matter of two people sharing the same name.

'So Caine knew him,' she whispered. 'They were second cousins. That's why Caine had to stay in France. That's why he didn't go home again.'

When Bradley and Caine arrived twenty miles outside Paris in the summer of 1942 they must have discovered that one of them had a direct connection to the heart of the Nazi war machine. A break like that could be invaluable to the Allies.

Mirabelle ran through the scenario. When the men realised von der Grün was newly stationed in the French capital – perhaps they had read the very newspaper article that Mirabelle had found in the library – they would have reported the information to London. Perhaps Christine Moreau had helped them. The Resistance was certainly their best chance of getting a message through. With that in hand, they must have settled down to wait for instructions. Mirabelle imagined Jack receiving the news at his large mahogany desk in the Whitehall office. It was a lucky break – a dream opportunity for anyone in covert operations – but of course it was also risky. Any action would have to be approved, so Jack would have gone to someone senior. In a back room somewhere, three or four British officers would have met around a table. Brandy and cigars, no doubt. What might they be able to make from such an opportunity? Could they trust that Caine's loyalty to his country was stronger than his family ties? As with any opportunity there were risks to weigh up.

On balance, she reckoned, Philip Caine would have been told to stay. Well, clearly he had been. And Bradley was more use at home, so Bulldog was sent back via Bilbao to a storm of press interest and a blackout on the news that he had escaped as part of a duo. Before the men parted, Caine made Bradley promise to look after his mother and Caroline. The

opportunity was so important to the war effort that it was worth abandoning his pregnant fiancée. Under orders, Caine would have had little choice in the matter. It must have been heartrending for him, she thought, and an act of selfless bravery. The men must have made a deal to ensure Caroline Bland wouldn't be humiliated by bearing Caine's illegitimate child. At home, Bulldog kept his word and married his friend's lover.

How tortuous, she thought, waiting for the news – lodging on the rue du Jour, in the care of Christine Moreau. Waiting for the woman he loved to marry his friend. But then, what he might be able to achieve for the Allies was so important . . . Mirabelle ran through the likely options – what had Jack decided Caine should do? There was no question the flight lieutenant would have been told to make contact with his cousin, but did Jack intend Caine to turn the Standartenführer for the Allies? Wilhelm, after all, had not been a member of the Nazi party in 1935. She wondered how late he had left it to join. Might he be considered vulnerable? Might Caine's mission have been to turn his cousin into a double agent? Or was the flight lieutenant simply instructed to position himself to gain inside information? There were other British officers who lasted out the war in Paris – one had famously won a fortune at the races and set himself up in an apartment in Saint-Cloud. Perhaps the plan was for Caine to throw himself on his cousin's mercy and lodge in the family house keeping his ears open. Or had Jack encouraged Caine to let his cousin think he had turned him against Britain by feeding false information to the Nazis while really being a triple agent and true to the Allies? Whatever his orders, she didn't envy Caine having to make the initial contact. Had he called at the rue de Siam or followed Wilhelm into a café one afternoon and slipped into a seat beside him? Wherever that first meeting took place it must have been terrifying – Caine couldn't have been sure how von der Grün would react. Despite their relationship, the

Standartenführer might simply have turned him over to the authorities and from there it would have been straight back to the Stalag at best. At worst Caine would have faced a firing squad, because as often as not a man out of uniform was a spy. In fact, from the moment Jack started to handle him, Caine wasn't just a serviceman any more – he *was* a spy. Mirabelle's fingers tingled at the thought.

'Are you all right?' McGregor asked, looking up from the menu. Mirabelle gulped in some air. She had been so busy thinking through the possibilities that she had forgotten where she was and with whom. The past engulfed her too easily. McGregor indicated the menu. 'I can't tell one dish from another. When I was a kid we learned a bit of French at school, but not enough, it seems.' He smiled. 'I fancy chicken, if there is any.'

Mirabelle blinked. Her stomach turned. 'I don't feel like eating.'

'Well, I'm ravenous.' McGregor motioned to the waiter and pointed to the card.

'*Poulet*?' he enquired.

'*Et pour madame*?' the waiter replied coldly.

Mirabelle shook her head. '*Encore du vin*?'

'*Oui.*' McGregor seemed to be able to make that out easily enough. As the waiter retreated he leaned over the table. 'I don't need ten years of experience on the force to see something's up, Mirabelle. Could you use a hand?'

Mirabelle looked doubtful. 'It's going to be important to blend in.'

McGregor laughed. 'Aah.' He peered down the side of the table, taking in her boots. 'I noticed you might be having some difficulty with that. Or have you been riding?'

She blushed. 'I'll need some shoes,' she admitted, 'but apart from that . . .'

'I probably look foreign, do I?' McGregor asked.

'A little.'

'I thought I'd done all right. Well, you could Frenchify me, if you like. It's always interesting about people, isn't it? I mean, they don't notice what fits, they notice what doesn't – the one tiny thing that's out of place. We get it all the time on the force. See, if I was describing you, I'd say five foot five, slender build, auburn shoulder-length hair, hazel eyes. Or the waiter – I'd say five ten, strawberry blond. No more than thirty-five. But a witness, they'd say the woman was, pardon me, ordinary enough but she was wearing riding boots with a dress. Course they would. They wouldn't have a clue how tall you were. They wouldn't think of that.'

'Point taken.'

'Let me give you a hand, eh? And perhaps tomorrow you could show me around. You must know the place. The Eiffel Tower? The cathedral of Notre Dame? Once you're finished your work?'

'I'm not sure how long this will take. And it might be danger-ous, Superintendent.'

McGregor lifted his glass. 'Enough of the "Superintendent"! It's Alan, please. And I owe you my life already, don't I?' he said referring to the year before when Mirabelle had freed him from a cellar on Queen's Road where he'd been tied up for the best part of twenty-four hours. 'You can tell me what's going on. What did Vesta send you?'

Mirabelle paused. She wasn't sure how to express it. Her mind was still churning the details. Was Philip Caine the reason Christine Moreau met Wilhelm von der Grün in the first place? Had she only encouraged the German as part of the scheme? Did she sleep with him for her country and then fall in love afterwards? Suddenly the whole situation seemed too compli-cated to unravel – whose side had everyone been on? It was impossible to tell. Perhaps that was why Jack had come here himself in 1944. Perhaps even he'd lost track of it all.

The waiter brought a basket of bread and a butter dish.

'You should try to eat something,' McGregor encouraged her.

Mirabelle picked up a slice without even looking at it. 'I wonder if they have soup,' she said.

McGregor's face split in an open grin. 'That's the spirit. Well, they probably have onion soup, won't they? With cheese on top? I believe that's standard rations around here.'

Mirabelle nodded. 'And afterwards I have to go and visit someone,' she said.

'So Vesta's papers were useful then?'

'Very.'

McGregor buttered a slice of bread liberally and decided not to push her any further. Mirabelle clearly wasn't going to give away anything willingly and he knew from experience that she was a tough nut to crack. Still, he wasn't prepared to give up entirely. 'Tell you what, you don't have to say a word. I'll just come with you. It's a nice night for an outing. You look as though you could use a hand.'

Mirabelle considered. The Russians hadn't seen McGregor yet. That of itself might be useful. If they were looking for her, a woman on her own, the addition of a male partner might buy some extra time.

'Of course you can come,' she said, relenting. 'Where I'm going we have to pass the Eiffel Tower so at least you'll get to see that.'

'Vesta said that it's a British airman you're looking for?'

'Missing since 1944,' she confirmed.

'Well, here's to a nice little holiday finding the old fellow,' he said.

Mirabelle sipped her wine and chose not to correct him.

Chapter 24

Of all the noises known to man, opera is the most expensive.

By the time they left the bistro it was well after nine o'clock and Mirabelle felt a lot better now she had eaten. The night air was refreshing as they hailed a taxi on the rue Saint-Honoré and Mirabelle gave the driver directions to the rue de Siam. It was late to make a social call, but the trail had led her back to Passy and, she reasoned, she'd rather return under the cover of darkness and as soon as possible. There was no advantage to be had from waiting till the following morning; in fact it only gave the Russians longer to find her.

After ten minutes driving through deserted streets, the taxi pulled in smoothly just round the corner from von der Grün's house. Quietened with a few francs, the driver turned off the engine. Mirabelle craned her neck to peer down the street to see if the house was being watched. The pavement was empty, not a single car parked along its length. Curtains were mostly drawn in the windows on both sides. Nevertheless, there was no harm in being careful. She directed McGregor to von der Grün's front door while she waited anxiously in the back of the taxi, watching from a distance as he loitered for a moment and then rang the bell. In the front seat, the driver lit a cigarette and rolled down the window to let out the smoke.

Von der Grün must know what had happened to his cousin, Mirabelle reasoned. He must at least know where Caine had been for the last ten years. And if Caine was dead he'd know where he was buried. Everything seemed to revolve around

this man: Christine's suffering, Caine's whereabouts and Jack's reason for being in Paris. Along the road McGregor stepped back slightly as the door opened and warm light flooded onto the pavement at his feet. Mirabelle could just make out the silhouette of the maid who had answered the door earlier. McGregor took a moment to enquire for the Comte de Vert.

'I won't have a clue what they're saying,' he had pointed out on the drive across town.

'It will be obvious,' Mirabelle retorted. 'And von der Grün probably speaks English. Besides, if he's there I'll follow you in.'

Now she leaned forward in her seat, clutching the edge of the leather upholstery, waiting for McGregor to disappear inside the black-and-white tiled hallway – her cue to follow him. The driver threw the butt of his cigarette onto the pavement and blew a last stream of smoke into the freezing night air. On the rue de Siam, McGregor turned. The door closed without admitting him, the street was returned to amber-lit semi-darkness and the superintendent walked back to the car.

'He's not in. I think she said he had gone to the opera.'

'The opera?'

McGregor nodded.

'If it's the national opera, it's close to where we just came from.' Mirabelle sounded annoyed.

McGregor checked his watch. 'It's only ten minutes back again.' He liked the idea of another ride across town sitting next to Mirabelle. They had been all but silent crossing the city. He had discounted reaching out to hold her hand – she seemed too distracted. She was wearing some kind of lavender perfume, or perhaps it was only the scent of soap that lingered on her skin. In the confined back seat of the taxi he could tell it was different from the musky perfume she normally wore in Brighton.

'They won't let us in.' Mirabelle cast her palm down her

outfit dismissively. 'I'd need a cocktail dress at least, and certainly not these ridiculous boots.'

McGregor regarded his tweed suit, which was no more acceptable. He'd never been to the opera – the most he'd ever stretched to was a Saturday matinee at the Lyceum and that was years ago. He realised that whenever he was with Mirabelle the world felt larger, more sophisticated.

'We could wait till he gets home,' he offered. 'It won't take more than a couple of hours, will it?'

Mirabelle said nothing and eyed the hotel sign at the other end of the rue de Siam. The street was known to the men in the Mackintoshes – she didn't want to spend more time there than she had to.

'No. I'm not giving up,' she said. 'We'll think of something.' She leaned over to give the driver instructions.

The Trocadero gardens were lit up as they passed. As in all cities with grand architecture, the night lent an extra air of glamour to the Parisian streets. Here and there an enticing arcade led off the main road, lit by ornate lamps like secret passageways. The paint was often flaking but the entrances were bordered by immaculately tended bay trees. The buildings seemed formal but the passages were more friendly, as if they were byways to the real life of the city.

As the taxi pulled up a hundred yards along from the opera house there was a crush of waiting cars ahead. At the front of the building a stall selling flowers spread along the pale stone steps leading to the entrance, its business in buttonholes and corsages over for the evening. An old woman bundled in a thick woollen coat fussed over a bucket of white lilies in anticipation of the orders for bouquets to be sent to the divas after the performance. Golden angels peered down from the rooftop at her wares and large buckets of red roses punctuated the sculpted columns.

McGregor paid the driver as Mirabelle took in the building,

considering the possibilities. *Tosca* was playing tonight. There were large posters on display along the front of it. As in London, the opera houses in Paris had stopped playing German music for a long time after the war. 'The devil has the best tunes, though. I miss Wagner,' Mirabelle remembered Jack saying. Italian composers had benefited from more willing forgiveness, though by now even Schumann and Mahler were back on the programme at Covent Garden. The French, it seemed, cut the Germans less slack – the posters here advertised Bizet and Berlioz, Rossini, Puccini and even Ralph Vaughan Williams, but nothing German.

Checking to one side, she wondered if she might be able to sneak in through the stage door. It flashed across her mind that she could buy a bunch of flowers and insist upon delivering them to one of the dressing rooms in person. From backstage it should be possible to make her way to the public areas. But before she could move, McGregor grabbed her hand and pulled her away from the entrance. He removed the blue scarf at his neck and bundled it into a ball.

'Put that down your dress,' he hissed.

'What?'

'Down the front of your dress,' he insisted. 'So you look pregnant.'

Mirabelle baulked. The dress was woollen. It would be stretched beyond recognition, the line completely ruined.

'I was planning to go in through the stage door,' she objected.

'This will work better. Honestly,' McGregor insisted. 'A pregnant tourist who needs to use the lavatory. It'll get both of us inside. And through the main entrance too.'

Mirabelle stared. He was probably right, but she would look even more ghastly than she did already. She tried not to think too much as she shoved the scarf in place.

McGregor inspected her. 'Higher,' he said.

Mirabelle looked confused.

'Haven't you ever seen a pregnant woman? The bump sits higher.'

'All right, all right.'

She shifted uncomfortably and presented herself for inspection once more. McGregor nodded, laid his hand on the bump to smooth it down and took Mirabelle's gloved hand in his, placing his other arm around her waist to help her climb the steps. At the entrance a doorman hovered.

'It's my wife,' he said. '*Ma femme.* She needs assistance. *Une toilette.*'

Mirabelle tried to look pained. The doorman maintained an even expression.

'The opera is for ticket holders only, monsieur,' he insisted in decisive English.

McGregor squared up. 'Look. My wife is unwell. She's having a baby.' He sounded genuinely concerned. 'You have to let us in. I'll buy a bloody ticket if that's what it takes.'

The doorman looked uncomfortable. He did not want to say anything about evening dress, given the circumstances, but still. Mirabelle let out a low moan to add a little pressure. She put her hand on the man's arm as if she could hardly stand upright. He clasped it.

'Please. I beg you,' she gasped in perfect French. That did the trick.

'All right.' The man relented, pushing open the door. 'Upstairs. But the interval is about to begin. Please, be quick.'

'Thank you.' McGregor led Mirabelle inside.

The hallway was magnificent. A wide carpeted stairway led upwards, splitting into two on a low landing, beyond which both sides rose to the height of the first balcony. Crystal chandeliers hung from the extensively muralled ceiling and lit the rows of pale columns that skirted the upper floor. The cornicing was gilded. Above they could just make out a crush bar

being set up, bottles of champagne popping in anticipation of the interval. McGregor firmly guided Mirabelle upwards, his hand on her arm. Von der Grün would have seats in the circle or perhaps a private box. Either way they had to get up to the first level – if he came out for a drink it would be there.

'What does this fellow look like?' McGregor asked.

Mirabelle laid her free hand on her belly. 'I'm not sure,' she admitted. 'I've seen a photograph that I think was him, but it was an old one.'

'Roughly?'

'He must be in his early forties. In the picture, he had dark hair.' Mirabelle grasped for more detail, realising that what McGregor had said about giving decent descriptions was entirely accurate. There had been nothing out of place in the old photograph – nothing unusual onto which she might hang the memory. 'He looked quite ordinary,' she admitted.

'That's no help to speak of.' McGregor smiled. 'Well, you have good enough recall for faces. Do you think you might recognise him?'

'I hope so.'

Keeping to the wall so that the doorman below wouldn't be able to make them out, they ignored the signs for the lavatories and edged towards a set of mahogany double doors leading to the auditorium. Without conferring, they both made for the one that would bring them out at the back on the left-hand side of the theatre – the best spot from which to survey any room without being noticed. Mirabelle noted that McGregor was better at this than she might have expected.

'Wait here,' she instructed, and he peeled off as she cracked the door and went inside. The sound of music hit her in a wave. In the hallway it had sounded like someone singing a long way away, but inside it was so all consuming you could drown in it. It was amazing the difference a door made. Mirabelle froze for a second as an usherette rose from a seat at

the end of the back row. It was dark and the girl didn't appear to notice Mirabelle's unusual footwear.

'*Madame?*'

'*Je cherche mon mari,*' Mirabelle explained. '*Il y a une urgence familiale.*'

The family emergency card generally worked. Slowly the girl took in Mirabelle's apparently swollen belly and then her eyes continued downwards to the boots. She pursed her lips.

'*Son nom?*' she asked coldly, and then enquired as to where Mirabelle's husband might be sitting.

'Le Comte de Vert,' Mirabelle tried, casting around for likely candidates, hoping that mentioning the title might lengthen the girl's patience. People made extraordinary allowances for the upper classes. There were hundreds of men in the auditorium, but the girl might remember a count. As she scanned the rows ahead she realised the male contingent of the audience formed a sea of black evening jackets between the gem-like chiffon and taffeta of the women. She didn't even know if she was looking for grey hair or dark brown, and easily half the men fell into the right age bracket. The action on stage was coming to a climax. The female singer dramatically stabbed a man at a desk and removed a document from his grip while belting out a stirring aria. Then the applause started as the curtain began to descend. One or two people got up from their seats and left quickly by the aisle, no doubt keen to be first in the queue for the lavatories. The applause, strong for a few seconds, petered out and the low hum of conversation swept the auditorium.

And then Mirabelle spotted something. Not von der Grün. It would be almost impossible to pick him out, she realised now. Instead, as the house lights came up, her eagle eyes lighted on a woman dressed in a beautiful gown, almost the same pansy purple as Vesta's wedding dress but fuller and cinched at the waist with a matching satin belt and diamante clasp. Her

hair was swept into an elegant chignon that set off her long diamond earrings to perfection, and as she rose to her feet and turned to leave the box where she was sitting with two men Mirabelle gasped. She was wearing a red rayon scarf, looped around her neck in a sheer slash the colour of blood. It was the scarf that Christine Moreau had delivered to the rue de Siam the night before, or one identical to it. Mirabelle turned back sharply into the hall with the usherette calling behind her.

'I think he's in a box with some friends.' She waved vaguely, dismissing the girl. 'I've spotted him.'

McGregor was waiting behind the door. He fell into step as Mirabelle made her way purposefully towards the right side of the hallway. The audience was flooding into the bar now, chattering and greeting each other as they bumped into acquaintances and made introductions. The opera, after all, was a social occasion as much as a cultural one. Voices rose in a heaving indistinguishable babble, discussing the performance, *le weekend*, the week's headlines in *Le Figaro* – the business of the day.

'Where is he?' McGregor's eyes darted across the sea of unfamiliar faces.

'It's the woman we need,' Mirabelle said without explaining further.

It was becoming difficult to move as the tide of people crashed onto the safe shore of the bar. Drinks were passed hand to hand, the rows of champagne glasses lined up on the marble surface disappearing like knitting unravelling into a single strand of wool. Behind the bar six men were serving at speed but even that wasn't enough to keep up.

'I can't see her. I need to be higher.' Mirabelle turned away, making for the stairs to the second balcony. From the vantage of the fourth step she could make out the crowd more easily. The woman in the purple dress was sipping a saucer of champagne on the far side of the bar. Her nails were painted a glossy

pillar-box red that was completely unchipped. Beside her, frustratingly, both the men in her party had their backs to the staircase. The little group was proving popular – people thronged around them, shaking hands and making conversation, and, Mirabelle reasoned, that meant they wouldn't move. She just had to fight her way over.

As she tried to do so she realised this would have been easier in appropriate attire. Women in cocktail dresses did not move out of the way for someone they considered their social inferior, even if that woman was heavily pregnant. McGregor proved an effective usher but it took a good five minutes to battle their way through the crowd. At last, only two or three layers away, the woman in the purple dress came into view. She was comforting a younger woman who had obviously joined the party. The newcomer was wearing taupe chiffon with a short fox fur cape slung over one arm, and was fanning herself furiously with a programme. Mirabelle observed that the girl was pink-eyed from crying, which Mirabelle assumed was on account of the performance. The opera appeared to have moved many people in the audience. Mirabelle had noticed a debutante at the bar with a watery stream of mascara down her cheek, and along from her a handsome man, in the requisite evening dress, comforted another man similarly moved by the music.

Beside the bar, the woman in purple was explaining something to her friend, both of them intent on whatever she was saying. Next to them the men were smoking and engaged in their own conversation, the low pulse of their voices just audible under the general hum of the crowd as Mirabelle and McGregor pushed closer. Although Mirabelle couldn't distinguish individual words, she could make out that they were speaking in French. Coming from the side she could also see their faces now. Of the two men, one was only in his thirties and the other must be at least in his late fifties – both the wrong

age for von der Grün. Where on earth was the man? She tried to work it out, and saw the woman in the purple dress put her hand on her friend's arm and whisper into her ear. Then she drew the slim red scarf from her neck and handed it over. The other woman dabbed her nose with it.

Mirabelle stopped in her tracks. Of course. It was the scarf. It must be. Somehow it contained information or signified something – a message, or at least a symbol. It had to be – there was no other way, and yet it seemed so innocuous, which was of course its strength. No one would think twice about a woman passing on a cheap rayon scarf – a mere item of fashion. It was small – easy to transport – only the size of a handkerchief. They were using the opera as a drop – and such an ingenious one. The young woman dried her tears and slipped the scarf into her satin clutch bag.

A bell sounded and the waiters at the bar served last orders. There was a shift in the crowd as people began to move back to their seats. Mirabelle tried to push forward but it was impossible against the tide. The group put down their glasses and started to return to their box. They were slipping away, back to the opera, out of reach.

'Wilhelm,' Mirabelle called, hoping a head might turn. 'Wilhelm.' Then she tried the name in French. 'Guillaume.'

Neither man responded.

Pushed along behind them by the tide of bodies, Mirabelle and McGregor were swept back towards the auditorium with the box party tantalisingly just out of reach. Then Mirabelle saw the girl who had been crying peel off. She was manoeuvring herself across the stream of people, away from the auditorium. Grabbing McGregor's hand tightly, Mirabelle heaved him in her wake, indicating the crown of the woman's head.

'You're taller. Can you see where she's going?'

McGregor strained. 'She's leaving. She's opened a door.' His voice was raised. 'I think it must be the back stairs.'

'Follow her.'

In less than a minute they were jammed against the wall with a sconce above them. McGregor reached for the brass handle and the door opened onto what must be a service stairway. A dull pale green light illuminated scuffed beige walls as Mirabelle squeezed through. Footsteps echoed from below as the young woman tottered downstairs in heels. Then the sound of the street echoed in their ears and a breeze whispered up the stairwell.

'I thought it was a man we were after,' McGregor objected, resisting the pressure of Mirabelle's pull on his arm. 'What about the matter in hand?'

Mirabelle shook her head. 'That woman has the information,' she whispered. 'I want to see where she takes it.'

Chapter 25

Curiosity is the lust of the mind.

Outside, the cold air stung and Mirabelle scanned the side street for any sign of taupe chiffon. McGregor looked left and right but they were too late to see which direction their quarry had taken.

'If she wants a taxi she'll make for the front,' he reasoned, but Mirabelle was already striding in that direction. The main street was better lit, and the flower woman and a couple of chauffeurs were milling about. One man passed a pewter hip flask to another as they inspected the tyres on his vehicle. Three men were playing cards in the back of a brand new Citroën Avant.

'Taxi!' McGregor put up his hand and whistled.

Mirabelle ran up the steps, and the vantage point afforded her a view of a short fox fur cape disappearing into a car further along. The doorman peered down at her. She waved at him, putting her other hand on her stomach as she realised that pushing through the crowd had left her with a misshapen baby bump. She pulled her jacket closed to obscure it from view. In the meantime the woman's car set off along the rue Auber with a smart chauffeur at the wheel. Mirabelle hurried back to the pavement and slipped into the back of the taxi McGregor had procured. She asked the driver to follow the car and sat forward on the edge of her seat. McGregor looked at Mirabelle's stomach, and then he smiled.

'Perhaps you'd better give me back my scarf.' His eyes

crinkled. Mirabelle undid a button to withdraw it. The action seemed too personal and McGregor looked away.

'Here.' She pushed the material into his hand.

'What do you think she's up to?' he enquired as he wound the scarf around his neck and they took the corner onto the boulevard Haussmann, heading towards Passy.

Mirabelle shook her head and cast her eyes towards the driver. You never knew, and after what had happened to her this afternoon it was as well to be careful. After three or four minutes the woman's car turned off the main road and drew up at a bar on a grubby-looking side street. Mirabelle directed the taxi driver to keep going and they passed just as the woman got out, waved away her chauffeur and disappeared inside. On the street the bells of a nearby church struck the half-hour. Ten thirty. It was getting late. Mirabelle peered at the bar's picture window. The woman was overdressed for the venue. Formica tables lined one room, while the wooden bar itself was housed in another adjacent to it. Apart from the woman and the barman, the place was deserted. Mirabelle instructed the driver to pull up a few yards further on, McGregor paid the fare, and the couple walked back towards the dimly lit entrance. Mirabelle felt very aware that her outfit looked even worse than when she'd started now the ruse with the scarf had stretched it.

'You look fine,' McGregor comforted her.

How did he know what was on her mind? Were her concerns so transparent? She felt suddenly, inexplicably cross as McGregor held open the door and they entered the bar. The woman in taupe was sitting by herself in the other room. She had taken a table at the window. In front of her was a glass of brandy and a cup of coffee. She was scrabbling inside her handbag and Mirabelle peered to see what she might be looking for, but the woman only withdrew a packet of cigarettes and a slim gold Rolex lighter. She lit up and inhaled deeply.

McGregor ordered a beer. 'What can I get you?'

'A glass of red,' Mirabelle said curtly and left him at the bar, wandering through and settling at the table behind the woman, who she could now see was even younger than she had thought. Before he could follow her, she leaned over and asked for a cigarette. The woman spoke French with a Parisian accent, indistinguishable from Mirabelle's own.

'That's a beautiful dress,' Mirabelle complimented her.

The woman smiled and said thank you as she held up a flame so that Mirabelle could light the Gitane. In England Mirabelle's remark would have felt unbearably personal, but in France women expected to be admired – they accepted it. 'I like the colour,' the woman admitted, 'the blandness of it. It means you can shine.'

This furnished no clues as to her identity or who she might be working for but it confirmed to Mirabelle that she was French. Such self-confidence was the reason that French women were considered sexy worldwide.

'Cold night,' was Mirabelle's attempt to continue the conversation, and she inwardly cursed herself for being so very English as McGregor arrived with the drinks.

The young woman wasn't interested in the weather. She shrugged lazily and turned towards the window. She took a sip of coffee and checked her watch, then got up and disappeared in the direction of the lavatory.

'Is it true what they say about the toilets in places like this?' McGregor whispered. 'The French don't mind if it's just a hole in the ground?'

Mirabelle didn't answer. Instead she reached over smoothly and scooped up the satin clutch bag the woman had left on the table beside her drink. With one eye on the bar and the other on the route to the lavatory, she clicked the bag open. There was nothing inside but the cigarettes – not even the gold lighter or a few francs to pay for drinks. The lining was secure and

there was nothing secreted inside. Most important, the red rayon scarf was missing. The woman must have put everything of value into her pockets and left the bag to make it look as if she'd be coming back.

In the other room, the barman switched out the light over the doorway, then wandered through with a greying cloth in his hand. Mirabelle hid the satin clutch bag down the side of her chair.

'We're closing now. Drink up. You have to leave.' He reached out to remove the coffee cup and brandy glass from the young woman's now vacated table, and ran the rag over the surface in a half-hearted attempt to clean it. Mirabelle lifted her glass of wine and took a sip.

'I better go and fetch my friend,' she said. 'She's in the toilet. I don't think she's finished her drink.'

'You have to leave now,' the barman repeated steadily, holding Mirabelle's eye.

Mirabelle got to her feet. She wasn't letting the other woman disappear that easily, but the barman blocked her way.

'Now look here,' McGregor cut in.

'We're closed,' the barman repeated, and indicated the exit. McGregor didn't argue – he just muscled the fellow out of the way to let Mirabelle dart in the other direction. Leaving McGregor to it, she checked through the door that lay beyond but there was no sign of the woman in the chiffon evening gown.

'Hello,' she called.

No answer. Further along the corridor some empty drinks crates were piled at the top of a flight of stairs. She took the stairs down into what seemed to be a cellar, but it was too dark to make out anything properly. Cursing, she wished she had brought her torch. She recalled last seeing it on the table in the hallway of her flat. She'd bought new batteries only a couple of weeks ago. Above, she could hear a chair scrape along the

café floor. Were the men fighting? She pushed on, her eyes becoming accustomed to the darkness. The cellar smelled of stale beer and the floor was uneven.

'Hello. Is anybody down here?' Nothing. She tried again in French. '*Il y a quelqu'un?*'

Silence. She checked behind a couple of large barrels that were piled to one side but the cellar was completely unoccupied.

At the back she pushed open a door that led onto an alley. Looking left and right only confirmed that the place was deserted. There was no sound of heels clicking on the tarmac, not even a car engine. But on the ground was a solitary button, covered in taupe chiffon. It must have fallen off the girl's dress as she left.

She's made a run for it, thought Mirabelle as she picked it up. Then she paused. She walked down the alley to the corner and turned back onto the side street where they'd come into the bar. Strolling towards the entrance, she saw through the window that the barman and McGregor were still tussling at the table. McGregor's beer had toppled and the missing woman's coffee cup had smashed, trailing a brown milky smear across the floor. As she watched, McGregor grabbed hold of the barman by the collar and pushed him against the wall. He pulled back his fist. His lips were moving, but Mirabelle couldn't hear what he was saying. She rapped sharply on the window and motioned for him to join her. He held off the barman, dropped his fist to his side and looking slightly disappointed backed out to the street.

'Did you find her?'

Mirabelle shook her head. The barman kept an eye on them as he surveyed the debris of the fight. Then he locked the door.

'Did you get anything out of him?' she asked.

'No time . . . Where do you think the woman has gone?'

'We need to find her car. The chauffeur will have waited,

don't you think? If she intends to go home, she wouldn't send him away for the night. Parking directly outside would be far too obvious – round here a car with a liveried chauffeur would attract attention – but he must be somewhere.'

'Unless she was expecting a lift from whoever she intended to meet,' McGregor hazarded.

'Either way, we need to look for her car. If it's gone then she's either run for it because we scared her or taken a lift with whoever she was meeting. But if the car's still waiting and she hasn't gone back to it, then it's likely she's been taken.'

'Taken?'

'Picked up.'

'By whom?'

Mirabelle didn't like to say. 'Come on. The chauffeur drove in this direction.' She touched McGregor's arm to encourage him to fall into step along the uneven paving stones.

'How long do you reckon we were inside?'

'Five minutes. Maybe seven. Tops.'

'And how long might you leave, if you were booking a driver to come back and get you after a drop . . .' McGregor looked dubious. He had never made a drop, but Mirabelle seemed to know a good deal about it. 'Ten minutes? Quarter of an hour? How long do you think it takes?'

'Not long,' Mirabelle replied decisively. 'And you want to leave immediately after if you can. Especially here. There's no one else about, which makes it easy to spot intruders like us. But it also makes the drop highly visible.'

McGregor looked at her sideways. She really was extraordinary. The sound of an acoustic guitar and a woman singing snaked across the pavement from a dimly lit bistro with candles in its window. Mirabelle ignored McGregor's look of admiration and peered inside, but the woman wasn't there. Almost at the main street they passed a hairdresser's and a jewellery shop – both closed. Mirabelle was aware that her steps were quieter

than usual, the soft thump of the boots' soles on the pavement matching that of McGregor's sensible shoes. An elderly woman wearing a heavy winter coat and a headscarf let herself out of a door and crossed the road. A taxi stopped at a red light and then zoomed off in the direction of Opéra.

'Left or right?'

'Right is the more natural turn. They drive on the right,' Mirabelle decided.

The streets were spaced randomly – Paris was not laid out on a recognisable grid. Here and there a dark passage linked the side streets. The iron gates were open but the shops inside were closed. They turned right and right again, and then from the other end of the street a familiar car chugged towards them.

'There,' Mirabelle said.

No one was sitting in the back. Mirabelle waved down the chauffeur but he didn't slow until McGregor stepped off the pavement and interposed his body. He raised one hand and pulled out his police badge with the other. The car came to a halt. Mirabelle was impressed. She felt a glow flush her skin. McGregor was surprisingly competent for a man who couldn't speak the language and had never worked undercover.

The driver rolled down the window and Mirabelle leaned in and spoke in swift French. 'Are you going back to pick up the young lady you dropped at the bar?'

The chauffeur didn't respond to the question. 'Who is he?' he said, casting his eyes towards McGregor.

'Police, of course.'

You could tell a lot by threatening people with the police. It occurred to her that if the chauffeur had been paid off by someone he'd show some sign of panic – a twitch or a flicker in his eyes. Instead the man nodded stoutly at McGregor and drew himself up in his seat. Mirabelle pulled the woman's clutch bag from her pocket.

'Your mistress left this in the bar. She seems to have disappeared. Where were you due to meet her? When?'

The chauffeur's eyes narrowed.

'It's important,' Mirabelle insisted. 'She may be in danger.'

The man stared at the clutch bag for a moment, weighing things up. 'She should be there now. Get in,' he said finally. 'You can give it back to her yourself.'

'How long have you worked for her?'

'I work for her father,' the chauffeur admitted. 'The family.'

'For long?'

'Since I came to Paris after the war.'

'So you know her well?'

'I don't know Mademoiselle Durand at all. I am a servant, madame.'

Mirabelle noted the name and opened the car door. McGregor followed her onto the back seat.

'This is risky,' he murmured. 'We don't know anything about this man.'

'It's less risky with you here,' Mirabelle whispered. 'I had no idea you were so handy.' Besides, the fellow was a family retainer. The driver pulled back onto the main road and overshot the turning for the bar, taking a left beyond it and then turning left again. He pulled up short of the next corner, parking tight into the kerb.

'Mademoiselle Durand didn't walk in this direction,' Mirabelle pointed out. 'She'd have had to pass us sitting in the window if she was heading here.'

'She might have gone round the block the other way,' McGregor said.

The little street was as deserted as the rest of the area. McGregor got out of the car and walked to the end of the road, stopping on the corner and peering in the direction of the bar. The windows were black and the light over the door was switched off. He gestured towards Mirabelle, shrugging

his shoulders. A ginger cat stalked across his path and stopped to look at this stranger.

'Where were you going to take her?' Mirabelle asked the driver.

'Mademoiselle Durand didn't say, madame.' He checked his watch. 'But it is customary to wait.'

'Where does she live?'

She could feel the chauffeur prickle. It was an unseemly question. The French were private, and even in England for a servant to reveal the address of his employer would be considered indiscreet. It was too much of an intrusion. Mirabelle tried another tack.

'Have you brought her here before? To that bar?'

The man's eyes burned in the mirror. McGregor opened the rear door and slipped back inside.

'Where does the woman live?' he said.

'You really think she is in some kind of trouble?' the chauffeur asked.

'Mademoiselle Durand has disappeared. Without her handbag,' Mirabelle pointed out. 'Yes. I believe she might well be in trouble.'

'Then surely we should start a proper search,' the man said. 'You are right – she is usually back in the car by now. One policeman . . . surely we should report the matter properly.' He eyed McGregor with dubiety.

'How often have you brought her here?'

'Three times. Perhaps four.'

'In how long?'

'The last few months. The first time was last summer.'

'I take it she doesn't make a habit of visiting dives late at night? But she comes here sometimes – always from the opera?'

The man nodded. 'Ten minutes,' he said. 'It takes ten minutes. A quarter of an hour at most.'

'And then?'

'She goes home.' The driver looked worried. 'If Mademoiselle Durand is missing, the master has to be told. I always wondered about bringing her here, but she insisted and it was always quick. He'll be angry, but if Mademoiselle is in trouble it's my duty to let Monsieur Durand know.'

Mirabelle cut in. 'Let's see if we can find her first, yes? That would make less trouble. I'm sure her father wouldn't be happy with her for coming here, nor with you for bringing her.'

The chauffeur's eyes softened. Mirabelle continued.

'Tell me, there aren't normally customers in the bar, are there? Not at this time of night. Have you ever seen anyone else inside when Mademoiselle Durand made her visits?'

The chauffeur shook his head.

'We scared her. We changed the transaction. She got up from the table because she knew it wouldn't go ahead. She wanted to get away.'

'Then you think someone kidnapped her because of us?' McGregor sat back.

'No. I think we were a symptom not the cause. She wasn't going to make the drop so she left her bag on the table to make it look as if she intended to return and instead she slipped out the back. She must have shoved everything important into a pocket – the scarf, her lighter, any money she was carrying. She secreted it all. The person she intended to meet might well have been watching from somewhere outside. When we arrived he would have left as well. The drop wasn't to go ahead if there was anyone else in the bar, you see. My guess is that if she's been taken it wasn't by her contact.' Mirabelle drew the little button from her pocket. 'She snagged her dress on the way out of the door. I found this on the cobbles. I'm wondering if she was grabbed by a third party. Someone who wanted the information she was carrying. Someone who was desperate for it. I might have an inkling of who they are and where they'd go.'

McGregor's eyes narrowed. 'What makes you say that?'

'They took me, too. Earlier today. But I got away.'

'What on earth have you got yourself mixed up in? What do you mean, they took you?' McGregor reached for her hand. It was too intimate a gesture. Mirabelle pushed him off.

'I need to think. But if Mademoiselle Durand has been taken I think she might be in the rue de Courcelles. Do you know where that is?' she asked the driver.

'Yes, madame. But Monsieur Durand would want to be informed. Mademoiselle Evangeline is his daughter.'

'In due course,' Mirabelle said decisively. 'First let's go and see if we can find her. Take us to the rue de Courcelles and park on the corner. We don't want to make it too easy for them to see us coming.'

Chapter 26

More law, less justice.

Mirabelle had no idea how to get into the building. In England when she was on a special case, she broke into private residences with the frequency of a cat burglar. But in France the architecture was a lot more difficult to negotiate. The terrace on the rue de Courcelles was no different and the balcony that had made it possible for her to escape from number 8 was too high to facilitate her return. There was no hotel or restaurant on the row through which she might access the rear of the buildings, and for the most part the street looked as if it was asleep. Of the few lights illuminating the windows, the top floor of number 8 burned brightest, firing her belief that Mademoiselle Durand might well have been brought to the house by Albert or one of his associates. Someone was up there, anyway. McGregor had managed to stay silent during the short drive as Mirabelle stared out of the window thinking it through. Now they had parked and were surveying the location from the safety of the back of the car, he could no longer contain his concern.

'So someone kidnapped you?' he said. 'And you were kept here?'

Mirabelle nodded. 'Earlier today. I got out over the roof. If they've taken this girl to the same place then she's behind that window on the fifth floor. They probably have other safe houses, but the men we're looking for were set up here this afternoon. Please, Alan, don't make anything of it. I'm

perfectly all right. I got out.' If he offered her sympathy she knew it would weaken her resolve, and the important thing at the moment was finding Mademoiselle Durand.

McGregor squared up. 'All right,' he said. 'I'll be pragmatic. Do you think they know you're gone?'

Mirabelle shrugged. It had been several hours. It seemed unlikely they had not checked on her in that time. 'I imagine so. On balance of probability.'

'So your theory runs that having lost you, they went out and took another woman. Is that what you're saying? It seems rather random, Mirabelle, and I don't understand how you're mixed up in all this. What's the connection between you and this Durand woman?'

Mirabelle cast a glance at the chauffeur, who showed no sign that he was eavesdropping on their conversation or for that matter was able to understand English.

'We should walk around the block and get the lie of the land,' she suggested. 'And as for you,' she addressed the driver in French, 'keep an eye on the door of number 8. We won't be long.'

Outside she put up a hand to stop McGregor interrupting her thoughts. They turned left along the main street. McGregor had made a good point without realising its significance. When Albert had interrogated her earlier in the day, he had no idea how Christine Moreau had been passing on the information in her possession, or even exactly what it was. So how had he known about Mademoiselle Durand's assignation? And if he had that piece of the puzzle, why had he spent time and effort picking up Mirabelle in the graveyard at Passy? No, she realised, it had happened the other way around. This was her fault. She cursed herself for being so slow. When she thought it through, what had happened was obvious.

The first thing Albert would have done when he found Mirabelle missing was to check everywhere he associated with her. There was already a watch on Christine Moreau's

flat but it would be only natural for him to return to the rue de Siam – the address Mirabelle had visited directly before she'd been taken. And there, if they waited, they'd have seen von der Grün and his wife leave for the opera, assuming that was the woman in the purple dress. They'd have recognised Christine Moreau's scarf just as Mirabelle had. From that point on all the Russians had to do was keep the party under surveillance. During the interval they'd have seen Frau von der Grün pass on the red scarf and they'd have followed Mademoiselle Durand, and for that matter Mirabelle and McGregor. Her lips pursed. She was out of practice, it seemed. She had only been looking ahead, not checking behind, and that meant that whatever had happened to poor Mademoiselle Durand was her fault as surely as if she'd pointed the girl out to Albert in the crowd.

'Were we followed?' She clasped McGregor's arm. 'I didn't notice us being followed, did you?'

'No. I told you when I arrived. There was no one on my tail.'

Mirabelle's voice was insistent. 'I don't mean at the Bistro Florentine. I mean at the opera. Were we the only people tailing Mademoiselle Durand?'

'There wasn't another car at the bar she went to. The streets were deserted, remember? If there'd been any traffic we'd have seen it.'

Mirabelle tried to focus. McGregor was right, but there had been plenty of cars on the main road. Stupidly, she had been so busy removing the scarf from her clothing and so focused on Mademoiselle's Durand's car ahead that like a rookie she hadn't paid attention to the rest of the traffic. She might know the drill, but her lack of practical experience was showing.

'They could have pulled over on the main road and cut down the back on foot,' she said.

McGregor shook his head. 'What, and just grabbed her

as she left? The woman would have screamed. She'd have resisted.'

Mirabelle recalled the effect of the chemicals on Albert's handkerchief. But if he had knocked out Mademoiselle Durand, he'd have had to get her body back to the main road. For a moment she felt weak – had the poor girl been left behind the casks in the cellar of the bar? Had she walked right past her body in the darkness? No, she reassured herself, surely Albert would want to interrogate her. That was the purpose of taking her. Getting hold of the scarf was only part of the mystery. There was little value in capturing an encrypted message if you couldn't decode it, or indeed find out its intended destination.

'He must have knocked her out. Then he'd have carried her. I wasn't quick enough, McGregor. He could have taken her in the other direction, back to a waiting car on the main road.'

'Who?' McGregor asked again. 'Who is it?'

'They're Russian,' said Mirabelle. 'And I led them right to her.'

By now they had made their way almost right round the block. There was a short run of shops, all of them closed, but no other obvious weak point that would afford easy access to the rear of the terrace. Together they turned onto the rue de Courcelles. Mirabelle looked up. The pane of glass she'd shattered during her escape had been taped up with what looked like newspaper. A light was on and the glowing newsprint made it look warm inside the top floor studio.

'But I thought you were looking for a wartime flying ace.' McGregor sounded genuinely mystified.

Mirabelle let out a sigh. It seemed rather long ago that she started out on Bulldog Bradley's mission and she still had no idea whether Philip Caine was alive or dead. Mademoiselle Durand's predicament was far more pressing. 'If I can get back up onto the roof . . .'

McGregor regarded her open-mouthed.

'If you give me a leg up I think I can do it. I got out that way so I can get in up there too.'

McGregor spluttered, unable to voice his objections because they came in such a rush. Mirabelle ignored him, and by the time he managed to say 'But that's preposterous' she had already rung the bell of number 2. The door was opened promptly by a housekeeper in a green housecoat. She looked most displeased.

'I want to speak to the man on the top floor,' Mirabelle said, 'the one with the broken window. I have something for him.'

The woman crossed her arms. 'It's very late for visitors.'

'This is a family emergency,' Mirabelle insisted.

The woman surveyed the couple and reluctantly stepped back to let them pass.

'I know the way,' Mirabelle assured her. 'We shan't be long.'

On the top floor they could hear the radio playing behind the closed door of the studio.

'He may not be pleased to see me,' Mirabelle warned McGregor. 'That's where you might have to come in.'

'Who is he?'

Mirabelle looked down. 'The owner of these boots,' she admitted as she rapped on the studio door.

Before McGregor could respond, the door opened on a domestic scene. Warm air wafted into the hall from behind the figure of an elderly man of military bearing who wore a thick moustache – the kind that had become unfashionable lately. His clothes betrayed that he'd seen better days. He had not tied his thick cashmere dressing gown in place properly over his wing-collared shirt, and his bow tie dangled round his neck. Behind him were the remnants of a lonely supper – an apple and some cheese lay half eaten on a chipped plate that he'd left on the chair in front of the stove.

'I'm sorry,' Mirabelle said in swift French. 'I'm afraid I'm the

person who broke in earlier this evening. My name is Mirabelle Bevan. I wanted to bring you back your boots. I left some money for the damage.'

The man's dark eyes surveyed her. 'You broke the window,' he said. 'How on earth did you get up here? No one breaks into the fifth floor from outside. You made a hell of a mess.'

'There's a story to it,' Mirabelle admitted. 'I came from an attic further along and now I need to go back there. I'm sorry. Would you let me use your window again? Please.'

The man eyed her feet. 'Those boots are worth a fortune, you know. I got them in de Sousa in Lisbon. There aren't even twenty pairs like them in Paris.'

'I was desperate,' Mirabelle apologised. 'And now I'm desperate again. Please would you help us? This is my friend, Superintendent McGregor. He's a British policeman. A detective.'

The man hesitated. 'It's most irregular,' he said, watching as Mirabelle peeled off the boots and the socks she'd stolen and laid them beside his bed. Her feet were filthy where she had escaped over the roof and her stockings sported enormous holes. She was aware that her woollen dress bulged at the waist, but just for the moment, how she looked really didn't matter.

'I'll be safer in bare feet. I've been clomping around all night with those boots hanging off me. I feel quite light on my feet without them. May I?' She indicated the newspaper that covered the window, which this time she opened using the catch. 'You'll need to give me a boost,' she said to McGregor over her shoulder.

The man broke in before McGregor could object. 'What are you doing? First you break in and now it seems you're breaking out. Are you burgling another apartment? You can't come into people's homes and just take things . . .'

Mirabelle turned. 'Look, there's a woman trapped in an

attic further along. The attic of number 8. At least I think that's where she is. I'm not a thief out of anything other than necessity, monsieur, and anyway I've brought back your things. I can't see any other way to help this girl. She's in trouble. Please, if you'll be patient, I'll see to it you're rewarded.'

'You should let me do this,' McGregor put in. 'It's dangerous.'

Mirabelle shook her head. 'I'm more agile,' she said. 'And I know where I'm going. I need to see if she's there.'

The man took a swig from a glass of port, which he'd left on the floor next to his chair, and gave a dismissive flap of his hand. 'Go on,' he said.

McGregor reached into his inside pocket and brought out a knife. 'Here,' he said, flicking it open. 'You might need this.' Mirabelle looked dubious. McGregor didn't normally carry a weapon.

'Why on earth did you bring that?'

'I'm abroad,' he said in explanation.

Mirabelle grinned. 'Thanks.' She slipped the serrated blade into her pocket so that the wool stretched even further. 'I hope it doesn't come in handy.'

Outside the air was chill. The iron grille of the balcony felt icy beneath her feet. She held her breath as McGregor's strong hands lifted her upwards and she scrambled onto the lead roof. Gingerly she crawled along the top until the skylight of number 8 was beneath her. When she peered in she saw the room was empty even of the chair and the rags she had been bound with. She squinted through the glass. The door to the hallway lay open as if the room had been hastily abandoned. Perhaps the Russians had moved. Safe houses could be switched in a moment.

Curious, she pulled at the skylight. It was more difficult from the outside than it had been from within, but slowly she managed to heave it open. Then she lowered herself onto the

bare wooden boards. Beyond the room where she'd been held, the hallway was deserted. Mirabelle crept on tiptoes to the top of the stairs and listened. There was no noise from below. Perhaps the Russians had gone. An eerie silence pervaded the apartment. Mirabelle started to turn back, but just as she did so there was a low moan from behind a closed door on the other side of the stair. Her heart flipped in her chest. It hadn't sunk in that there was another room up here.

Aware she must work silently, Mirabelle tentatively turned the key that had been left in the door and swung it open. The room smelled rancid. There was no ventilation – the men had clearly decided to use this side of the hallway after her escape because there was no skylight. Inside, Evangeline Durand was tied to the same chair Mirabelle been tied to earlier in the day with what looked like the same linen rag. Mirabelle checked over her shoulder before walking silently into the room. The girl was dripping with sweat and a thin line of vomit trailed down her beautiful dress. She was breathing heavily. Mirabelle took her hand. The skin felt clammy but Evangeline was conscious. She looked up at Mirabelle and smiled.

'I've come to get you. Can you stand up?'

The girl took a protracted breath that was painful to watch. She shook her head.

'He put it over my mouth,' she wheezed, enunciating each syllable slowly and with an effort. 'I have asthma. They say it's in the mind, but whatever he put over my mouth started it.'

Mirabelle wondered whether she might be able to carry the girl to safety, but it would take two pairs of hands to hoist her through the skylight. Perhaps the quickest way would be to fetch McGregor. Together they'd manage it. She was about to turn when she heard a heavy footfall on the wooden steps leading up to the attic. She froze, then whirled to close the door, realising she couldn't lock it from the inside. Someone was coming. Would they tumble to the fact that Evangeline

must have had company – someone who'd unlocked the door? With her heart thumping, she rolled out of sight under the only other piece of furniture in the room – a large upholstered chaise longue placed along the wall. The women's eyes met. Mirabelle put her fingers to her lips and Evangeline nodded. The door swung open and Albert strode in.

'You are an idiot, Pieter,' he said to someone outside. 'You didn't even lock it.'

'I did,' a second voice insisted.

Albert ignored him. He hovered over the girl. Clearly this time he'd decided to try different interrogation tactics. Perhaps her youth made him bold. Or maybe her once beautiful dress offended his political sensibilities. Without warning Albert pulled back his arm and struck her a full blow on the face.

'Where is it, Mademoiselle Evangeline? Where is the scarf? Who were you going to deliver it to?'

Mirabelle could only see the girl in profile now but the kid was plucky. The faintest smile flickered across her face as she heaved for breath, and her eyes were hard.

'That's my secret,' she managed. 'Fetch a doctor or you'll never know.'

Albert leaned over her. 'Don't tell me what to do,' he sneered. And to underline his point he shoved his hand into her face and held her mouth and nose spitefully so she couldn't breathe.

'I bet a daddy's girl like you is used to issuing orders. Well, Mademoiselle Durand, you're not in high society now. Did you think you were playing a game?'

Evangeline's face turned puce and her legs twitched. In her current state the poor girl was so completely vulnerable it was painful to watch. Mirabelle felt in her pocket for McGregor's knife as her anger rose. If she could take Albert by surprise, perhaps his greater height and weight wouldn't count too much against her. She'd need to slit his throat, she calculated.

That way he wouldn't be able to shout for help. Her mind rushed with a cocktail of terror and outrage and she visualised herself rolling from under the chaise longue and getting to her feet before he could react. The element of surprise would work in her favour. Albert let go of Evangeline's face as a second man came into the room. Mirabelle held herself back. She couldn't take both of them. The girl's wheezing resumed. She gasped desperately but clearly she wasn't getting enough air. Not nearly.

'If she dies we won't get anything out of her,' Pieter pointed out. From what Mirabelle could see this second man was younger. 'I could fetch the pharmacist we used when Max got shot. He'd be able to help.'

'Shut up,' Albert hissed.

'You gave her the stuff,' Pieter said. 'It's not my fault she can't breathe properly. How much did you use?'

Albert shoved the boy's shoulder. 'She's just panicking,' he snapped, and turned back to Evangeline. 'If you tell me where you put the scarf, I'll let him go for the pharmacist. He wants to go, mademoiselle. He's quite gallant, don't you think? Your knight in shining armour.'

Pieter stiffened. 'Do what you want,' he said. 'I'm only trying to help.'

Behind Albert Mirabelle could see that Evangeline was in some kind of altered state of mind. The lack of oxygen had clearly affected her. The girl didn't seem fully conscious. She began humming between wheezing.

'The scarf,' Albert insisted.

'I did my hair. I went to the opera,' she sang. It must be taking a huge effort to get the words out, Mirabelle thought.

'Where did you hide the scarf?'

'My mother prefers a chignon. But I like a full bun.'

Albert slapped the girl hard. 'I swear,' he said, 'you'd better tell me.'

Evangeline laughed. She turned towards the chaise longue, wheezing all the while, and stared Mirabelle right in the eye.

'Elnette,' she said, 'is the best hairspray.'

Albert lost his temper. He punched Evangeline in the stomach. Pieter pulled him off. 'Jesus,' he said. 'You'll kill her.'

'These women . . .' Albert was so angry that he couldn't bring himself to finish the sentence.

Evangeline was retching now. A slick dribble of vomit slid down her chin and onto the chiffon bodice. She heaved in as much air as she could, but it was only a trickle and it cost her dear. She stopped humming. She couldn't speak. Her arm jerked as she pulled against the linen rag that tied her to the chair. Mirabelle looked away. There was nothing she could do. She willed the girl to calm down – panic wouldn't help, though there was plenty to panic about.

'I'm getting the pharmacist,' Pieter said.

Mirabelle waited as his footsteps receded down the stairs. Albert paced to and fro in front of the girl. 'Where is the scarf?' he repeated.

Evangeline was clearly fading. Albert crossed his arms and stared at her. Then he put his hand around her throat. 'Where?' he demanded.

Mirabelle couldn't watch any more. She rolled out from the chaise longue and got to her feet, flicking open the knife in the same smooth movement. Albert turned too slowly. She remembered somebody saying that stabbing a man took strength and determination. Perhaps it was Bradley. Perhaps it was Jack. Whoever it was, they were wrong. Stabbing someone, she realised, took unadulterated fury. In her case, anyway.

She launched herself at him. Albert was so surprised that his immediate reaction was to laugh and lazily put up one arm in defence. It wasn't enough. McGregor's blade lashed into his throat and the laugh turned into a gurgle. She had missed his jugular, she thought as he punched her solidly in the face. That

meant there would be less blood. She reeled, vision blurred, as Albert tried to pull the blade out. He couldn't. It was lodged too deeply in his flesh and he was thick-fingered with shock. A strange cacophony of two people's gasps for breath assailed Mirabelle as her anger subsided. Still reeling, she made for Evangeline's side. The girl's eyes betrayed her terror.

'It's all right,' Mirabelle tried to soothe her. 'He's not going to hurt you any more.'

Albert fell to his knees and then onto the floor. A trickle of blood began to pool in front of him and the sound of his gasping stopped.

'He's dead,' Mirabelle said. 'You're perfectly safe. Just take your time. Calm down.'

But Evangeline's chest was raised as if she had taken a breath in and couldn't let it go. She reached up to her hair and slipped her fingers inside her bun, pulling out the corner of the rayon scarf that she had folded into a tiny square.

'You were trying to tell me?' Mirabelle whispered. 'You hid it there.'

The girl nodded. She squeezed Mirabelle's hand so tightly that it hurt. She couldn't speak any more. It was too late for that.

'I'll take it back to the rue de Siam, don't worry. We just need to get you out of here . . .'

But that wasn't going to be necessary. In only a few seconds Evangeline Durand's grip failed. She slumped into the seat, no longer struggling for breath, her eyes wide with horror at her own demise.

'No!' Mirabelle cried out. 'Don't.'

But the girl was gone. Mirabelle checked her pulse. Then she kicked the leg of the chair, her palm over her mouth. It had all happened so quickly. She wondered whether, if she'd been quicker, Evangeline might have recovered. But she couldn't have taken Pieter as well as Albert. Not even armed. Then she

remembered that Pieter was going to return. She wondered how long he might be.

'I'm sorry,' she whispered to Evangeline's body, as she tentatively pulled the rest of the scarf from the girl's hair. Then she turned her attention to Albert. She removed his wallet: his identity papers might prove useful. You always tried to provide proof of who you'd killed. Someone had told her that once. Gingerly she removed McGregor's knife from the wound. The slick scrape of metal against bone made her wince. Lastly, she fished her lock picks out of Albert's pocket and then, with a glance over her shoulder, Mirabelle fled across the hall and back through the skylight. Her heart was racing as she climbed the sloping part of the roof, but she tried to measure her pace. One slip was all it would take, quite literally. Once she was on the flat section she scrambled haphazardly towards number 2. Looking round, she picked out a large tree in a garden below. Then she threw the knife so it embedded itself towards the top of the trunk. No one would find it there. It was far better than dropping it down a drain or leaving it in a gutter. Looking around, somehow afraid that someone might have seen, she slid carefully down the lead roofing and braced herself.

'McGregor,' she hissed towards the window.

There was no response.

'McGregor.' Louder.

The superintendent's face appeared, peering upwards. 'Come on,' he said. 'I'm here.'

Mirabelle felt herself relax slightly. She'd never been so glad to see someone in her life. She gripped the edge of the gutter and let herself swing into his arms.

Chapter 27

Only the dead have seen the end of war.

Up at the corner, the driver had gone. His loyalty to the Durand family must have overwhelmed him. He was probably at their residence now, telling an outlandish tale about the backstreet bar and the untidy couple who thought Mademoiselle Evangeline had been taken to number 8 rue de Courcelles.

'It would have been a long time for him to wait,' said McGregor. 'The French police will want these fellows, you know. And you're a witness, Mirabelle. By rights we should go straight to the station and offer our evidence.'

'I can't do that,' Mirabelle replied under her breath. McGregor hadn't asked for his knife back and she hadn't told him what she'd done with it. All she'd said was that Evangeline was dead. 'There's no more we can do for the poor girl now. There's too much at stake to stay here. We have to press on.'

It had started to drizzle. McGregor stared at Mirabelle in the lamplight. She was always so perfect in Brighton, but tonight she had been through an immense ordeal and seeing her in disarray was somehow stirring. He wondered if this was how she must look in the morning – her hair dishevelled and her make-up worn away. The man in the studio had lent her a pair of velvet slippers that she deemed more comfortable than the riding boots and she had done away with the torn stockings. When she slid off the roof and into his arms he had wanted to kiss her. Or at least he had felt that way until he noticed that she was fighting back tears.

'Come on,' she said. 'We'll be lucky to find a taxi round here at this time. We'll have to walk at least as far as the Arc de Triomphe.'

'Where are we going?'

Mirabelle was finding it difficult to look McGregor in the eye. She wasn't sure how he would react when he discovered she was a murderer. Mirabelle had killed someone before, but only in self-defence. Afterwards a tribunal had cleared her. She tried not to think about the difference between that occasion and what had happened tonight. She'd been trying to save Evangeline Durand, but she'd failed. She couldn't tell McGregor about it – not yet, anyway.

'We need to find the woman who handed Evangeline the scarf in the first place. My guess is she's von der Grün's wife. At the very least von der Grün must know her. The scarf started out in his house.'

McGregor didn't like to ask. He told himself Mirabelle's judgement had always been sound in the past as he fell into step alongside her. Almost at the Arc de Triomphe they found, not a cab, but a rag and bone man driving a little wagon. Mirabelle flagged him down and agreed a fee in excess of what he would expect to make for a whole night's work, McGregor assumed, given the look on the man's face. At least they would get to their destination more quickly, he thought, as he sat on the edge of the cart and gawped down the Champs-Élysées like some kind of gypsy. This wasn't how he'd envisioned spending a few days in Paris with Mirabelle – soggy and on the run. The rain eased as the horse pulled up at the rue de Siam and they stepped down to the pavement. The driver gave a little salute and cracked the reins.

It was close to midnight. They could hear the hooves retreating down the street as the rag and bone man went back to his rounds. Mirabelle took a moment to compose herself on the doorstep of number 25 before ringing the bell. The fanlight

was bright but no one came to answer the door. Perhaps the von der Grüns had gone somewhere after the opera. Paris was a city that partied all night, even on a Sunday. After a weekend in the country maybe they had decided to kick up their heels. She tried the bell once more.

McGregor checked his watch. 'It's getting late.'

Mirabelle was on the point of deciding to take a room in the Hôtel Siam, although she feared that in her current attire the staff might treat her with less respect than they had shown the other night. It flitted across her mind that McGregor and she could check in as Mr and Mrs Horton. She shocked herself with the blasphemy of even considering it, and made up for the thought with the silent vow that if they did so McGregor would be sleeping on the floor. From there they would be able to keep an eye on the rear of number 25 in shifts, and if the lights came on they could move quickly. She was about to make the suggestion when the door swung open. Inside, the younger man who had attended the opera stood in his evening dress. The staff must have been dismissed for the night.

'*Oui*?' he enquired curtly.

Mirabelle wasn't sure where to start. The words came in a babble. She found herself gesticulating as she spoke – all in French. McGregor stared, only able to guess what she might be saying.

'I'm a friend of Evangeline Durand,' she started. 'It's been the most dreadful evening. I'm sorry but I need to speak to the woman in the purple dress, if she's here.'

'*La comtesse*?'

'I suppose so.' Mirabelle shrugged. 'I have bad news, I'm afraid. The worst. I know it's late but I must speak to her at once.'

The man paused for a second, but ultimately stood back from the threshold to let them in. He ushered his eccentric-looking visitors into the study, where a fire was burning in the

grate and a half-drunk bottle of champagne stood on a side table. The woman in the purple dress stood up with her glass in her hand. Mirabelle fumbled in her pocket and pulled out the scarf. The woman looked uneasy, her eyes lighting on the man who had opened the door as if to see if he understood the implication of the scarf's turning up in their house again.

'Evangeline Durand is dead,' Mirabelle said, in her brisk Parisian accent. 'I'm so sorry. She was followed. She was taken. I tried to rescue her but she was ill. She couldn't breathe and I couldn't save her.'

The man who had answered the door stepped forward. Unexpectedly, he had a cut-glass accent that wouldn't have been out of place in St James's. He probably thought speaking English made the conversation more private. Neither McGregor nor Mirabelle corrected him.

'Good God, Elizabeth, what is this woman talking about? What the hell have you been up to?'

Elizabeth took the scarf from Mirabelle's hand. 'We need to run this over to the American Embassy,' she said. 'Now.'

'Answer me! What have you got yourself involved in? You've been working, haven't you?' He sounded furious. 'After everything we said. What about the children? We can't do this kind of thing any more. The war is over, damn it. Dead and buried.'

'We can discuss it later.' The woman's voice remained even. She rang the service bell to the right of the fireplace 'I'll raise Javier and have him bring round the car. Please, Philip, calm down.'

Mirabelle turned towards the man in evening dress. 'Philip?' she repeated, staring at him as the name fell into place. 'Are you Philip? Philip Caine?'

He turned on her. 'And who the hell are you?'

Mirabelle cocked her head to one side. He was the right age. He was clearly English. 'What are you doing here?' she exclaimed. 'I've been looking for you. I thought you were dead.'

'Well, you've found me.' He gave a shallow bow. 'Philip, Comte de Vert.'

'Of course,' she said. 'Von der Grün was your cousin. But does that mean . . . excuse me, but did von der Grün die?'

Caine flipped open a cigarette box on a side table. He offered it round, lighting a Gitane and sucking hard as if he was taking out his anger on it.

'Yes. Wilhelm died. Kurt died. Everyone bloody died and I inherited in the end. I'm the survivor. I didn't catch your name.'

'Mirabelle Bevan.' She held out her hand. Stiffly, Caine shook it. 'I hope you don't mind my asking but when did von der Grün die? What happened?'

Caine hesitated before deciding that it was all right to continue. 'It was February 1944, if you must know. What is it that you want, Miss Bevan?'

It suddenly occurred to her that this meant Christine Moreau had lost her lover only a few months before the liberation of the city and had then had to endure being punished for the affair. Mirabelle tried to remember what had been happening in February 1944. She could not think of any obvious action in which Wilhelm von der Grün might have perished. The Resistance had struck out as it became obvious the Germans would have to quit the city. Perhaps von der Grün had fallen foul of that, though it was earlier in the year than she'd place the majority of the civil disobedience.

'He's buried in Passy cemetery, I imagine,' she said.

Caine nodded. 'A small gravestone, given the circumstances. No "Soldier and Great Man." No marble angels.'

'How did he die?'

'I don't see it's any of your business.'

'Tonight I watched Evangeline Durand die. She was very brave. I killed a man while I was trying to save her. I came to Paris to find you, Flight Lieutenant. Matthew Bradley asked me to. And I've ended up a murderer. So when I ask

you how Wilhelm von der Grün died, I consider it very much my business.'

'You've been taken for a ride, Miss Bevan. Matthew knows exactly where I am if he wants to find me.'

Mirabelle sank onto the edge of the sofa. 'He knows? You're sure?'

'It's not common knowledge. I couldn't go back. I don't want to. But Matthew knows. He knows everything. What does he want, anyway?'

'He wrote asking me to find out what happened to you.'

'Well, I don't understand that.'

'It was in his will. He died about a week ago, you see. I'm sorry.' Had it only been a week?

Caine stubbed out his cigarette. 'Right,' he said. 'I hope Caroline is all right. She and the girl.'

'They're fine,' Mirabelle replied.

The door opened and a butler entered the room. 'Duchamp,' the countess said. 'Could you have the car brought round? I know it's rather late. And raise Javier to drive it for us.'

The man bowed and retreated. Mirabelle found herself unable to take her eyes off Philip Caine, wondering if he'd succeeded in turning his cousin for the Allies and how much sensitive material he had managed to pass to Jack in the two years he'd spent undercover in Paris. Had it all been worth it?

The countess scooped up a fur wrap that was slung over a chair. 'May I have that?' She put out her hand, and Mirabelle handed over the scarf in a daze. Philip Caine glared at his wife.

'Elizabeth, I wish you wouldn't.'

'It's too late now. I have to. Poor Evangeline Durand gave her life. Do you expect me just to burn it? To ignore it? They need this, Philip. It will be the last. I promise.'

'You shouldn't go alone.' Mirabelle got to her feet. 'It isn't safe.'

'Let me,' McGregor insisted. 'You look done in, Mirabelle. Do you mind, monsieur? It's been a hell of a night.'

Philip Caine nodded curtly. 'I'll keep her here till you get back,' he said. 'Miss Bevan, may I offer you some champagne?'

Mirabelle couldn't help thinking that what she'd really like was a cup of tea but she nodded, accepting the glass that Caine put into her hand. When she sipped it was certainly reviving.

'Well, that's settled.' The countess swished past in a cloud of Dior.

McGregor followed her, and Mirabelle's gaze fell to her feet and the damp velvet slippers as the door clicked closed. On the hem of her dress was a dark splatter that had sunk into the brown wool. Only now did she realise it must be blood.

'You can rest here,' Caine said, scrambling in his desk and pulling out a box of cigars. 'I wouldn't smoke one of these in front of a lady. I'll go up to the drawing room.'

Mirabelle stood up. He wasn't getting away that easily. In the hallway she heard the front door closing behind McGregor and the countess. The car would be along directly.

'I love the smell of cigar smoke,' she said. 'I don't like cigarettes, but I enjoy a Cuban now and then. Please let me join you.'

Chapter 28

Being good is easy, what is difficult is being just.

Eddie was right about Churchill and the stogies. Smoking cigars was difficult. Mirabelle had seen many men over the years cutting the cap and lighting up, but she'd never done it herself. Upstairs, Caine handed her the box and she took one. Then he handed her the cutter and watched, smiling, as she made a valiant attempt to use it, before offering a lit match. Mirabelle leaned in and puffed. She didn't want to say she'd been in the room before – when she broke in the other night and had seen Christine Moreau from the window.

'It's a lovely house,' she managed just before the smoke made her cough. It was strong and it caught in her gullet. Caine's smile widened into a grin as he prepared his own cigar.

'You're an unusual woman,' he said, taking a seat on a leather chair by the fire and reaching for his champagne. 'Tell me, what did you do during the war?'

Mirabelle sank onto the sofa.

'I worked in Whitehall. For Jack Duggan. I was only a secretary. I never went into the field, like you.' She saw Caine register Jack's name.

'It was a long time ago,' he said. 'How is Jack?'

'He died. Some years ago. In Brighton, where he lived.'

Caine's gaze was drawn to the fire. 'They're gone, then. Both Jack Duggan and Matthew Bradley?'

She nodded.

'They seemed indestructible. Almost inhuman. I can't believe I'm the one who's left.'

'You fell out with them, didn't you? When they came to Longchamp?'

Caine took a deep draw. 'You better keep puffing on that or it'll go out.'

Mirabelle drew the cigar to her lips and tried again. 'I read the medical records,' she said. 'You were the one who left them bruised.'

Caine nodded. 'My mother had died and then I was furious about what had happened to Christine. She was . . .'

'Von der Grün's mistress. I know. I can't imagine being bereaved like that and then punished anyway once the man you loved was gone.'

'She's still in the same little studio. She won't accept any help. They tried to send her away but she wouldn't have it. I offered to set her up somewhere else but she turned me down. She looked after me, you know. All those years ago. But she's a proud woman. Tell me, Miss Bevan, you said earlier that you were a murderer. That you killed someone.' His gaze fell to the splatter on Mirabelle's dress. She felt suddenly glad that she hadn't gone for Albert's jugular.

'Yes. It was a Russian agent. He was hurting Evangeline Durand. I came at him from behind.'

'You shouldn't think of it as murder. They're not real people,' Caine said. 'Anyone in covert operations. They're not subject to the same rules or the same rights. Do you understand?'

'You were a covert operative.'

'Yes. I was.'

Mirabelle rolled the cigar between her lips. 'So who did you kill?' she asked.

Caine sat forward. 'Very good. That's excellent. I'm surprised Jack didn't deploy you in the field. It's not often old

Duggan missed a trick.' Mirabelle must have flinched, and Caine laughed. 'Oh, I see,' he said. 'So that was you, was it?'

'What do you mean?'

'I knew he was sweet on someone. He never used the story on me, of course. I'd lost the woman I loved, and I didn't love again until . . . well, you can see. Elizabeth and I were supposed to quit all of that. Clearly she hasn't kept her side of that deal. I maintain it doesn't do to love someone if you're in the service. But Jack used to say he'd found someone who was worth winning the war for. He'd use the story when he wanted to inspire someone. Some poor idiot who still believed in goodness.'

Mirabelle's stomach sank. 'You don't think he really loved me?'

'I don't think anyone knew what Jack Duggan really felt.'

Mirabelle remembered the day Jack had declared his love. He'd insisted that he hadn't expected it. It had been a bolt from the blue. She'd been his black swan, he said. For years he'd only seen white birds on the water and then suddenly he'd found something he didn't believe existed and everything had changed.

'It felt as though he loved me.'

Caine puffed. 'Maybe he did.'

This was beginning to feel like a game of chess. Mirabelle turned the table. 'I must say, I admire what you did – leaving Caroline Bland behind. You must have been very committed to the service. Did you succeed in your mission? Did you get what you wanted out of your cousin?'

Caine nodded. 'I was as inhuman as the best of them. One of Duggan's finest. Paris fell a good three months earlier than it would have if it hadn't been for me.'

'But you never went home?'

Caine spread his arms. 'This is my home.'

'Not Pity Me in County Durham? To see your mother's grave?'

'Inhuman, aren't I? They trained me well.'

Mirabelle stood up and walked to the window. 'I don't

believe you're inhuman, Flight Lieutenant. I think you were too upset. I think you're a man who loved his family so much you couldn't bear it. But you did your duty.'

'I hope you aren't expecting me to break down and tell you everything, Miss Bevan, because I won't. I worked hard. I've seen what I've seen. I think I deserve a normal life now.'

'Your wife doesn't want to give up, though, does she?'

Caine's jaw stiffened. 'I can't imagine what she's thinking. We have children to consider.'

'Perhaps that's precisely what's on her mind.'

Caine's eyes narrowed. 'Oh, the bigger picture. Contributing to a better world? Yes. I see what you mean. I'm not sure there is a bigger world. I'll admit it. There. The bigger picture wasn't worth it. If I'd realised that, my mother would have been alive to meet her grandchildren. She didn't deserve what happened to her. Dying alone that way, not knowing that I was safe, or even alive. Thinking she had no one any more. She took sleeping pills, did you know? They said it was an accident but my mother was an accurate kind of person and if she took extra sleeping pills it was because she intended to. She didn't want to go on. My brother was shot down and she thought I was dead. A man feels a duty, you see, to his country and to his family. During the war I had to choose which of those was more important. Life is in the small things, Miss Bevan, and I chose badly. I as good as pulled the trigger on the old lady. If I had honoured what was really important she'd be alive today. And so would my cousin.'

'You think you killed your cousin?'

'I know I bloody well did. And on your precious Jack Duggan's orders. Wilhelm was on to us. It was me or him. Actually it was me and Christine or him. Though I'm not sure Wilhelm would have turned in Christine. He loved her, you see. Perhaps he'd have let her get away. Anyway, I shot him. He died in the street. Coming out of a little bar he liked, only just

up the road. He was alone – no escort. I'm under no illusions. He would have shot me too. Cousin against cousin. That's what war does to people. That's family for you. Sometimes agents in the field have to make split-second decisions. Sometimes you find out a lot about yourself in a millisecond. The Germans thought it was the Resistance who killed him, of course – and in a way it was. So they rounded up a hundred men and shot them. I must have killed thousands if you count all that, because I was a very accomplished Nazi-murderer in my day. Covert and inhuman at once – the SOE's dream. The truth is that of all the men I killed, it's only Wilhelm's death I regret. I'll bear that till the day I die, Miss Bevan – the sight of him lying there in the street, bleeding to death. And look at me now, sitting here, smoking a cigar in our comfortable family home. Are you surprised I couldn't bear to go back to England and pretend to be a war hero? Our children are asleep upstairs and every night when I check on them I think I don't deserve this. I don't deserve any of it. If Duggan and Bradley came today to try to take me home, I'd wallop them again. Is that what you came here to find out?'

Caine stubbed out his cigar and checked his watch. He stared past her out of the window.

'Christine says it's always the women,' Mirabelle said.

'Yes. She's right. A lot of the time it is.'

'But you found love again? You made it come right.'

'Yes. Elizabeth and I.'

'I'm curious. Would you marry Caroline if you had 1942 to live again?'

Caine's eyes hardened. 'And have Jack Duggan court martial me, the bastard? ' He shook his head. 'I'd get a message to my mother. I'd make sure Wilhelm didn't tumble. But who the hell has a real choice? A man could go mad. We did what we had to do.' He finished the conversation as if a shutter had rolled down. 'Look, we'd better go back to the study. They'll be home soon.'

Chapter 29

There is pleasure in the pathless woods.

The American Embassy wasn't far. The countess slid into the back seat of the car and McGregor followed. She gave the chauffeur instructions in swift French and then turned back to McGregor as if he was her guest at a cocktail party.

'Have you visited Paris before?'

'No. It's my first time.'

'Well, you must see the sights. The Eiffel Tower and the Arc de Triomphe.'

'I expect it would be best to get Miss Bevan home. She's had a shock.'

'Is it the first time she's faced this kind of situation?'

'No.' McGregor surprised himself with the thought that if anything this kind of experience seemed to follow Mirabelle around, and yet, every time, he treated it as if she was the rookie and he knew best. 'I think perhaps she did something of this nature during the war.'

'Ah.' The countess nodded. 'I see. That's how my husband and I met, though we didn't discover our feelings until after the peace. He used to say that fighting the Nazis focused the mind, but I think it was living in fear. Have you ever lived in fear, Superintendent?'

McGregor shifted uncomfortably. During the war he'd worked in Leith, at the dockyard. He'd tried to enlist in the army but he hadn't passed the medical. Stories of wartime

derring do always left him feeling inadequate. 'I suppose I haven't,' he admitted.

'Philip is angry,' the countess continued, oblivious, her attention focused no doubt on the argument that would face her when she got home. 'After the war we swore never again. Who would have thought that not ten years later the Germans would be our friends and the Russians would be the enemy? They are a formidable enemy, too. Stalin has split Europe just as surely as Hitler did. The Americans call them the Reds.' The countess pulled the scarf from her purse. 'Reds, you see. It's a little joke.'

'And apart from its colour, what is it about the scarf? Why is it so important?'

The countess pulled the material smoothly between her fingers. 'I suppose I can tell you. It's over now, or almost. It's the pattern. Pretty, isn't it? The material is delivered to the seamstress, you see, and in one section of the roll the pattern is very slightly different. No one would notice in the normal run of things. People would simply think that the print was misaligned, but it means something if you can read it. The rest of the roll is just cheap frippery for downmarket shops. The seamstress cuts the material into squares, hems them and makes her money on the rest of the scarves, but this one is priceless. They paint the message by hand. It's this one that contains the code.'

'What does it say?'

'I have no idea. I'm not a codebreaker. I'm a mule. I always have been. The thing they're most concerned about, though, is atomic energy. I read the newspapers. Europe is lining itself up in a series of alliances fuelled by the H-bomb.'

'And you work for the Americans?'

The countess nodded. 'They are generous, but they have no sense of humour. None at all.'

'Do you always deliver the scarf to the Embassy?'

'Never. I give it to Evangeline at the opera and she meets a man from the Embassy and gives it to him. I don't know where. Poor Evangeline.'

'She met him at a bar not far from the opera house.'

'Ah,' the countess nodded, 'I see. Hand to hand. Different places that are difficult to connect.'

'Well, they have connected them.'

'All good things come to an end. It's been almost a year.'

There was a wistful tone in the way she said this. It came to McGregor that there was something feral about the countess despite her tailored dress and immaculate make-up. When she said 'Poor Evangeline' she hadn't really meant it.

'You've enjoyed being back in the game?'

The woman parted her lips. 'It's not that I don't love my husband and my children. But one becomes accustomed to adventure, you know. The war was a golden time. One feels most alive when one is facing death. The thrill of the forbidden, I expect. One looks evil in the face – badness, you might say – and one is never sure of getting away. Do you enjoy forbidden pleasures, Superintendent?' The countess's gaze landed on McGregor's thigh. Then she ran her eyes upwards suggestively and lingered. The superintendent shifted uncomfortably.

'We must be almost there,' he said.

'Yes. At the end of the street and to the right.'

'I hope Mirabelle is all right.'

'She is your lover?'

'No,' McGregor said quickly. 'A friend. A good one.'

It occurred to him that he wanted much more than that. Even in a stretched wool dress and men's slippers, he found Mirabelle far more enticing than any other woman. Her goodness went all the way through.

'I'm sure Miss Bevan will recover,' the countess said dismissively, turning her gaze back onto the street outside. 'A good night's sleep works wonders.'

McGregor was about to form a question about whether Mirabelle's killing the man in the safe house was really murder in French law when the chauffeur cried out, the car jerked and they came to a sudden halt. The superintendent was jettisoned from his seat and the countess landed on top of him. As they disentangled themselves he looked out of the window and saw that a car, speeding onto the main road from a side street, had run straight into them. Now a young man had emerged from the other vehicle and was walking towards them.

'Drive on,' the countess hissed at the chauffeur. 'Quickly. Go round him.'

In the front, the man was conscious but clearly concussed. 'Madame,' he murmured woozily, pawing at the steering wheel.

McGregor pushed the countess out of the way and scrambled over to the front seat, hauling the chauffeur to one side. He slammed the car into reverse and backed up, ignoring the sound of scraping metal. Then, in the rear-view mirror he saw another car behind them blocking the road. A man had emerged from it and was approaching from the rear. His mind raced. The fellow from the crashed car was straight ahead, and coming closer. Now McGregor could see that the boy was holding a gun.

'Drive!' the countess shouted.

The engine was still running, but with no way forward and no way back the superintendent hesitated. The boy had almost reached them now. The muzzle of the weapon clicked against the side window, pointing straight at the countess. 'Roll down the window and give the scarf to me,' he said. 'Now.'

In the mirror McGregor saw her shaking hand reach out to do so. He gritted his teeth. They had come so far and risked so much – Mirabelle had killed a man. He wasn't going to let her down at the last pass.

In a movement so smooth it surprised him, he reached over and grabbed the scarf from the countess's hand while at the

same time opening the driver's door. He hit the pavement and began to run. With the car between him and the assassin he reckoned he must have at least a second or two's grace. He cleared the other vehicle just as the first shot rang out. The end of the street and to the right, she'd said. He kept going. The men must be following but he couldn't hear the clatter of their feet, only the pounding of his heart. He had almost made the corner when he heard the second gunshot. This time he felt it – a sharp stab in his shoulder, but not enough to stop him. If the men were shooting at him, he reckoned, at least they must have left the countess alone. If she'd any gumption she'd get herself and the chauffeur out of there. He swerved right just as another shot rang out. This time he couldn't say for sure if it had hit him. If anything it gave him a burst of energy and he ran faster. If they kill me I'll never hold her again. I'll never kiss her again.

Around the corner, like a smack in the face, he realised Paris was on a scale so much larger than Brighton or Edinburgh. He gulped in a breath, taking in the avenue Gabriel as he sprinted. A huge park ran along the street and the wide road was curved. The embassy must be here somewhere, but there seemed to be a dearth of buildings. Everything was just open space. Behind him another shot rang out and then he heard a siren. Somewhere nearby a police car was coming, alerted by the gunshots. For the first time in his life, he realised, he didn't want the police to arrive. Anything that tied him to these men potentially also tied Mirabelle to the agent she'd killed. One of the cars rounded the corner and he heard another shot. It didn't slow him. Then he heard the sound of metal on metal. The car must have crashed, he thought. He pushed himself harder, and at last he saw a guard box and the corner of an American flag. He made straight for it, stumbling. A man caught him as he went over.

'The Reds,' he gasped. 'They mustn't get it.' He fumbled the

scarf into the soldier's hand. Then from the ground he saw the wheels of a car pull up and a flash of purple fabric. His shoulder stung and he felt his body shaking. The air was suddenly unbearably cold.

'Quickly.' The countess's voice was insistent. 'We have to get him inside.'

'She's not my wife,' he said out of nowhere.

And then everything faded to black.

Chapter 30

*Every person above the ordinary has a certain
mission that they are called to fulfill.*

Caine's car chugged slowly to a halt at the bottom of the
rue de Jour and Mirabelle opened the door. The sky clung
on to its last hour of darkness. It had been a long night. A
pigeon flapped overhead, settling on the gutter at the top of
Christine Moreau's building and staring down. Elizabeth Caine
gave swift instructions to Javier, the driver, before she stepped
onto the pavement and clicked shut the door. She seemed very
fresh for a woman who had been up all night. Mirabelle dug
deep to dredge up some energy. There was no sign that Christine's studio was being watched now – the Russians who had
followed the red scarf were either dead or in custody. She took
a bracing breath of pre-dawn air and the women crossed the
road and rang the bell to Christine's studio, stepping back from
the door so that if she looked out of the window she'd be able
to see them. A shadow shifted above them and a few seconds
later the door opened and Christine hovered barefoot on the
threshold in a thin cotton nightgown.

'What are you doing here?' she hissed, her eyes darting
between the two women and up to the top of the road.

'Can we come in?'

Christine stepped back and the three of them climbed the stairs
in silence. In the studio Christine lit a lamp. Elizabeth Caine sat at
the dressmaker's work table. Mirabelle hovered. It occurred to her
that when it came down to it, it was all between the women.

'Well?' Christine fumbled for a woollen wrap, which she pulled around her shoulders.

'Evangeline Durand is dead,' Elizabeth started, 'but the scarf was delivered. The last scarf.'

'I'd hoped we'd get longer,' Christine admitted.

'It's quite some ruse,' Mirabelle said.

'It's so difficult to get anything out, you see. But they're desperate for trade with the western nations. And we need to know. The Russians have some of the most advanced German scientists. Who knows what they're building?'

'Our Germans and their Germans.' Mirabelle smiled crookedly. 'Did even one scientist remain in Germany after the war?'

Christine sat down. 'I'm sorry to hear about Evangeline.'

'I killed the Russian responsible.'

Christine nodded. 'Good,' she said, and Mirabelle felt a kind of acceptance settle on her shoulders.

'But the real reason we came is for your sake,' she said. 'Oh, the men had their falling out, and Philip Caine had to do some dreadful things, but they each made a new life, Christine. Caine, Duggan and Bradley. And you are still here, scarred inside and out. I had to come back to do what I can. I want to help you.'

'It's none of your business.'

'I disagree. It is my business. I loved Jack Duggan. I'm part of what little is left of him. And Jack wounded you. He insulted you. He didn't understand. But I do.'

'I'm not the only one who suffered. Philip . . .'

Elizabeth Caine stood up. She moved towards the stove and crossed her arms. 'My husband will never get over what he had to do. But he has me and our children. If he ever forgives me, that is.'

'He has a temper,' Christine said sagely. 'It would have been better if he hadn't found out that you were involved.'

Elizabeth shrugged her shoulders. 'I am what I am,' she

said. 'If you're asking me if I regret it, it's like asking a wolf if she regrets hunting with the pack or a gull if it regrets diving for fish. I came alive during the war. I don't want to live without the thrill of it.'

'Were you in Paris?' Mirabelle asked, suddenly curious.

'No. I was with the Maquis – in the countryside. I was in charge of a hundred men. Between us we saw the Germans off. Now what the Soviets are doing is just as bad. I'm glad I have taken some small part in fighting them.'

Mirabelle was silently grateful that she didn't have the countess's need for an enemy. Some people only blossomed in conflict, defined by their opponents. 'We looked evil in the face.' Elizabeth reached for a packet of cigarettes on the mantel and lit one without offering the packet round.

Christine, Mirabelle decided, was cut from different cloth. Elizabeth Caine was addicted to danger. She sought it out. But Christine was a victim of it. She had got lost somehow, unable to move on. Who could blame her? Mirabelle had come close enough to that herself.

'You've had enough, haven't you?' she asked the dressmaker. 'You'd like to put it behind you.'

Christine nodded.

'I have an idea that might help.'

'I don't want money. I have money.'

'Money is the least of it.' Mirabelle smiled. 'No, what I suggest is something altogether more civilised. I've sent for someone – he's coming from London.'

'The British!' Christine spat.

'I know we let you down. But aren't you curious? Don't you want us to make it up to you? Really?'

Christine's lips pursed. 'Why would they? Duggan is dead. He's the one who knew what it was like. He's the one who knew everything.'

Mirabelle shifted. She was taking a risk, but it was time to

put her cards on the table. 'They'll do it because you still have the information, Christine, don't you?'

Elizabeth Caine glared at her friend. 'But that's ridiculous!' she declared. 'You never keep a copy. That's the first rule. What if it falls into the wrong hands?'

Christine's jaw shifted. She surveyed Mirabelle carefully, her eyes hard and shrewd. 'How did you know?' she asked slowly.

'You can't let anything go, Christine. None of it. Not a memory, not a single wound. Working for the Americans is your revenge on the British, isn't it? You don't trust anyone. It stands to reason.'

Elizabeth spluttered, and stubbed out her cigarette. Christine moved to the sideboard and took down a leather-bound book, part of a set of three. 'The words of Voltaire,' she said. 'Now he was a spy.'

'It will take courage to let things go,' Mirabelle said, 'but if there's one thing I've learned it's that we are all owed a fresh start. No matter what we've done.'

Christine opened the book. She pulled back the inside leaf of the binding. 'I copied the patterns and I coded the dates they came in and went out.'

Mirabelle grinned. 'I'm going to need something to wear,' she said.

Christine eyed the stretched woollen dress and the slippers. 'It's far too late to make anything. You'll have to buy off the rail.'

Elizabeth Caine looked blank.

'I know somewhere that isn't too bad,' Christine offered.

Elizabeth nodded. 'All right. Let's go round to the *Cochon* for breakfast and then I'll have Javier drop you two off.'

Chapter 31

Romance should never begin with sentiment.

Mirabelle crossed at the Palais Royal and dodged into the Louvre. She checked her watch. It was just past one o'clock but she wanted to make him wait. A black man in a well-cut suit cast his gaze over her and tried to catch her eye. He wouldn't have done so the evening before, she told herself, but a new pair of heels and a jade-green suit procured earlier that morning from the boutique Christine recommended on the rue du Faubourg Saint-Honoré had worked wonders. The only thing that could make her look more Parisian was the addition of a small dog on a lead. Looking slightly haughty, Mirabelle swept past. Then, turning into the courtyard, she fumbled in her bag for her sunglasses. It was bright and cold – the perfect winter's day. The Eiffel Tower punctuated the skyline and she wished McGregor could see it.

A woman in a stovepipe hat was standing at the entrance. Mirabelle waved, and when she reached her, kissed her on both cheeks.

'Do you have it?'

Christine Moreau nodded.

'Good.' Mirabelle took her friend's arm and guided her into the entrance hallway. 'Lunch,' she said. But they both knew it was more than that.

In the restaurant the waiter fussed over the women, showing them to the table where Eddie Brandon was already waiting, smoking a cigarette and sipping a lethal-looking cocktail.

'Ah, there you are.' He got to his feet. 'Who's this?' He inclined his head towards Christine.

'Christine Moreau. So, you two haven't met before?'

'No, but I know your name, of course, Mademoiselle Moreau. Might I order you a glass of champagne?'

'That would be lovely,' Mirabelle answered for them both, thinking that it would be better to have something light. Christine's propensity for a gin before breakfast might land them in trouble when there was negotiation afoot.

'And three soles meunière.' Eddie waved off the waiter. 'That's the thing, isn't it?'

'Quite.' Mirabelle removed her gloves.

'Well, I must say, you're looking rather smart.'

'Thank you.'

'I hadn't expected you to. After what happened, I mean.'

'Oh, I brush up.'

There was a silence. Mirabelle let it be. Christine studied Eddie; Mirabelle hoped she wouldn't bolt.

'Well, I expect you contacted me for a reason,' Eddie said petulantly, the first to break the silence. 'It's quite some mystery. And I'm under no illusion there won't be a price.'

The waiter delivered the champagne and the women both took a sip. 'Goodness. You do think us mercenary, Eddie,' Mirabelle said.

'At least you haven't been shot this time.'

'My friend was.'

'The black girl?'

'No. Another friend.'

'I see. Well, go on. What am I getting and what will it cost me?'

Mirabelle nodded at Christine, who pulled the sheaf of papers from her handbag and handed it over. 'From Russia with our best regards,' Mirabelle said. 'The Americans have these already.'

'We share information with the Yanks.'

'You share the information you're both prepared to share. Honestly, Eddie, I'm not an idiot. They got the last of these messages last night. As you can see, there have been six. Miss Moreau wisely made copies of the earlier missives. Given the energy the Russians put into trying to recover this last one, I expect they pertain to something terribly serious. It was atomic energy in which you were most interested, as I recall.'

Christine Moreau nodded. 'They are up to something. They are definitely up to something,' she said. 'And I overheard something about a secret announcement, but I don't know how to read it, I'm afraid.'

Eddie looked at the drawings more closely. 'And the code used?'

'We have no idea. But you have men who devote themselves to nothing but cracking this kind of thing.'

Eddie had to acknowledge that she was right. British code-breakers were the envy of the world. 'But, Miss Moreau, you are only prepared to disclose this information to us now. It's somewhat late, don't you think?'

Mirabelle cut in to defend her friend. 'Christine rather suffered at our hands after the war. I consider it jolly generous of her to give us another chance.'

'All I'm saying is, had you come earlier I'd have been able to get you more. What are you after, Mirabelle?'

'Me? I'm only doing my duty. I might need a little hand with the French police over a medical matter.' She slid Albert's ID over the table. 'This fellow won't be recovering, you see.'

'Did you shoot him?'

'I used a knife.'

Eddie raised his eyebrows only a fraction. 'Well, at least that kind of thing is easier to sweep under the carpet if it occurs abroad. And you, Miss Moreau?'

Christine shifted in her chair. 'I'd like an apology. An official one,' she said.

Eddie smiled. 'Money is far easier.'

'Yes. It is.'

He sighed. 'The press won't pick it up, you know. No one's interested in the war any more. The only thing from 1945 that makes the news these days is unexploded bombs.'

Christine nodded. 'I know. It's only for me, and I'd like it in writing, please.'

'But you were a covert agent.'

'And you abandoned me.'

'Hardly.'

'Now, Eddie.' Mirabelle's tone was that of a nanny chastising a naughty child. 'The SOE won't issue a letter. Nor should they. But I'm sure that there must be a government department somewhere willing to recognise a brave friend of the Allies.'

Eddie finished his drink and motioned to the waiter for another. 'All right, all right. Well, it's going to be cheaper than I expected, at least.' He leaned towards Christine. 'Last time Mirabelle negotiated a costly education programme out of me.'

'A music school,' Mirabelle corrected him.

'Yes, yes. But, Miss Moreau, if I get you this apology, this recognition . . .'

'A proper sorry and a proper thank you,' Mirabelle cut in.

'Exactly. What will you do with it?'

Christine smiled. The women had discussed this at some length as dawn lit the Parisian sky and they tucked into their breakfast steak. Now she took a breath. 'I will live again,' she said simply. 'I will be able to live.'

The waiter arrived with the fish. Mirabelle picked up a wedge of lemon wrapped in muslin and squeezed juice over her plate, before inspecting the sautéed spinach and potatoes that had been left for them to share.

'So you won't work for us again, Miss Moreau?' Eddie enquired.

Christine shook her head. 'It is time for me to retire.'

Eddie picked up his cutlery. 'We're damn short of women, you see, if you fancy Berlin. Things are hotting up in Berlin just now. I could place either of you very well in the Soviet sector.'

Christine shook her head. Mirabelle smirked.

'So that's what you're really working on, Eddie,' she said. 'Well, if it's women you want, I would certainly suggest you approach Elizabeth Caine. She is . . .'

'An addict,' Christine finished the sentence.

Eddie took a forkful of fish. 'Oh my! The French, I swear, are culinary geniuses. You can't get fish like this at home. Not even at the Café de Paris.'

Mirabelle smiled. 'Well, that's that settled,' she said. 'Let's enjoy our lunch, shall we?'

That evening, when McGregor came to, Mirabelle was reading *Le Monde* beside his bed. He looked around. The pale walls were a giveaway.

'Hospital,' he rasped.

Mirabelle took the glass of water from the side table and held it up for him to drink. He tried to take it from her but the pain made it impossible. She helped him gulp a little down.

'That's better, isn't it?' she said. 'You were quite the hero, Superintendent.' There was a swish of lavender soap as she sat back.

'Not as good as a decent whisky,' he said with a smile.

'I think I might be going off whisky,' Mirabelle admitted. 'I'm developing a taste for gin.'

'Really? We made it then, Belle?'

'You were tremendously brave.'

'There was a police car . . .'

'Don't worry about that. It's all settled. The diplomats saw to it. You did marvellously, Alan.'

He took this in. He wouldn't like it much if there was a misdemeanor on his patch and some diplomat tried to hush it up. Yet here he was, safe and sound, with Mirabelle at his bedside.

'I thought of you,' he admitted.

'When you got shot?'

'When I had to keep going.' He reached out and took her hand. The movement sent a pain shooting across his chest but it was worth it. Mirabelle didn't pull away. The pain settled into a dull ache. 'Some little holiday. When do they say we can go home?'

'In a few days.'

'Will you wait for me?'

'Of course.'

'All this has made me realise, Mirabelle, that it's you I want.' She looked down.

'I know you can't get over him. The man who died . . .'

'No,' she cut in. 'I think I am. Getting over him, I mean. It's unexpected, I know, but he's going. He's been going since that night in Brighton. The truth is Jack belonged to a different time.'

'So would you consider me, Mirabelle? Please consider me.'

He strained forward and kissed her. Her lips parted and she moved closer. His hand touched her thigh and he stroked the skin, latching his finger on the top of her stockings. She tasted sweet and his heart jumped as she gave a little sigh.

'*Alors!*' a voice exclaimed behind them before babbling in a rush of incomprehensible French. Mirabelle pulled back. A nurse in a starched wimple clapped her hands as if she was scaring a flock of birds. Whatever she was saying, she certainly didn't approve of the scene she'd just witnessed. Blushing, Mirabelle apologised, or at least, McGregor thought, it sounded like an apology. The nurse picked up the medical notes hooked on the end of the bed and left the room briskly. McGregor grinned.

'You look like the cat who got the cream.' Mirabelle sounded like a schoolmistress.

'Well, I don't care about this any more,' he indicated his bandages, 'not if I get to do that again.' His eyes lingered. He could look at her for a long time. She seemed so Parisian in her green suit.

'I don't know,' she said. 'I'm sorry. I can't rush.'

'I'll wait. I don't mind waiting.'

Mirabelle slipped her hand across the bedsheet. Her fingers stroked his palm and McGregor considered it settled.

'I don't suppose anyone thought that the hero might like some grapes?'

Mirabelle grinned, and reached into a shopping basket at her feet. 'I bought some at Les Halles. I hoped you might rally.'

'Nothing like a spot of shopping to pass the time. What else have you been up to?'

'Oh, just some sightseeing,' she said casually. 'And I had lunch at the Louvre.'

Epilogue

The futire is purchased by the present.

The snow was still lying in Durham as Mirabelle and Vesta got off the train. They took a taxi from the station to their destination. It crawled carefully up the hill at no more than ten miles an hour.

'We should have walked,' Vesta complained. 'It would have been quicker.'

Mirabelle paid off the cab. The pavements had mostly been cleared but there were still some patches of ice. From where they stood they could see the cathedral towering over them, fringed in white. It was where Bulldog Bradley had married Caroline Bland and where he was probably buried. Below them the river was frozen over and a group of children were skating on it, only distinguishable one from the other by the colour of their hats and scarves.

'I think York might have been better,' Vesta pronounced.

'Well, we can hop off the train there on the way home. Why don't you have a look around while I deal with things here?' Now Vesta had set her wedding date there were endless chores to see to. Today's was to find shoes to match her dress.

'You don't mind?'

'Not at all.'

Vesta hooked her handbag over her arm as if she was going into battle and disappeared into a promising-looking boutique, leaving Mirabelle to compose herself before she entered the offices of Lovatt and Stone. In the reception area a young secretary sat at a desk, typing furiously. She looked up.

'May I help you?'

'I've come to see Mr Lovatt.'

'Do you have an appointment?' The girl cast her eyes over the diary that was propped to one side.

'No. But he'll see me,' Mirabelle said steadily. 'My name is Mirabelle Bevan.'

'I'm afraid Mr Lovatt is with someone at present.' The secretary crossed her arms.

'Please tell him I'm here.'

'He's in a meeting, Miss Bevan. I can't disturb him.'

'I think you should.'

The girl was torn. She got up though, smoothed her skirt, and left the room. A few seconds later she returned. 'He'll see you now,' she said coldly. No one liked being overruled.

In the hallway a man tipped his hat to Mirabelle as he passed her on his way to the door.

'I'm sorry,' she said. 'I disturbed your meeting.'

'You can't help an emergency, love,' he replied pleasantly. 'I'll pop back later.'

Lovatt's office was panelled in oak. It smelled of respectability – a mixture of thick paper, ink and just a whiff of spirits. A row of embossers teetered on the edge of a set of bookshelves, and every available surface was covered in leather-bound law books and sheafs of paper.

'Miss Bevan.' Lovatt sprang eagerly to his feet with his hand held out. Mirabelle shook it and took him in. She remembered the scent of his aftershave. He was as well presented as he had been in Brighton but she'd never trust him now. Never again. He had seemed so above board. It just showed you.

'I don't know exactly what you've been playing at, Mr Lovatt, but I can't imagine the Law Society will approve.'

Lovatt blanched. 'Did you find out what happened to him?'

Mirabelle nodded.

'Is he . . . ?'

'Flight Lieutenant Philip Caine is alive, Mr Lovatt. But I can't imagine what he means to you that you'd be prepared to risk your whole career to find that out.'

'Mr Bradley . . .'

'Now, now. Mr Bradley didn't enjoin me to search for Caine. You did. And I think you owe me an explanation.'

Lovatt sank into his seat. 'The bequest . . .' he said weakly.

'There was no bequest. Please don't treat me like a fool.'

'Where is Caine?'

'He doesn't want to be found, Mr Lovatt. He doesn't want to come back.'

'But he's alive?'

'Yes.'

'And you're going to turn me in?'

'You altered a client's will, Mr Lovatt. You tried to misappropriate a client's money.' Mirabelle was furious. She despised dishonesty. When he replied, it surprised her to realise that Lovatt's anger matched her own.

'Bradley had enough money,' he spat. 'And none of it made any difference to him. He was still a bastard.'

Mirabelle stopped in her tracks. To her mind Bradley was a hero, but anyone she met who knew him seemed to disagree. 'What on earth did he do?' she asked.

'Bradley? He did everything. With his bluff manner and his titled wife. We knew each other as children. We all knew each other – Duggan, Bradley, Caine and I. Let me tell you, it's no surprise that Bradley ended up being called Bulldog. He was a vicious bloody bastard and once he had his teeth in you he never let go.'

'A bully, you mean?'

Lovatt's skin was pink in his fury. He looked as if he might attack any moment. 'A bully. Yes. And after the war . . . I mean, I was here. I didn't see any service. Bradley became this ridiculous hero and Philip just disappeared. Matthew said he'd signed

the Official Secrets Act and couldn't tell me anything. Jack Duggan neither. Bradley held it over me, though. He kept hinting at one thing and another. I thought he'd killed Philip, Miss Bevan. I thought he'd murdered Philip and married his girl. It wouldn't have surprised me. He hadn't changed from when we were all at school. That's exactly what he was like till the day he died. And in the end it was an irony – all his money couldn't save him. When he knew he was dying I visited him and begged him just to tell me what had happened. Philip was a friend, you see. But Matthew just laughed. "I left him in France in 1942," he said. "And you're not cleared to know any more than that. I'm taking it to the grave," he said. And I could never understand, if Caine was alive, why he didn't come back.'

'So you altered Bradley's will?'

Lovatt nodded. 'God help me, yes. I added the clause and I wrote that letter.'

'And you thought ten thousand guineas would . . .'

'Hold your interest. Duggan mentioned you once or twice, what a marvel you were. And then I saw you in *The Times*. I'd tried to look into it myself but so many people had died that I got nowhere. I thought if I just tried to commission you, you'd turn me down.'

'I would have.'

'I've been desperate, you see, all these years. And I still don't understand. Why didn't Caine come back, Miss Bevan?'

Mirabelle regarded her shoes for a moment. 'Well, I suppose he'd been bullied too in a way, and he turned his back on it all. After his mother's death he blamed Matthew Bradley and Jack Duggan as well as himself. He didn't want to come home. He was ashamed of what he had to do. He changed his name.'

'But he's all right?'

'Yes, he's all right. And he has no idea that you have been thinking of him all this time.'

'After Bradley died I thought that he might want Caroline. I

thought if you found him he'd know she was free and maybe . . .'

'He's married, Mr Lovatt. He married someone else. He has children. Two, I think.'

'And if I were to write to him?'

'I could pass on a letter if you like. One letter.'

Lovatt nodded. 'Thank you. And I'll see to it that Bradley's bequest is paid to you. Please don't concern yourself.'

'I can't accept that. It's stolen money,' Mirabelle exclaimed. 'No. That will never do. I shall submit my invoice, Mr Lovatt, on a generous daily rate plus expenses.' She paused, thinking of the money she'd paid the old main in the attic and her eventual, rather costly hotel bill. And also a sum for donation to the Red Cross. I shall expect you to pay it yourself.'

She stared out of the window onto the street. People were picking their way along the pavement. It was on the tip of her tongue to ask Lovatt exactly what Jack had said about her, but then she realised it didn't matter any more. Jack had either loved her or he hadn't. He'd either intended to leave his wife or he'd intended to stay. There was no point in dwelling on the past. She didn't want to end up strangled by all the endless ifs. If Christine Moreau could move on, so could she.

'I do hope you don't make a habit of swindling your clients' estates,' she managed.

'Are you going to make a complaint?'

Mirabelle considered. If everything came out in court it would embarrass Mrs Bradley and her daughter, and it would expose Philip Caine. It might even expose her affair with Jack.

'No,' she said. She might as well be honest.

Lovatt looked as if he might burst into tears. 'Thank you,' he breathed.

'I'm not doing it for you,' Mirabelle snapped. 'I'm doing it for everybody else.' She got to her feet trying not to think of Evangeline Durand's funeral and the scars on Christine Moreau's arms. 'Good day,' she said.

Back out in the street she followed Vesta into the boutique. Inside, Vesta was arguing with the shop assistant.

'I want to try them on.' She indicated a pair of satin heels.

The shop girl's jaw was set. 'We can't have nignogs trying things on in here.' She sounded at the end of her tether. 'You'll get them dirty.'

Mirabelle drew herself up. Her eyes were like Medusa's as she swung in. 'Are you aware of the solicitor's office across the road, young woman? Lovatt and Stone?' she asked.

The girl nodded, abashed at this well put together woman cutting in on Vesta's behalf. She seemed to have come out of nowhere.

'Mr Lovatt is a personal friend of Miss Churchill's,' she said. 'Now you don't want to end up in court, do you? Over a pair of shoes? Miss Churchill is a size five, I believe.'

'But,' the girl stuttered, 'she's a darkie.'

Vesta bit her lip.

'But you'd let me try on the shoes, wouldn't you?' Mirabelle spat.

'Oh, if they're for you, madam, that's fine.' The girl sounded relieved.

Vesta sighed. 'Blow it,' she said. 'I can't be bothered with this.'

'I don't blame you.' Mirabelle put her hand on her friend's arm. 'It's ridiculous. We fought a war . . .' She struggled to contain her fury. 'We fought a war against this kind of prejudice.'

As they turned to go Mirabelle noticed a display of scarves. Red ones, with a familiar tag that said *Made in Paris*. Vesta followed her eyes.

'That colour would suit you,' she said.

'I wouldn't shop here.' Mirabelle sounded shocked. 'Places like this should be closed down.'

Vesta gripped her hand tightly. 'Good,' she said. 'Let's go and catch the train.'

Questions for readers' groups

1. Is McGregor good enough for Mirabelle? Is she treating him fairly?
2. How much of any character is the sum of that character's history? Can you ever transcend your past?
3. In the 1950s did women keep more secrets than men? Do they still?
4. Should information about military personnel be on a family-only basis? Does Mirabelle's connection to Jack entitle her to the information she uncovers? When Mrs Bradley warns her off, should she respect her views?
5. At what point should a war criminal become a civilian?
6. *Mieux Hitler que Stalin*? Better Hitler than Stalin?
7. Does Mirabelle have a death wish?
8. Was World War II a greater conflict than World War I?
9. After a bereavement or a betrayal do those affected have a duty to recover?
10. If you were Catherine the seamstress, would you have returned to Paris?
11. How far would you go for a friend?
12. Are we ever justified in not reporting a crime?

The quotations and misquotations used to open each chapter are taken from the following sources: 'Character is formed in the stormy billows of the world' (Goethe); 'A thing is not necessarily true just because a man dies for it' (Oscar Wilde); 'Where there is mystery there must also be evil' (Byron); 'Life can only be understood backwards but it must be lived forwards' (Kierkegaard); 'Being a woman is a terribly difficult task' (Joseph Conrad); 'One who makes no mistakes, makes nothing' (Casanova); 'I want to be with those who know secret things' (Rilke); 'There is nothing like a dream to create the future' (Victor Hugo); 'Happiness is a choice that requires effort' (Aeschylus); 'One should take good care not to grow too wise for so great a pleasure of life as laughter' (Joseph Addison); 'The price of anything is the amount of life you exchange for it' (Henry David Thoreau); 'Say what you will, 'tis better to be left than never to have been loved' (William Congreve); 'Suspicion always haunts the guilty mind' (Shakespeare); 'The greater the obstacle, the more glory in overcoming it' (Molière); 'If we don't know life, how can we know death' (Confucius); '*Timing*: judgement of when something should be done' (generic dictionary definition); 'Good clothes open all doors' (traditional saying); 'Curiosity is one of the permanent and certain characteristics of a vigorous intellect' (Samuel Johnson); 'The real voyage of discovery consists not in seeking new landscapes, but in having new eyes' (Marcel Proust); 'I know what I'm fleeing from but not what I'm searching for' (Michel de Montaigne); 'Knowing is not enough' (Goethe); 'One cannot answer for his courage when he has never been in danger' (François de La Rochefoucauld); 'Adversity is the first path to truth' (Byron); 'Man is made by his belief' (Goethe); 'Let food be thy medicine and medicine be thy food' (Hippocrates); 'Of all the noises known to man, opera is the most expensive' (Molière); 'Curiosity is the lust of the mind' (Thomas Hobbes); 'More law, less justice' (Cicero);

'Only the dead have seen the end of war' (Plato); 'Being good is easy, what is difficult is being just' (Victor Hugo); 'There is pleasure in the pathless woods' (Byron); 'Every person above the ordinary has a certain mission that they are called to fulfill' (Goethe); 'Romance should never begin with sentiment' (Oscar Wilde); 'The future is purchased by the present' (Samuel Johnson).

Don't let the story stop here

www.sarasheridan.com

Join Sara and her fans online for the latest
news, events, competitions and more